Someone *Bad* and Something *Blue*

Also by Miranda Parker

A Good Excuse to Be Bad

Published by Kensington Publishing Corporation

Someone *Bad* and Something *Blue*

Miranda Parker

Kensington Publishing Corp.

http://www.kensingtonbooks.com

DAFINA BOOKS are published by

Kensington Publishing Corp.
119 West 40th Street
New York, NY 10018

All Kensington Titles, Imprints, and Distributed Lines are available at special quantity discounts for bulk purchases for sales promotions, premiums, fund-raising, and educational or institutional use. Special book excerpts or customized printings can also be created to fit specific needs. For details, write or phone the office of the Kensington special sales manager: Kensington Publishing Corp., 119 West 40th Street, New York, NY 10018, attn: Special Sales Department, Phone: 1-800-221-2647.

Dafina and the Dafina logo Reg. U.S. Pat. & TM Off.

ISBN-13: 978-0-7582-5952-3
ISBN-10: 0-7582-5952-2

First Dafina trade paperback printing: July 2012

10 9 8 7 6 5 4 3 2 1

Printed in the United States of America

To Maggie and Suzette—your lives are inspiration infinity, rest in peace.
To my mom, Dorothy, for taking cancer down by the throat.
And to Selah for all that is good in my life.

Acknowledgments

If this is your first time reading Angel's story, let me first tell you that I'm not as smart/dumb (circle best answer) as you may think. If it weren't for the village that is Miranda Parker, *Someone Bad and Something Blue* would not be in your hands.

So let me acknowledge the truth about what went down getting this book published and who did the most work:

Kensington/Dafina Books:
- To my editor, Selena James: If there was an award for Most Dedicated Editor, Selena James should get it. When I wrote this novel I had written the first chapter fifteen times and fifteen different ways. And after each draft my vision for this story blurred. To make matters worse, there were so many challenges going on in my personal life I didn't have the time or energy to get back on track. Thank God for Selena. She emailed me her thoughts of my manuscript and stated one sentence that turned a switch on inside me. It put *Someone Bad and Something Blue* back into full view for me. I became excited again. I am very, very grateful for that. I also thank her for being so patient with me.
- To Mercedes Fernandez: Thanks for calming me down when I really almost chucked this book outside.
- To my cover designer, Kristine Mills-Noble. Again?! I was happy about the concept for *A Good Excuse To Be Bad* and then I received this cover. I jumped. I leaped.

It's like you plucked a dream out of my head. Thank you.

- To my book cover photographer, George Kerrigan. Thank you for your great work and for Donna Bradley. My readers have told me how much they loved the cover.

- To Adeola Saul/Publicity: Thank you for taking care of me at NBCC and Black Pearl Magazine's Chocolate Social, for sending such a great letter to Dekalb County Public Library on my behalf, for introducing me to ITW, for making me look good, and for answering the phone every time I called.

- To Alexandra Nicolajsen/Digital Content/Marketing Manager: Thank you for helping me with my book trailer and tweeting everything I got myself into. It was very sweet of you.

- Dafina's Sales Team: Thank you for getting my book in Publix Supermarket. I cried when I put my own book in my shopping cart. ☺

I did a lot of research when writing *Someone Bad and Something Blue* and had the pleasure to chat with some interesting people:

- The Honorable Robert Moore, retired United States Marshal
- Patricia Boudrot, PR at Filene's Basement
- To my Ex aka Papi Chulo for all things buck, hooch, life behind bars, and the prison system, thanks for being a sport and telling me more than I probably needed to know.
- To Prohibition Speakeasy Bar in Atlanta. I'll keep your secret.

Now that I've gotten that out of the way, I need to acknowledge a few people who sacrificed themselves for me, while I wrote this novel.

- Selah: My lovely daughter, who somehow grew up, while I was writing. Please don't grow that fast between Book 2 and Book 3. I love your sweetness and sass. You teach me more than I teach you.
- Mom: This has been a whirlwind year. I thank God you are here with me. When I was exhausted and wanted to ditch Angel and her crazy manhunt you inspired me. If you could grin and bear it through radiation treatments and biopsies, I could dig in and stop whining. You're also the best direct seller on my planet and keep me on my toes about monthly sales goals. I'll do better with this one, promise. I pray for your continued health and love you!
- MeLana: My inspiration for Whitney and my real little sister. You are my ride or die chick. When I thought no one would show up to my book signing, not only did you come, but you made my signings look fabulous. Thanks for watching our girl for me.
- David: My twin. Ava is definitely not you. LOL. Thank you for getting male readers behind my book. I think I have more men fans then women. You are the best brother.
- Eric and Derrick Phillips: Thanks for making my book a hit with firemen. Wonder Twins definitely united. I love you, brothers.
- Daddy: Thank you for making sure Angel held her gun properly and planted her feet. It's indeed a blessing to have a former U.S. Marine sharp shooter help me write these books. I love you.
- To my Ace: Dr. Natasha B. for talking me out of another

year of bad decisions. You became a mom this year and yet had time for me and Miranda. Thank you for encouraging me to move forward with this writing thing when I was still stuck in who I used to be. Love you and Aria.

- To Cathy Blair: Although you're Angel's nonexistent personal assistant, you're my good friend, book buddy, prayer pal, and movie maven. Thanks for watching Selah for me when I had to do a book event, needed to write in peace, needed to know someone cared.
- To Daren Gayle: My brother in Spirit. Thank you for being the best booking agent on the planet and treating Selah like the princess she is.
- To Gaspard: Thanks for loving me and Selah unconditionally.
- To Doctor David Song: Again you saved my life this year.
- To Bernadette Davis for being my cohost in #blacklitchat on Twitter.

Now this part gets tricky, because if I miss someone, someone may get offended. I tried to name most of you in *Angel On the Back Pew*, so double check that. However, I want to give a special pen up to some people who stood out on helping me through this book:

- Rhonda McKnight for being more excited at times than I was about my book.
- Tayari Jones for coming out to see me speak at Decatur Book Festival. If that wasn't the best book promotion for me. You made me impo'ant.
- Creston Mapes who wrote the nice endorsement on the front. I heart you.
- Tiffany Warren for all things books, comedy, and side eye.

- Tia McCollors for glamorizing my world and saying good things to book clubs about me.
- ReShonda Tate Billingsley for getting this book into so many readers' hands. Had you not wrote the blurb for *A Good Excuse to be Bad* they may not have picked it up.
- Victoria Christopher Murray for commenting on every blog post about my book, Facebook status, have supported my efforts and shared my book with her fans.
- Booker T. Mattison for those long chats on Facebook and being a great escort at NBCC.
- Trice Hickman for making me look good in front of some of the largest book clubs on the planet. Thanks for getting me that great spot in front of Tyrese and Jeff Johnson. ☺
- To Shelia Goss for being crazy enough to host a writing workshop with me.
- To my International Thriller Writer Family: Jenny Milchman, Allan Leverone, Gary Kriss, and Ethan Cross. Thanks for adding me to the family.
- To my sisters in The Atlanta Georgia Peach Authors: Marissa Monteilh, Dwan Abrams, Electa Rome Parks, Gail McFarland, Jean Holloway, and D.L. Sparks. I'm Peachy and Proud.

To the Literati:
- Ella Curry for calling me when I'm not well, for telling everyone she knows about Miranda Parker, and for sharing your world with me.
- Tashmir Parks for supporting me when only two people knew my name.
- Tasha Martin for treating me like an honorary Sistahfriend before I became Miranda P.
- Tee C. Royal for holding Gwinnett down now that I'm

gone and for championing me every RAWSISTAZ tread. Also thanks for checking my website for malware.

- Martin Pratt for calling me late at night and smiling through the phone. My friend.
- To Myguail Chappel at DeKalb County Public Library. I was honored to have you read my story out loud.
- Nyisha Ferguson of Houston Public Library. What you did for me and library acquisitions in rural Georgia is amazing. Thank you.
- Linda Jordan at Atlanta Fulton for becoming my cheerleader in the library system.
- The Friends of South Georgia Regional Library for making me feel like royalty in my hometown.
- The Atlanta Press Club for covering me all summer and then inviting me to the prestigious holiday party. I'm still pinching myself.
- To Troy Johnson for hooking me up on AALBC.Com.
- I'm sorry. I forgot you. I promise I will get you in Book Three.

Miranda P.

1

Friday, 8:00 AM
Greyhound Bus Terminal, Atlanta, Georgia

Just as I was about to cuff Misty Wetherington for ditching DUI court for the fifth time so she could hit the slots at Harrah's casino with her book club buddies, my phone buzzed. I looked down. It was my calendar app, reminding me that I had to be at Bella's school in ninety minutes.

"Crap, I forgot." I sighed.

My daughter, Bella, had asked me if I could join her at Sugar Hill Elementary School today for Doughnuts for Dads. It was a PTA event to celebrate fathers, more like a backdoor way to get men into the classroom without them feeling awkward. However, Bella's best friend Lacy's mom came to the last one and, according to my friends at the Sugar Hill Church Ladies' Brunch, no one seemed to mind.

And . . . today was Bella's seventh birthday. I had to be there.

However, I was a little under an hour's drive from the school. If I could punch it without getting a speeding ticket, I would make it in time. The only problem was I didn't know what to do with Misty.

With the exhaustively long lines at the City of Atlanta's

traffic court, who knew how long it would take to process her? I wondered as I looked down at her bleached, moppy hair.

She was still on the parking lot ground, face to the gritty, piss-stained pavement while I straddled her back. My handcuffs dangled in my hands.

"Misty, you have been caught on a particularly good day for you. . . ."

I placed the cuffs on the ground near her face so she could see them. I waited until she turned her head in the cuff's direction before I continued.

"Look. It's my daughter's birthday and I need to be with her. We both know that what I'll make for hauling your butt to jail is about the cost of two tickets to the Atlanta Aquarium, the Coke Museum, and one night's stay in the Georgian Terrace. So here's my proposition. Today, I let you go. I'll have Big Tiger finesse the city into giving you another FTA hearing, but on one condition: You fork over the money you were about to spend at the casino. I can surprise my girl with a kid-cation in Atlanta. What do you say?"

Big Tiger was the bail bondsman who kept me under contract. He introduced me to bail recovery and taught me the tools of the trade.

"And if I don't?" She grunted.

"How confident are you that the City of Atlanta will grant you a new FTA hearing after five no-shows without some help from Big Tiger? How confident are you that some other bail recovery agent isn't lurking behind any of these cars out here, waiting for the chance to take you from me? And uh . . . where are your gambling buddies when you need them?"

Her gaze searched the parking lot. "Did they leave?"

"Darling, they are the ones who turned you in. Now those

are friends to keep. I can be your friend, too. Just say the magic words."

She sighed. "The money's in my front pocket, Angel."

"Bingo." I hopped off her and flipped her over.

She reluctantly pulled the money out. I stretched out my palm until she placed the money into my hand. Misty was carrying five hundred dollars.

I placed the money in my back pocket and smiled. "Happy Birthday to Bella."

Friday, 10:10 AM
Sugar Hill Elementary School, Sugar Hill, Georgia

Sugar Hill Elementary School was unusually packed when I pulled into the parking lot. "I can't believe this many men are here to eat doughnuts," I said to myself as I sped up the boardwalk to the school's entrance.

When I walked into the foyer, Dale Baker, the president of our homeowners' association, waved me down and mouthed *good morning*. I waved back and continued toward the front office. Inside, I spotted the parents' sign-in sheet, pulled a pen out of the flowerpot pen holder, and signed my name.

The front office manager, whose name I could never remember because the constant scowl on her face reminded me of the taste of a bitter honeysuckle, pulled her glasses down her nose and shook her head at me. I called her Mrs. Bitter behind her back.

She pointed to the sign-in sheet. Her aged fingers seemed swollen, even for someone her age. "Uh . . . Miss Crawford, you don't sign in here. This is for Doughnuts for Dads."

"I know that," I said with a don't-start-with-me smile.

"Honey, I know you're rough-and-tumble. I see you on the news, bursting down doors and pushing men around. But here at Sugar Hill we don't need that kind of confusion for Isabella."

"No offense, but I know what I'm doing." I brushed her off.

This wasn't the first time an older Southern woman had tried to tell me how to parent. It didn't offend me, but today I didn't have the time to extend her more kindness than the fake smile I'd already offered. Doughnuts for Dads lasted thirty minutes. Ten minutes had already passed and Bella was still waiting in her homeroom class to be called.

"Can you please call Isabella Crawford up to the front before it's too late?" I checked my watch and turned away from her.

She huffed. "I'm sure you think you know what you're doing, but have you thought of how *what you* do affects Isabella?"

And she didn't shut up. While I watched her mouth moving, my fingers curled into a ball. This was the first time since I became a single mom that I felt inadequate. It angered me. Thus, my resolve to be good faded the more she preached. Mrs. Bitter was about five seconds from getting her feelings hurt. I counted to ten real slow and hoped for some miracle to stop me from knocking the taste out of her big, meddling mouth.

"Mrs. Montgomery, I'm afraid this young lady has plans for Ms. Crawford." Justus Morgan's voice made me tremble.

I turned around. He stood in the front office threshold and looked down. Bella was in front of him. Her smile was as wide as the summer days were long. The shame I'd just felt faded away with every second of her presence in the room.

"Surprise, sweetie!" I knelt down and hugged Bella.

She broke free and grabbed my hand. "Come on, Mommy.

Mr. Baker has saved us the biggest sprinkled cupcakes in the entire world because it's my birthday."

I mouthed *thank you* to Justus as Bella whisked me away from Mrs. Bitter. When I glanced back, I noticed her head had dropped. Justus was saying something to her that made her cower.

After Doughnuts for Dads, I thanked Dale and the rest of the PTA Room Moms' Committee for putting this together and walked toward Justus. He had just completed a conversation with Principal Boyd.

He must have seen me coming, because his face lit up bright. It made me blush.

Justus was my pastor and once my secret crush. Now I avoided him when I could, because apparently he had a thing for me, too, which was even scarier than pining for him from afar. The last man I loved died in my arms and left me his daughter to parent on my own. I was still gun shy of good love and terrified of Justus To Hot to Be Holy Morgan.

"Thank you," I spat out before I lost the nerve.

"For what?" He grinned. His deep right dimple humbled me even more.

"For coming to my rescue with Mrs. Bi—Mrs. Montgomery."

He looked down and chuckled. "I finally get to be the hero."

"Look around this place, Justus. You're always the hero."

He didn't respond, just looked at me in that way that made me feverish around my lips.

"What are you doing here? Trish's boys needed a stand-in?"

Justus's sister, Trish, was a military wife. Her husband, Mike, was deployed overseas more than he stayed stateside.

Yet they managed to have three children despite his long stays away. They had a teenage drama queen daughter named Kelly and twin sons who were about Bella's age. But rumor around Sugar Hill Community Church was that Trish had a new bun in the oven.

"No, actually Mike was here. He couldn't stay long. You probably missed him when you were chatting with Mrs. Montgomery."

"Good news for them." I smiled.

He stopped smiling. "He's being called to Afghanistan."

"Wow."

"Wow indeed." He nodded. "I'm here because I came to invite the dads to the North Georgia Bike and Car show."

"Bike and Car show?" I stepped back in surprise. "You bike."

"Among other things. Since you keep giving me rain checks on our date, you miss out on these cool things about me."

Our date? I folded my arms over my chest. *Are we still on that subject?*

The last time Justus and I were together was at my brother-in-law Devon's homegoing celebration. I had admitted that I had considered a relationship with him, but the reality of our situations didn't seem like they would ever mesh. He's a minister and I'm . . . well, I need a lot of prayer. He had brushed off my excuse as if I'd never said it, while I'd dodged him every chance I'd gotten since then.

Today, after what he'd done for me, I owed him at least a straight answer.

"Justus—"

"Wait before you come up with another weak excuse why you can't date me. Let me stop you by telling you that I'm letting you off the hook. You don't owe me anything," he said.

"Good, because I don't want to date you. . . ."

The fire in his cheeks had gone out. "I understand."

I walked closer toward him and stood short of his boots. "I want to know if we could have a future together."

His eyes blazed. His smile outdid Bella's. "What if I already know the answer is yes?"

"Then I'm giving you the chance to prove it."

"No time like the present," he said. "Tonight we begin."

"You make that sound really, really, really hot, but I don't have a babysitter for tonight. It's Bella's birthday. Besides, Whitney has plans. Her bestie is getting married and the bridal team is getting together to powwow about the wedding plans. Ava is taking the kids to spend time with Devon's family, and Momma . . . hopefully she's on her honeymoon with my quiet-is-as-kept, new step daddy."

"You want to know if I can fit into your world. That world includes Bella and her perfect birthday. Let's do her up big. Let's take her to the circus. They're in town."

"Last-minute tickets for something like that is killer," I said while those five hundred dollars burned holes in my pocket.

"My treat," he said.

"That's sweet, but a night at the circus with a kindergartner doesn't sound like hot date material."

"Who says I want a hot date?" He touched my hand. "I want you. That's all. Any time with you is blue hot in my book."

There was something about his hand squeeze, the sincere look in his eyes, and his way with words that made me wish very hard that was true.

"Okay, then. Tonight we begin," I said, but it didn't sound as cute as when Justus had said it.

2

My flexible work schedule was the main reason I became a bail recovery agent. My former job at the *Atlanta Sentinel* had so much structure, so many rules, and that feeling of an invisible thumb on your back that it was driving me batty. But now I set my own hours. Now I was the boss. I slept in and hit the clubs at night. I could bop into Bella's school for Doughnuts for Dads, hop over to Big Tiger's to skim through his current jackets, and then take a quick run to the Decatur Hotel, the nickname for the Dekalb County jail.

Today, because it was my designated day to run Bella's car pool, I was on my way to GCDC. That jail was twenty minutes from Sugar Hill Elementary. So I had a solid ninety minutes to get in, get what I needed, and get out of there with time to spare.

I needed to check through the inmate list to see if one of my skips was already inside. Although both the national warrant and the prison system intranet service did decent jobs connecting charges, sometimes they missed a few. Especially if the prison was a private institution or the inmate had a common name like Miguel Lopez, Kim Li, Mike Jones, or my current skip's name, Cesar Cruz.

Cesar had an FTA jacket that was ten skips deep. At the bottom of the habitual bail-jumper's barrel was Big Tiger's $25,000 Fulton County, newly forfeited bail bond. If I found Mr. Cruz in less than 150 days, then I would take home five thousand dollars. That was my mortgage for almost six months.

Since Gwinnett County had a large immigrant population, this was the best place to start. I also had a snitch on the inside, Rosary DiChristina. Her ex-husband was related to Cesar. She needed a few dollars on her commissary. If she gave me a good lead, I would take care of her toiletries for a few months.

After I checked in as an inmate visitor, I took a seat in the lobby, waited for my last name to be called, and scanned the place for the familiars and the newbies. I could spot a newbie within seconds of them entering the jail: the dropped jaw, the turned-up nostrils from the part urine/part bleach/part stank stench, and the realization in their eyes that this nightmare actually existed. For the rest of us, the ones who've grown accustomed to the fluorescent lighting, beige cement walls, exposed pipe ceiling, and air so cold and stale your nose and fingers numb on impact, we know to wear our worst jeans and a bomber jacket.

I had spotted at least four newbies when my name was called.

"Hey, Angel." One of the women correctional officers on call today waved at me. She had a tiny crush on Tiger.

"Hey, girl. You got time after I come down? I need to check on some folk."

"It depends. I'm off the clock in forty."

I nodded as I passed by. "I'll see you before then."

"Who you come to see?" She reached for the sign-in clipboard. "Aw, lawd, not her."

I stopped short of the elevators leading to Rosary's living pod, but didn't turn around. "What's wrong with Rosary?"

"Your girl has gotten into some more trouble. I can get her out of it, but she's not cooperating. Maybe you can talk some sense into her before it's too late."

I pursed my lips. I was confused. Rosary didn't seem like the bad-girl type. There must be more to this than she was telling me.

I pushed the elevator button. "She's a good girl. Don't worry. She'll listen to me."

"She better or she's going to catch a new case." The officer scoffed.

"A new case?!" I spun around and sighed. "What do you want me to do exactly?"

If you've been in one county jail's inmates' quarters, you've been to them all. They were quartered off in polygons with the officers' station planted smack-dab in the middle. This way, they could keep their eyes on the prisoners, whose rooms resembled glassed-off pet rat cages. My best definition for county jail at GCDC was a cross between a science lab and a day care, except the baby rats wore blue jumpers.

Rosary entered the visitation chamber about two minutes after I arrived. We were separated by a scratched glass partition. Both our cubes had a phone nailed to the wall, a steel table attached to the glass, and a beige piper stack chair. The I-don't-know-what-it-is-but-it-burns-my-nose smell was the only odor in the room.

She sat down. Before she lifted her phone to her head, I knew what the officer meant. Rosary appeared groggy and listless. I crossed my arms over my chest and didn't pick up the phone receiver. What was the point, since my informant was drunk off buck?

Buck is the term for moonshine made from fermented

fruit. Most prison inmates used bread, orange peels, and orange slices to concoct their brew. They would put that nasty mess in a plastic bag and let it sit for days until the bag popped. The pop indicated the alcohol was ready.

Therefore, fruit peels were forbidden inside, so Rosary was in trouble. If I didn't get her straight and find out who brought her the orange peels, she would have another charge tacked onto her current DWI charge.

I huffed. *I didn't come here for this.*

She tapped the window to get me to pick up my receiver so we could talk.

I snatched the phone off the wall and didn't put the receiver on my ear. You would be surprised what some of these visitors do to that thing.

I spoke into the receiver. "Looks like you began the party without me."

"No, just sleepy." Rosary lisped. Her tongue was heavy from drinking hooch. "They keep it so cold in here."

"Rosie, don't play. You're drunk and you just wasted my time today."

"It's cold in here. I need something to keep me warm."

"I would have put enough money on your account for you to buy some long johns, but now . . ." I shook my head. "I'm not wasting my money."

She sat up straighter. "¿Qué estás diciendo? You're not putting any money on my commissary?"

"Why should I? And your Spanish is getting rusty."

"Not fair, and my Spanish is just fine." She pouted.

"Not fair? Let me tell you what's not fair. I came straight from my daughter's school to see you and you're drunk. You knew I was coming, yet you insult me."

She giggled. "This stuff doesn't get you drunk. I'm just a little buzzed."

"Honey, even through these thick walls I can smell orange

hooch on you. Let me tell you something . . . the staff is on to you, too. If you don't tell me who brought you the orange rinds, then they're going to stack another case on. More than likely you won't get out of here until after Christmas, if they do. That's not going to look good to your boss, who's been nice enough to hold your job for you. Plus . . . how do you think little Lucia is going to feel about having an alchi for a mom?"

"I don't want that. I promised her she wouldn't go through what I went through." She began to tear up. "Help me, Angel. I'll tell you who's supplying us. It's Day Day, one of the servers in the cafeteria. He gave it to me in exchange for cases of Pop's cigarettes."

I gasped. "Pop's cigarettes?!"

Rosary's dad, Pop Calhoun, made a name for himself with the alphabet agencies (ATF, IRS, and GBI) and the prison world because of his creation, sale, and distribution of both illegal cigarettes and apple pie flavored moonshine.

"When you called me and told me you were in here, and that you didn't want to be bailed out so you can get cleaned up, I thought you had learned your lesson about your father. I thought you finally got it in your head that he doesn't care about you."

"Well, he sent Day Day the cigarettes, so he must care a little." Her eyes were so dilated I shook my head in disgust and disappointment. "Don't look at me like that."

I sat back and placed the phone on the steel table. This conversation had gotten darker by the minute. I checked my watch. I needed to line up for Bella's car pool within the hour. I picked the phone back up.

"I'm sorry, Angel. I won't do it again," she whispered. "What else do you need from me to get my commissary back?"

"Nothing. Right now, I can't trust anything that comes out your mouth."

"Come on, Angel. It's hard in here. You know how it is. . . ."

"No, I don't know how it is. I'm on the other side of the law, the right side."

"Okay. I'm about to be on the good side soon."

"You could've fooled me," I said.

"For real. I'll prove it. Who are you searching for right now? Who do you need me to help you find? I got connections."

"Your cousin Cesar Cruz." I pulled out a picture of him from my back pocket. "He's changed his hair, but that's still him."

She observed the picture and nodded. "I saw him at Big Tiger's a while back."

"Yeah, you did. Is that all you got?"

"Cesar's new girlfriend is Tara Tina Ramirez. They live in Doraville, off Peachtree Industrial. She works as a hostess at Grits Draft House in Johns Creek. Want the number?"

"No, and I don't need anyone tipping her off either."

She threw her hands up. "I won't tell."

"All right, I'll check this out."

"You gon' hook me up now, manita?"

"If you agree to more rehab, then yeah. I got you."

"I don't need to do more rehab."

"Then you can kiss your job goodbye, because they'll take your bartending license for good if you don't go, and you definitely won't get my money. Matter fact, maybe you shouldn't be working in a bar. Have you ever thought of that?"

"I have. I got a plan for something better," she said.

"Good." I stood up and got out of there before the stench made me pass out.

3

Justus arrived at my home at six sharp for our blue-hot date. He held a single white rose in one hand; I noticed a bouquet of red ones behind his back. I blushed in excitement.

He smiled as he stepped inside my foyer. "Where's the birthday girl?"

I stepped aside. "Primping in the restroom."

"Of course she is." He chuckled.

"When I told her you were taking her birthday up a notch, she became ecstatic." I folded my arms over my chest and gave him my flirty side glance.

He touched my arm. "Please tell me that I didn't ruin any plans you had for her."

"No . . ." I shook my head. "Last year, when she was in kindergarten, we decided that when her birthday fell on a school night we would do something simple like dinner and a Disney movie, then have a party on the weekend with her friends."

"It's Friday." He looked up then his brows furrowed. "So do I need more tickets to accommodate her friends?"

"No, she's having a slumber party tomorrow night at

Ava's. Taylor wants to attend this year and Bella wants her friends to experience the McMansion."

"The McMansion" was my nickname for my sister Ava's million-dollar starter mansion in Atlanta. Taylor was Ava's eight-year-old daughter and my very prim and proper niece.

"This is her first time sharing her birthday with her cousins isn't it?" He smiled.

"Yep, but I don't know . . . Bella's been spending a lot of time over there, since Ava and I are now on good terms. But Ava's lifestyle is more extravagant than mine. I'm already competing with Bella's classmates. I refuse to compete with Ava. Shoot. I can't."

"Why do you see it as a competition?" he asked.

"Because it's always been a competition between us."

"So is this why you agreed to our date? To one-up Ava?"

"As many times as I've tried to lie to you, I can't do it." I paused. "I didn't agree to this date because I wanted to use you. I wanted to spend time with you. However, your plans for tonight put me in a great spot. It's shameful, but I must admit that."

"Glad you shared that with me. I know that was hard for you." He grinned.

"It is. I love Bella. I don't want anything or anyone to harm her, including myself."

"You won't, Angel. The ladies at church can't stop singing your praises. Remember, I was with you when you stuck your neck out to save Ava. You're a great woman, a great sister, a great mom."

"You didn't say great girlfriend." More of my side glance.

"Woman, don't play with me. We were in the middle of having a serious moment together and then you threw a joke in there."

"I wasn't trying to joke. That was my bad attempt at flirting with someone I actually wasn't paid to pretend to like."

"I see." He pulled me closer to him and then . . . "Would you mind if I kissed you now?"

"I don't mind." I nodded, while my knees became jelly as he leaned toward my lips.

"Are those roses for me?" Bella asked and scared the Goodness Gracious out of me.

The back of my head hit the wall. "Ouch."

"Are you all right?" Justus grabbed me up.

Bella grabbed my knees. "Sorry, Mommy."

"It's all good, everyone. I just lost my head for a minute." I blushed, after glancing at Justus. "So are you finally ready, birthday girl?"

"I am, but I have to ask Mr. Morgan a question in private." Bella wrinkled her nose. "Is that okay, Mommy?"

I smiled at her, trying to hide my curiosity. "It's your day. Whatever you want, but don't take too long. You still have to honor your bedtime schedule."

She rolled her eyes, then smiled. My little sister, Whitney, who also lives with us, does the same thing. When Whitney does it, she pisses me off, but when Bella does the same thing, it tickles me. The Mom Double Standard was my term for my hypocrisy.

I left the foyer for the living room so that Bella and Justus could talk. While I waited, my smart phone buzzed. I checked the caller ID. It was Big Tiger, my favorite contractor, honorary big brother, and the best bail bondsman on my planet.

"Hi, Tiger. I don't have much time. We're about to take Bella out for her birthday."

"Cool. Tell Little Princess happy birthday and I have a gift for her at Mama's. . . ."

Mama's referred to BT Trusted Bail Bonds main office in Decatur, which also doubled as Mama D's Soul Kitchen

Restaurant in the back. His mom, Mama D, was also co-owner of the bail bondsman office.

"Why don't you, Whitney, and Bella stop through? You know it's Fish Fry Friday. Mama serves Bella's favorite peach cobbler. I'll make sure that Mama holds a pan for the baby."

"That's sweet, but actually Whitney isn't coming with us. Justus is."

Silence.

More silence.

Last summer when I was investigating my brother-in-law Devon's murder, Big Tiger and I were almost killed. Tiger blamed Justus for the near-death experience. For a short while I did, too, but that was my ego talking. Needless to say, Tiger hadn't liked Justus since then.

"Tiger, are you there?" I asked.

"I thought you weren't going to give the pastor the time of day," he said. His voice had changed to deep and selfish.

But I wasn't going to let him get away with it. Tiger was the poster child for bad relationship advice. "Tiberious Jones, don't start with me. Anyway . . . why did you call?"

"A few tips have come in about your personal project."

He referred to the mysterious postcard I received the day after Devon's homegoing celebration. Someone had sent me a box of roses. The note card attached to it was a picture of Bella and me at Devon's funeral. On the back there was a note, more like a question. *Do you still love me?* When I read the question, the first thing that came to my mind was Gabe, Bella's father. He was dead and those were his last words to me before he was murdered. I don't believe in coincidences. Therefore, the card had creeped me out so bad I fainted. Whitney found me on the doorstep. I gave her some lame excuse about me being exhausted. She bought it and I called Tiger about the card. We had been scrubbing the streets for answers. I even put up money to give to tipsters who could give us solid leads. Unfortunately, all of them had led nowhere and my budget for more tips ran out last month.

I leaned back on the couch. "You know what, Tiger? I don't want to deal with this today. In fact, I think I should let it go. It's been months and nothing. Whoever sent the flowers is ghost, too. I think it was a prank, some disgruntled skip I sent back to jail, trying to scare me. Let's just hang this whole thing up."

"Angel Soft, you received three tips today from different people saying the same thing."

I perked up and sat up. "What was it?"

"Some girl named Marlo made the postcard."

"Do they know who she made it for?"

"Nope. She does wedding invitations and fancy paper stuff for a few event planners and businesses around town. Who knows? All I can say for sure is she made it."

"So why hadn't she called me then?" I shook my head. "Nope. Sounds like another crazy dead end to me."

"She read about you in the paper and got scared. Now that's funny." He chuckled. "You've managed to get more of a bad-girl reputation since helping your sister." He laughed even harder.

"Not funny." I checked my watch and stood up. We needed to get out of here if we were going to make the show on time. "Text me the deets on this Marlo chick."

"I'm going to do you one better. She's night manager at Grits Draft House tonight. Let's roll up there and talk with her."

Grits Draft House? That's the same place Rosary talked about when I was looking for Cesar.

"I can't see her tonight. It's Bella's birthday. I promised quality time with her."

"Girl, you're full of it. 'Cause if that was the case, Justus wouldn't be tagging along." He scoffed.

"Get used to Justus in my life. Okay?"

"Oh, it's like that?" he asked. His voice had raised an octave.

"It's like that, so tonight is out."

"You know good and well we can go there tonight. You can drop Bella at Ava's early instead of Saturday morning and get Justus back to Sugar Hill before he turns into a pumpkin."

"Ha ha . . ." Then I thought about what he had just said. "What do you know about Bella's birthday party tomorrow anyway?"

"Your sister and I are friendly now. She tells me things." His voice softened a little.

I threw my head back. "Oh God."

"What's wrong with that?" I heard the frown in his voice.

"Leave my sister alone, Tiger."

"Only if you leave Reverend Romance alone first."

"Sounds like you're jealous."

"Nope, just trying to save you from heartache."

"And I'm doing the same for you." I began walking toward the foyer. "You don't know my sister like I do."

"For the sake of our friendship, let's just get back on the subject," he said.

"Yep, let's. . . ." I peeked in on Bella and Justus. They were still talking about God knows what. "If Whitney comes home before Draft House closes, then we can go. Otherwise, I have to stay here because there's no one here to watch Bella while we're gone."

"That's understandable," Tiger said.

"And I have other plans tonight, too." I referred to my alone time with Justus.

"I guarantee Reverend Romance will disappear by midnight with the pumpkin and the glass slipper. He has an early start on Saturdays: hospice visitations, soup kitchen, being a superhero . . ."

I laughed. "You know way too much about the people in my life."

"See you at midnight."

I chuckled. "I seriously doubt that."

"We're ready," Justus called out.

"And we have a surprise," Bella squealed.

"Bye, Tiger." I hung up and walked into the foyer to join Justus and Bella. "What happened? What are we doing now?"

"We have a change of plans," Justus said.

"What? No circus?" I asked.

"No, Mommy . . ." She jumped up and clapped. "We're going to see The Muppets at the super-duper fabulous Fox Theatre. I can't believe it!"

She began jumping again. She squealed louder with each jump.

"Bella, calm down." I chuckled, then looked at Justus. "Are you crazy?"

"Someone owed me a favor. It's no problem."

"What about your nephews? Do you think they want to come?" I asked.

"They will be there. Mike and Trish scored the extra tickets for us. I promised to treat them to cake at Broadway Diner. Bella says she's never been."

"I haven't either."

His eyes lit up. "So there's a place in Atlanta that you don't know."

"Yep, the wholesome ones always escape me."

He took my coat off the hanger by the front door, then helped me into mine and Bella into hers. "Ladies, shall we?"

I gave Justus a smooch on the cheek. "Thank you."

He smiled. "Thank me later tonight with some one-on-one time."

I nodded, then hugged him. Although I knew I shouldn't, I checked my watch and wondered how much one-on-one time we could have before Grits Draft House closed.

Friday, 11:00 PM
Home, Sugar Hill, Georgia

Justus, Bella, and I arrived back home a little before eleven. Bella had fallen asleep on the drive home. She'd eaten a ridiculously large slice of Oreo cake.

"I hope we didn't ruin her appetite for tomorrow's slumber party," I said to Justus as he carried her up the stairs.

He laid Bella in her bed and tucked her under the bedcovers. "She'll be fine."

I observed Bella's dollhouse clock and then texted Whitney. While at the show, she had sent me a message that she would be home by midnight. That gave Justus and me thirty minutes of alone time together.

Justus escorted me downstairs and into my sunroom. We could see the stars from there.

When I'd bought this place, the sunroom was a part of the large wraparound porch. However, I'd wanted a room I could rock Bella to sleep in, take long naps in, and forget the troubles I left behind in Atlanta. We walled it off with windows and white pine. I never considered this room to be romantic until tonight. I blamed it on the company I kept.

Justus sat down beside me on my ginger-colored suede sofa. This would feel nice if I weren't on pins and needles.

He smiled; I smiled back.

"What plans have you and Tiger made for after I leave?"

My shoulders tensed. My jaw clenched. "How did you know?"

"You've been eying clocks and watches all evening."

I lowered my head. "I'm a bad girlfriend. Aren't I?"

"I don't know. You've never defined what we are to each other."

I dropped my head. "Does this conversation have to be so serious?"

"Nope." He laughed. "Tell me about this case that will cut our time together."

Justus's reaction to my plans with Tiger surprised me. However, I wasn't going to tell him the truth. He knew I was slightly off my rocker, but this card issue would make me look fruitier than a Broadway Diner fruitcake.

"It's just a locator project I've been working on for the past few months. This is our first real lead. If we don't act on it tonight, it may go cold."

He sighed and lay back on the sofa. "I can get used to you dipping out late at night, as long as you come back to Bella and me every night."

"We, huh?" I blushed.

"I know what I'm getting into with you."

"But I can't keep doing this to you."

"No." He shook his head. "But we'll figure out a solution that will make the both of us happy. That is, if you want to work at this with me."

"I do." I smiled. "Tomorrow we could pick up where we left off. Bella will be at Ava's after breakfast, I have the weekly roundup meeting at Big Tiger's at ten, and then I have no plans after that."

"I need to prepare for Sunday's sermon."

"Oh, that's right." I rubbed his strong arms. "Will that take all day?"

Just before he replied, I heard someone shutting the kitchen door and dangling keys. It was Whitney.

Justus followed my eyes and then exhaled. "The date is over."

He stood up.

I caught his arm. "No, it's not over."

"It's fine." He removed my arm.

"No, it isn't." I hopped up. "I don't want you to go just yet."

"I think this is the best time for me to go."

"Why?"

"Because I may change my mind about letting you leave later." He looked at me in a way that made me want to call Tiger back to cancel.

I reached for my phone.

He put his hands over it. "Don't. I'm fine about this. Really."

"But you made time for me today. I'm stupid. Stay here. I'll call Tiger off."

"No, you just want another kiss from me." He grinned. "However, it's late. I don't want to disrespect you. I shouldn't be here this long alone with you anyway."

"What? Why?!" I hopped up. "It's only been about fifteen minutes."

He kissed me and shut me up. "Thank you for a nice evening."

"You never answered my question earlier. Will you be working on your sermon all day and night? Because if not, we could have more of this tomorrow night."

He grinned. "Are you ready for this?"

I nodded. "I'm prepared to have my mind blown."

4

Grits Draft House was a Southern revival cocktail bar located in an affluent part of the North Atlanta area. It was a twenty-minute drive from my home. The good thing about Grits Draft House was that you didn't have to dress up in a cocktail dress to enjoy yourself. It was more like a stylish watering hole: peanut hulls covering the floor, whiskey barrels made into bar tables, and antler barstools—real country. Of course, most of the people there wore four-hundred-dollar jeans and one-hundred-dollar T-shirts, but I didn't have a problem fitting in. The Johns Creek Goodwill had some of the best bargain couture redneck wear in the state. I wore a pair of black jeans, a button-down white cotton shirt, and black cowboy boots I found in a boutique shop in Buford. I placed my bounty hunter's badge on a black leather belt and brushed my hair back into a two-twist chignon. I was looking Southern charming and country chic. If I could kick my heels, I would have.

Tiger, however, looked straight up and down South Dekalb. He rolled up in there with a black leather jacket, a blinged out black T-shirt that read BIG BAD BOY, black jeans that hugged his ripped thighs, military boots, and a black beanie on his head. If I didn't know him, I would have run out of the place the moment he stomped in there.

"So . . . dressing like a body double for The Rock is going to warm this Marlo chick over to us?"

"Angel Soft, this isn't my territory. Too many ole Georgia Boys up in here for me to dress soft. I mean business. I want to look like I mean business."

I stepped back. "Fine, Mr. Business. Just lead the way."

I spotted Marlo around the same time she saw me. She was a petite, brunette bob-wearing freckle-faced young lady. She was cute as a button and probably did better in tips than I did on most hunts. Before I could extend my hand toward her, her eyes bulged and her face changed into a crazed banshee. She lifted a large white ceramic boilermaker shaker from the bar and cracked me across my head with it.

I hit the floor. Before I passed out, I heard Tiger's sawed off shotgun cock. The sound of that gun jolted me back to the day Gabe died and why I remembered the detail of that note card.

Seven years ago . . .
The parking garage outside Buffalo Wild Wings Bar &
Grill, Buckhead Atlanta

It had been too cold for March mornings in Atlanta. Fortunately for me, it had also been too wet to do the first part of my assignment covering Filene's Basement's annual Running of the Brides event for the *Atlanta Sentinel*.

The storm had been so torrential that all the bridal teams camped out in their cars instead of clogging the sidewalks like usual. We, Gabe and I, hung back in a parking garage within view of the department store. Actually, we were making out.

Although lightning flashed around us and thunder made the car windows rattle, being with Gabe made me feel safe. I didn't want it to end, but Gabe pulled back from our embrace and scrunched his nose.

"Did lightning strike?" he asked.

Although there was lightning close to where we parked, I knew that smell wasn't lightning striking. Lightning smelled like ozone. This was gunpowder.

My eyes widened at the revelation. I sat up, looked at the rearview window, then shouted, "Gabe, duck!"

The right side of the car shook something furious and a loud crackling sound jolted me forward.

"Get down!" Gabe pushed me onto the floorboard and covered me with his body.

I grunted, then smelled more gun smoke, red Georgia clay, and Gabe's peppermint shampoo. The shampoo smell almost calmed me. However, bullets pelted his Candy Painted Blue Ford 150 like a surprise hailstorm in September. My heart fell to my feet. I grabbed Gabe's chest and screamed.

Something fell out of his jacket, a black note card with the words DO YOU STILL LOVE ME? written in bold white typeface across the back. My eyes bulged at the sight of it.

When I reached down to pick it up, a bullet rocketed through the car and zipped into the backseat. Another one had dropped and I had dropped to the floor along with it.

The medium pitched thunk of Whitney's cell phone hitting the hospital floor brought me back to consciousness, along with more questions about Gabe and who hired Marlo to make that card.

Saturday, 4:00 AM
Emory Johns Creek Hospital, Johns Creek, Georgia

I blinked a few times and let my mind settle on the fact that I was back in the hospital before I let anyone know I was awake.

"Is your phone working?" Ava asked Whitney.

"Yeah, Angel bought me this cool phone guard that protects it from anything," Whitney said.

"How nice," Ava said. "But I wish our sister did a better job at protecting herself."

"Ava, please don't make me hurt you." Whitney scoffed.

"If you do, then she's in the best place to recover." I mumbled. "Don't mean to interrupt, but can someone tell me where my baby is?"

"Mama has her," my sisters both said at the same time.

"How do you feel?" Ava asked.

"Confused. Why am I in a hospital bed and not in the ER?"

"You got into a bar fight and suffered a mild concussion. Since you have a history of getting popped in the head, the doctor on call wanted to keep you in the hospital overnight for further observation," Whitney said.

I tried to sit up, but couldn't. My body lay trapped under bed sheets in a crowded hospital bed, because Ava and Whitney didn't prefer the chairs. Whitney snuggled on top of the sheets beside me and Ava sat at the foot of the bed wagging her red stiletto sling backs.

Although I didn't understand why Marlo had decked me at first sight, I understood my twin sister quite well. That nervous ankle tic was the precursor to a sticky favor request. Unfortunately, whatever it was usually meant another hospital stay for me or worse. I shivered despite the heat.

The last time Ava had asked me for one of those favors was eight months ago, and the result of that was me finding her holding her husband, Devon, dead in her arms, she being accused of his murder, and myself a head-butt away from getting macheted by the real killer. Like I said before . . . that twitch of hers was bad business.

Whitney crawled off the bed, kissed my forehead, and

stepped out of the room to procure some choice treats. She knew I hated hospital food. As the door closed behind her, I waited for Ava to drop the bomb on me.

Ava continued thumbing through a pamphlet, then forced it into my hands. I read the title: GEORGIA STATE BOARD OF PRIVATE DETECTIVES AND SECURITY AGENCIES LICENSING APPLICATION PROCEDURES.

I looked at her and frowned. "Don't start this again."

I had assumed that after I saved Ava from going to jail for Devon's murder a few months ago she would respect my career as a bail recovery agent. I was wrong. Now she thought I would be a better private detective. It had become her new mission and distraction from mourning for Devon.

"You know I'm always concerned about you and the life you've chosen . . ." She patted my arm.

She continued to tell me in the nicest way that she could how she thought that this episode, which landed me in the hospital, was God's way of telling me that I needed to slow down. I threw the pamphlet back at her and reached for my hospital service remote. I needed the nurse ward clerk. It was hot in this room and Ava's overpriced gardenia cologne clashed with the smell of recycled, hospital bleach water.

"This license would legitimize your company far better than that other thing you do." Ava scrunched her nose at "that other thing," as if it were the thing stinking up my room.

"But 'that other thing' kept you from going to jail. . . ." I rolled my neck in self-satisfaction. "Besides, what just happened was a fluke. It happens to the best of them. But it's okay. I will make it up to her when I catch her."

"You're incorrigible." She stood up and straightened her skirt suit with a hard tug.

"It's not the first time someone called me that and it won't be the last."

"That's a sad way to be," she said.

"I don't care."

"Yes, you do, especially when it comes to Bella. She's begun kindergarten. She's going to meet friends. Their parents are going to want to know you, but all they have to go on is what they see on television or read in your old paper, because you can't participate in PTA because you spent all night on a stakeout in some seedy hotel."

"I'll have you know that I attended Doughnuts for Dads yesterday." I licked my tongue at her.

Ava shook her head. "Oh, brother. . . . Why am I not surprised?"

"There were other mothers in attendance, too, so what's the problem?"

"The problem is you. Look at you, Evangeline Grace Crawford." She pointed at me.

It must have been serious, since she used my full name. I reached for the mirror and slowly raised it toward my face. My head had a skid mark that ran between my temple and my cowlick.

I dropped the mirror in my lap and gasped. "What happened to my hair?"

"Stitches. Your assailant put a gash in your head. The attending physician had to shave a patch of hair off your head in order to stitch the wound," Ava said.

"I look horrible!"

"He was thoughtful. It could have been worse, but don't worry about your hair. I've already made an appointment with Halle for an early salon visit. She'll give you a fresh new haircut, while Whitney and I deal with Bella's slumber party."

"I think you'll look real cute with a pixie hair cut." Whitney slid back inside the room.

"I agree." Ava sat down beside me and placed the brochure in my hand again. "It would be befitting: a new do for a new you."

"It wouldn't hurt to get some continuing education," I mumbled. "This could apply to my state renewal anyway."

"So you're going to do it?" Ava asked.

"I haven't agreed to it yet. But I've been thinking about doing some skip tracing work for some attorneys. I could charge a higher fee with the certification."

Ava almost hopped into my lap and hugged me. "I'm so happy we finally see eye to eye!"

I searched for Whitney's face. She was balled up on the hospital floor laughing. I didn't find Ava funny at all.

"Remember, I didn't agree to this just yet." I still needed to chat with Tiger about what happened. "By the way, where's Tiger?"

"He's outside." Whitney looked at Ava then at me. ". . . raising Hell."

5

"Let me tell you what you gon' do," Tiger shouted to someone through his earpiece while using his hands to text someone else.

He stood outside my hospital room door just like Whitney and Ava said. However, they didn't tell me that he was out there terrorizing the triage nurses, too. His strong voice boomed through the air like the sound of thunder rattling my bedroom windows or what an oak tree sounded like once lightning split it in half. Crisp, hard edged, powerful, and dangerous—with a twinge of Southern ghetto—was what Tiger sounded like with my eyes closed. I tried to get his attention, to get him to whisper, but he was in his zone.

"You gon' bring me my money or you're going to bring me my money. However you dissect that, take it apart, put it back together, and formulate it, what I just said had better come out to fifty thou wows in my hands. You got me? Or you can save yourself the headache and give me Torrance. Let him be a man for once. How else is he going to grow up?"

I thought about what Tiger had just said and felt guilty. At the rate I was going, I wouldn't see Bella graduate kindergarten, let alone grow up. This Marlo chick had me twisted. I felt dizzy.

"Bet." Tiger nodded. "Bet. We can do that. Tell me when and where. Just don't play me. Don't make me send my boys after you. They don't care that we're cousins."

I got tired of waiting. I got out of bed and tapped his shoulder. "So, are you going to continue terrorizing your cousin or did you come to see me?"

"Who said I was coming to see you?" He turned around and smiled.

"Don't think that because Marlo caught me off guard that I'll let you get the best of my twin sister."

"The best deserves the best, Angel Soft."

I tried to playfully swing at his jaw, but stumbled back mid-swing. He slid his phone into his black leather jacket, scooped me up, and carried me back to my medical cot.

Ava gasped. "Let me call the nurse."

"I'm all right," I mumbled. "The medicine has me a little groggy."

"If that's the case, then you need to sit yourself down and stay down," he said.

I could tell by the hesitation in Tiger's voice when he spoke that he was working hard not to curse in front of Ava.

I giggled at him and turned away. "Stop being ridiculous."

He grinned. "Ladies, I need a minute alone with my friend before the docs kick her out."

If Tiger wasn't such a bad boy, I would have snuck him a kiss years ago. A man like Tiger, of course, was a fine, tall, long, thick bowlegged hottie, the color of homemade chocolate icing. He wasn't bald, but kept a shadow of fuzz on the top of his head, around his contoured nape and goatee that gave his look some swagger. He oozed the urban coolness of a Decatur man and held a mischievous grin that could made you change your life's compass if you were not careful. It was a good thing his old torch for me had diverted its attention to Ava. I wasn't built for love triangles.

"What's this about, Tiger?" I said, while gathering my things.

"Stay down." He grunted. "You do too much and it's my fault. I push you too hard."

"You push me?" I scoffed and leaned back against my pillow. "Like I said before, you're being ridiculous."

"No, I'm not. I was ridiculous when I didn't listen to you earlier about waiting to visit Marlo. . . ." He sat down beside me.

Thank goodness the bed wheels were locked. His 6'3" muscular body would have catapulted me toward a wall.

"I messed up, baby girl."

"It's spilled milk, Tiger." I patted his massive back. "After I get my hair done and Bella birthday fabulous, we'll talk and regroup. Obviously, we're on the right road now."

"No, that's what I'm telling you. The road is closed. There is no road. We're done. And as much as I hate to say this, you have a date with Reverend Romance tonight. Yeah, Ava told me that, too. That's what you need to focus on." He brushed past my bald patch with his hand. "First, take care of the baby, then this head needs to be priority numero dos. When was the last time you took a vacation?"

"Vacation? You're crazy if you think I'm not hunting this Marlo girl down and beating the truth out of her the first chance I get."

"Stop it," he said. "Stop it right now, Angel."

"No. . . ." I jerked away from him and stood. "You can't make me!"

He grabbed my arms and lifted me back onto the bed. I kicked my legs in defiance. He held them down with his hands. They felt like grips. I couldn't move below my knee.

I huffed. "Let me go."

"Not until you listen and listen good." His eyes were red. He was tired and tired of me. "You're taking a vacation, as of now. I'll pay you to stay home, rest, spend time with Bella, or go to that PI class that Ava has set up for you."

"Wow, you're talking to Ava way too much." I frowned. "She's not going to be your woman. You do know that. Right?"

"I'm serious, Angel. There's nothing wrong with taking a break."

"What are you talking about? I can't take a break after what just happened. Would you?"

"Nothing happened, not like what you think."

"There's nothing you can say that will change my mind. I know what I saw."

"Why don't you listen?" He cursed and pulled his beanie off his head. "Look, I didn't want to tell you this because I'm pissed about the whole thing and now I have to do something I swore I would never do again. . . . I'm gonna tell you the truth about what happened last night so that you can leave the Gabe nonsense in this room and you can take this vacation in peace."

"I know the truth and I'm not taking a vacation." I crossed my arms over my chest.

"After Marlo cracked your head, my rifle made her spill her guts," he said. "She didn't know anything about a Gabriel Hwang."

"Then who sent it?" I asked.

"Riddick." He shook his head and mumbled something.

Riddick Avery was another independent bail recovery agent, who worked with Tiger. He owned A1 Recovery Agents and mainly worked the far northern counties in the Atlanta area. I didn't think much of him.

"That doesn't make sense for him to do that, Tiger."

"It is, if you're competition." He lowered his head and

sighed. "Riddick doesn't like the fact that you became a local celebrity after what you did for Ava. You've been stealing his thunder."

"But I only work for you, Tiger."

"He works for me, too, but that's not the point." Tiger said. "He's been pitching a television show to one of those cable networks. Rumor has it the network was more interested in you, because they kept reading about you in the paper."

"Is the title of the show 'Do you Still Love Me?'?"

"How do you know?" He wrinkled his nose. "It's the stupidest thing I've ever heard. The show is supposed to be about how he convinces skips' loved ones, you know their girlfriends, baby mamas, and mothers, to give them up. Like he's some kind of Convict Whisperer."

"Real dumb, just like Riddick." I chuckled. "So instead of pulling more skips off the streets, so he could get in the paper, he decides to send me roses and a stalker photo?"

"No, I think he was congratulating you on getting Ava off that murder charge and also thanking you for being so distracted with her case that you dropped the ball on the bounty hunting."

I shook my head "I still don't believe it. He needs to tell me that crap to my face."

"I don't know where Riddick is, but you can ask Marlo. She'll be spending the weekend in the piss chamber at the Dunwoody Jail. Let it go and move on with your life." He stood up and reached for my bag. A nurse stood at the door with a wheelchair. "And let's get out of here before the doc changes his mind and admits you for being a hardhead."

"Where are the girls?"

"Your sisters are waiting for you outside. Ava's taking you home with her, because Whitney has bridesmaid duties."

"Yeah, Lana's having a bridesmaid brunch today."

"Whew, there's a lot to do today."

"Right." He huffed. "It's too big a day to be dealing with foolishness."

"I agree, but I am going to see Marlo this morning. I need to end this today."

"And how will you do that? Ava's not letting you out of her sight."

"My head might be bruised, but I still can outsmart her."

6

Who would have thought it would be hard sneaking out of a mansion? After all, it was ginormous. Yet I couldn't, because my sisters had a nosy nose like our mother.

I had carefully made Ava's guest bed without making a peep, which was a feat in itself. The white queen-sized canopy had a heavy, white duvet that was a nightmare to lay down quietly. But I did it. Just because I was sneaking out for a few hours didn't mean I would leave the room messy.

I didn't shower, because the sound of the water would tip them off. But I should have. There was a blood stain on my white shirt.

The trouble came when I couldn't find my car keys. Ava had driven me here, but Whitney had driven my car here, since she and Ava had come together to retrieve me at Johns Creek. However, the keys weren't in the guest room Whitney slept in. They weren't in her purse, on the nightstand, in the bathroom, or on a key rack in the garage. I stood in the garage dumbfounded.

"I knew you would try to leave without telling us."

Mama's voice made me back into Ava's Maybach. I had to

keep myself from flipping over its hood. Nonetheless I lost my footing and stumbled into the rack. A few keys fell on my head.

Ouch! I caressed my head. The scarf Ava had given me to cover my jacked-up head now covered my face. Mama slid it off. The expression on her face made me pull the scarf out of her hands and put it back on my face.

She snatched it, then grabbed my ear. "Cut it out."

Let me tell you something . . . the ear pinch hurt worse as an adult. I quailed on my knees and stood up on wobbly legs.

"Mama?!" I groaned.

"Don't 'Mama' me. You were about to get into more trouble, weren't you?"

Mom, like my twin Ava, was beautiful, privileged, and in some weird way, entitled. Dad had thought her Southern-belle-gone-persnickety personality had to do with the fact that she looked like movie legend Diahann Carroll. Same petite form, high cheekbones, penchant to wear kitten heels even in winter, caramel skin, feline-shaped eyes, and a sophisticated golden coif created to spotlight the expensive jewelry around her neck and on her ears or a church hat big enough to sail in Lake Lanier. Don't get me wrong. My mom had her bad days, but she always had the company of a good man to carry her through them.

She had married and buried two ministers before she wed my new step daddy, El Capitan (my nickname for him). She thought it would be disrespectful if she didn't introduce herself as "Mrs. Crawford Curtis Carter, widow of Bishop B.T. Crawford of Calvary United Church of Valdosta, Georgia, widow of Reverend Dr. Augustus Curtis of Piney Grove Community Church of Lithonia, Georgia, and now wife of retired Fulton County Chief of Police, Carrolton Taylor Carter." I thought she placed too much of her identity on who her husbands were. But then again, back then—and even now to a certain extent—wives made good men greater. So I guessed she had the right to let the world know that she was the wind that blew their sails.

"I didn't get into trouble last night. My attacker did and that's why she is in jail," I said.

Mom squinted at me and pursed her lips. She had her arms folded over her chest, with one hand—the one revealing her gaudy wedding ring and band—propping up her chin. "Is that where you were going . . . to see that woman in jail?"

I nodded. I had enough good sense to not lie to my mom. She frowned. "Looking like that?"

"No." I felt my lower lip protrude. I was pouting. "I was going home to get cleaned up first. My shirt's all bloody."

"Ava has clothes you can wear."

"We don't share the same taste in clothes."

"Are you aware that your daughter is sleeping upstairs, anticipating her *grande soirée pyjama?*"

"Did I miss the memo when we begin speaking French?"

She slapped the back of my head with that ringed hand. "Did you get it? I just sent it."

I wanted to roll my eyes, but I was afraid she would slap me, pinch my ear, or something worse, so I stood still. "Yes, ma'am."

"Now that we've cleared the air . . ." She sighed and flattened her beige silk blouse.

The blouse had a huge bow that wasn't big enough to hide the pearl choker around her neck. I looked down to see her black pencil skirt, fishnet stockings, and black suede Mary Jane pumps. She was dressed way too affluently for a child's sleepover. Something was up.

"I'm going to take you to see this idiot woman," Mom said.

I perked up. I'm pretty sure my eyes were bulging out of their sockets. "You're what?"

"You heard me." She looked around the garage, then back to me. "I knew you before you were born, Evangeline

Grace Crawford. When your mind is set on something, you will scorch the earth until you get it. Today is not the day for that kind of foolishness. Don't you agree?"

I nodded.

"I'm going to take you to see this crazy woman and maybe wrap my hands around her neck, if I can get that close. Then once you're done, you have a standing appointment at Halle-Do-Ya Spa & Salon. That hair will do fine at jail, but not another minute in my presence. And then . . . I'm taking you shopping. You have a date with the best man this side of happy and I don't want you to screw it up."

"Okay, but, um . . . when will I get my car keys back?"

"Do you want me to wring your neck this morning?" Her eyes blazed.

She stepped forward; I cowered back.

Mom grinned and then revealed my keys. They'd been in her other hand the entire time. "You'll get them when I give them to you. Now let's go before everyone wakes up. JJ's been waiting outside in this cold for at least ten minutes."

"Yes, ma'am." I chuckled and let her lead the way.

Saturday, 9:15 AM
Dunwoody Detention Center, Dunwoody, Georgia

Since Johns Creek was a newly incorporated city, inmates were housed at the city of Dunwoody Jail. It was about a half hour drive from the McMansion when you were riding in style.

Mom's Cadillac rode so well I couldn't feel the tires kiss the road. Jean Jacques, her driver, was a Haitian transplant from New York. He'd been a part of the family for at least ten years. I think Mom hired him so she could practice her French. I liked JJ, although he rarely smiled.

I had him chauffeur us to the back side of the jail. It was where the bail recovery agents brought in skips. I knew prison visitation didn't start until ten o'clock and there was no way that Marlo would have me down on her approved visitor's list. To be honest, I didn't think she would be admitted into the population. If she had an affiliation with A1 Recovery Agents, they would more than likely be back here preparing to take her out in their custody. I hoped I had beaten them to the punch.

I turned to Mama. "This is the part of today's story where you stay in the car with JJ."

JJ nodded.

"That's not the plan." Mom shook her head. "I'm going. My mind's made up."

"All right. Come on," I grumbled.

JJ opened our door, then whispered to me. "Do you need my gun?"

I stuck out my hand and slid his pistol underneath my shirt and placed it into the holster strap I kept in the back of my jeans. "Mesi."

"You're welcome." He still didn't smile.

I tightened the silk scarf around my head as Mom and I approached the back door to the jail. I wasn't shocked to see Marlo and Riddick Avery, the owner of A1 Recovery Agents, walking out. Riddick looked like the textbook definition of a bounty hunter. I had heard rumors that he ran with the U.S. marshals. He was rugged, white, blond, wore a ten-gallon hat, and had blue eyes that cut a hole through you, depending on the way he looked at you. He had women lined up to try out his handcuffs on their bedrails all over this state. Bad men here were often pretty.

Riddick pushed Marlo behind him. "What are you doing here, Angel?"

"Why are you trying to scare my baby, Mr. Avery?" Mama asked.

My eyes finally rolled in embarrassment.

His brows wrinkled as he observed my mom, then he smiled. "Angel, is this your mom?"

"Yes, it is. So obviously I didn't come here to start any trouble."

"Fair enough . . ." He sucked his teeth, looked at Marlo, then back at me. "But I'm the one you need to be talking to, not her. She only did what I asked her to do."

"You asked her to hit my daughter on the head?"

"My apologies, ma'am. Now, that was a mistake. Marlo got worked up when Big Tiger showed up. She's not accustomed to guys that look like that over here." He turned to me. "You understand?"

"Nope, not so sure," I said. "If Tiger wasn't here? What were you going to do to me?"

"Nothing, I didn't know you would be searching for Marlo about the lovely roses I sent. If anything, I was expecting a 'you're welcome' from you."

"I would have, if you would've put your name on the card, but you didn't. I think you did that on purpose. You were trying to scare me."

"Scare you?" He folded his arms over his chest and pursed his lips. "It was a picture of you and Bella on my note card. What's scary about that?"

"You know what I'm talking about. I'm talking about Gabriel Hwang."

"Bella's father?" He looked at me then at Mom. "Am I missing something here? What does he have to do with this?"

I huffed, but Mom touched my shoulder before I could go off.

She stepped forward. "Angel took your gift the wrong way. She's had a lot on her plate lately. Wouldn't you agree?"

"I didn't mean to ruffle your feathers like that, Angel." He had a genuine look of concern on his face. "But you have to wonder whether or not you're cut out for this line of work."

"What does that supposed to mean?" I asked.

"You've always had a problem with boundaries. That's really why you're not a reporter anymore. The sooner you realize you can't do everything, the better off you'll be."

"So I shouldn't pitch my own television show to some of my former media peers?"

"Tiger can't keep his mouth closed to save his life." He grinned.

"He was sticking up for you, but I don't care what he says. I don't like you."

"Angel, darling, you don't need to like me, but you do need to mind your business. You have the Chocolate cities. There are more than enough criminals there for you. But this is my territory. North Fulton and people like Cesar Cruz aren't meant for someone like you. So since we're on the subject, back off, because Tiger isn't paying you to bring him in."

"He will if I bring him in first. In fact, lately I'm bringing them in faster than you. Perhaps this isn't the place for someone like you anymore," I said. "Step into the twenty-first century with the rest of the world."

He frowned. "You shouldn't have brought Tiger."

"You should have signed the card like normal people do."

"That was my fault." Marlo interrupted. "I forgot to include it on the card."

"Okay, well now that that is settled. It sounds like miscommunication, because of the business rivalry between you two," Mom said.

"Exactly, Ma'am," Riddick said. "And again I apologize for what happened."

"And I'm suing your ass for the medical bills," I said to Riddick and then turned to Marlo. "And as for you . . . I don't know you, but I now know what you look like. I won't hurt you like I want to, because my mom is here and we're standing outside the jail, but one day we'll cross paths again and you're mine. Come on, Mama, let's go."

Mom and I turned around and began walking back to her car.

"Is that it?" Riddick yelled from behind. "You didn't come here for playground mediation. You want to know how I know about you and Gabe Hwang."

I stopped; Mom caught my arm. "Keep walking."

I whispered, "I can't."

"Let the dead bury the dead and move on. If he was alive, you wouldn't be raising Bella on your own."

There was truth in what she said. Gabe wouldn't do that to me.

After all, Riddick had just admitted he didn't want me hunting Cesar Cruz. The only way he could have known I was searching for Cesar was from Rosary, though. I shook my head. He must have bailed her out for a favor. Dang, he got my snitch. I hated how cutthroat bail recovery could get sometimes.

I squeezed Mom's hand and began walking again.

On the drive to Halle's, Mom touched my arm with one hand and wiped her eyes with a hankie with the other. "Angel, I have to say . . ."

"You don't have to say it." I stopped her.

"Oh, but I do. It's important."

I smiled. "Mom, I thought about what you said and agreed. I've been holding on too tight. It's time that I let Gabe go."

"Well, that's good, but that isn't what I was about to say." She removed the hankie, looked down at my clothes, and sniffed. "You need a shower before we do anything else."

7

Mom lived well. It wasn't just the affluence. There were plenty of people in Atlanta with money. However, the way Mom maneuvered through the city, her daily routine, the places she would go, and the people she knew were always world class. Taking a hot shower in Renew exemplified the fabulosity of Mom's life.

From the outside, Renew looked like an old white and brick Victorian doctor's office. Inside, however, it was text-book bliss: an actual waterfall instead of a hippy soundtrack; quiet staff with genuine smiles; genteel blue and white magnolia interior; cucumber water; cheese and crackers; hot stone massage; rose-scented body cream; and Vichy showers with lavender body wash.

After I toweled off and sniffed my delicious-smelling skin with great satisfaction for the thousandth time, I put on a robe and shuffled my feet in terry shower slippers to my locker room. I couldn't find Mom or my clothes. There was a note on the wooden bench in front of me with a tray of more fruit and cheese. I sat down, nibbled, and read it.

Megan at the front desk sent your clothes to the cleaners. They'll be delivered to my house next week once they remove those stains from your shirt. Apparently, blood splatter was everywhere. Megan has a new outfit for you. Join us in the lobby. Mom.

"Us?" I peeked around my locker. "Who else is here?"

I opened the locker to see what Megan had for me and then gasped. There was a gold metallic doctor's bag. It contained a bounty of lip glosses, blushes, and love potions. There were a few wrinkle free floral rompers I assumed were just my size, a matching head scarf, and some golden sling back kitten heels to round out the I-would-never-be-caught-dead-in-this look.

I put it on.

When I walked out to greet Mom and Megan, I saw Whitney stuffing rolled turkey on toothpicks into her mouth.

"What are you doing here?" I asked.

Whitney looked at me, her eyes widened, and she almost spat out her food. She swallowed, then laughed. "I'm here with Lana and the bridesmaids. . . ."

Whitney had befriended my old college mentor, U.S. Congresswoman of the Great State of Georgia, the Honorable Elaine Turner's only daughter, Lana. All the bridal hoopla events Whitney had been attending were for Lana. I assumed this was another event.

"What's so funny?" I frowned.

"You look like Ava, except for that missing patch of hair." I touched my head and realized I forgot to put that scarf back on my head.

"Say that again and we're not sisters."

"Not saying what's on my mind has never been my thing. You know that," she said.

"It needs to be, if you intend to get married," Mom said

to Whitney, then she looked at the both of us. "Let's go. I'm treating everyone to brunch and then Angel has a meeting with a haircut."

Whitney nudged me. "What kind of haircut are you getting?"

I shook my head. "Whatever makes me not look like Ava."

Whitney giggled.

"Angel, you could paint yourself blue, but you and Ava will always be lonesome doves until you find a way to forgive each other." Mama eyeballed us both, then sauntered toward the lobby. "Ladies, let's go . . . joie de vivre this Saturday."

"Lonesome doves? What is that supposed to mean?" I asked, ignoring her nod to French again.

Whitney's nose wrinkled. She threw up her hands. "I don't pay Mama much attention, especially when she's talking Old South."

"You and me both." I smiled at Whitney. "Tell Mom I'm coming. I need to call Bella first. Where are we going for brunch, by the way?"

"Douceur de France."

"Lord have mercy. She got you speaking French, too?" I chuckled, then pulled out my phone and began to dial. "Since we're going there I might as well pick up some petit fours for Bella's sleepover."

Ava picked up on the first ring. "Hey, Mommy!"

It was Bella's voice. I was caught off guard.

"Hey! Did your auntie hand you the phone when I called?"

Bella said nothing.

"Are you nodding? If so, say yes."

"Yes, Mommy."

I chuckled. "Grandma and Aunt Whitney are with me. We're going to bring you a great surprise for your birthday party."

"Cool," she said. Her high-pitched voice tickled my ears. "Aunt Ava needs to speak to you, Mommy. I love youuuu."

"I love you, too," I said.

"You have a funny way of showing it, by sneaking out the house this morning." Now Ava's voice was on the line.

"Ava, I needed to get some things done before my hair appointment."

"And that's why I called Mom after we left the ER. I knew you would need some help."

I frowned. "You called her?"

"She was coming over anyway and I needed her busy."

"No, you wanted her off your back, so you used me."

"Same difference. You know how she can get," she said. The tone in her voice was matter of fact. I didn't like it when she sounded cold like this. She was hiding something.

"I do, but you won't believe that she has been very motherish today, not the glam diva who rules with an iron fist that we know and fear so well."

"Wow." She chuckled. "Prayer does work."

"It does, but is it working on you?" I asked.

"What do you mean?"

"Ava, we're twins. I know your tics just like you know mine. What gives?"

She sighed. "Tiger has been here three times looking for you. He said he's been calling, but you haven't answered your phone. He's pissed."

Ava never said "pissed." It was against her religion. This had to be bad.

"I'll call him. Thanks for telling me."

"No offense, Angel, but what did you get yourself into this morning?"

"Nothing I can't fix." I checked my watch. This conversation had gone on too long. I began to race-walk out of the spa. "Anyway . . . kiss my baby for me. I don't know how long Mama will keep me as her Prisoner of Beauty."

8

Saturday, 11:30 AM
Douceur de France, Marietta, Georgia

Douceur de France sat around the corner from DuPre's Antique Market in Marietta in the shopping center that used to house Kirk's Supermarket. The building had been painted powdered-sugar white and navy blue. It was very clean, minimalist, and chic. Now, the Marietta loop didn't look so Southern, but like a snapshot of Paris. The outside café tables further enhanced the ambience. However, it was too cold in March to be having brunch outside.

We went inside and it looked like puff pastry palace: éclairs, Napoleons, tiramisu, petit fours, just from first glance. My mouth watered at the sight of a huge white chocolate and raspberry sour cream pound cake.

Lana waved us over. She and the rest of the bridal party (three other girls whose names escaped me) had already found two tables for us. Everyone else ordered something with eggs and heavy cream, but I ordered le pain perdu, French toast. However, this breakfast wasn't the kind you stuck in a toaster. No. It was a slice of brioche hand-dipped in crème brûlée butter, then topped with strawberries, bananas, and whipped cream. Ooh la la!

While I enjoyed my meal, Lana touched my shoulder. "Angel, do you want to be a bridesmaid in my wedding?"

Lana was Elaine's only daughter. I had baby-sat her while I was in undergrad. She and Whitney became best friends after that. However, since we'd moved away from the perimeter, I hadn't seen her as much. Now she was getting married. Time flies stupid fast.

I shook my head. My mouth, tongue, and thoughts were all on that French toast. "No."

"But why?" She pouted.

I looked over at her. Fruit syrup dripped from my lip. I stopped chewing. "Because I'm too old to be a bridesmaid."

"You're not old and you definitely don't look it."

"I accept that compliment. Thank you." I wiped my mouth with a handkerchief. "But weddings and I aren't friends."

"Why?" Lana looked from me to Whitney and back. Her blond ponytail bobbed every time she turned.

Whitney chimed in. "For some reason she's always seated by snooty women who flaunt their marital status around her as if she should feel bad for being single."

"Gee, thanks. I need my little sister to defend me . . . er . . . embarrass me," I scoffed.

"I'm sorry, Angel," Lana continued. "But if I make sure you're seated by people more down to earth, would you at least come to the wedding?"

"Is the reception adult only?" I asked.

"It is, but we're having a separate party for the children. Mom's procured a magician, an au pair, puppets, and a live band to keep them entertained. Isabella would have a ball."

Wow. Big money Elaine. "How could I pass that up? Send me an invitation."

Lana clapped using her fingertips. Her blue eyes blazed in

delight. "Should I add a plus one for Reverend Justus Morgan?"

"Put him down," Mom said.

The girls squealed; Mom squealed the loudest. My heart fluttered at the thought of Justus in a tux.

"But if he sees your hair like this, he'll say 'no' for sure," Whitney reminded us.

I threw my hands over my head. "Mama . . ."

"Oh dear. We need to go." Mom threw her napkin on her plate and hopped up. "Let me clear the tab. Girls, you can hang here as long as you like. . . . Whitney, you, too."

Whitney rolled her eyes. "Thank you, Mama."

"Angel, can you join us for The Running of the Brides? It would be fun."

The Running of the Brides or ROTB began in 1947 in Boston when the retailer Filene's decided to host a one-day bridal gown sale. Brides who participated in the event got the chance to purchase designer wedding gowns at a fraction of the cost. So of course the ROTB was a hit. Now the event was a national treasure and sprinkled in stores across the country like Buckhead Atlanta, where Gabe was murdered.

"Oh, nooo." I chuckled dryly. "Besides, since I'm not working this Saturday, I'll have double duty next weekend."

My phone buzzed. I looked down. It was Tiger. A chill ran down my spine.

"Speak of the devil." I stood up. "Ladies, it's been real, but I need to get this."

They waved good-bye. I walked outside to take his call while Mom finished up inside.

I put the phone to my ear. "Hey, Tiger. Look, I know you're mad—"

"Angel, didn't I tell you to leave it alone?" he shouted. "Didn't I tell you it was handled?"

"I heard you, but you know me. I needed to see Marlo. I needed to see myself."

"Yourself? Yourself?!" His voice grew louder. I moved the phone from my ear and put him on speaker instead. "See, that's your problem. You're not a lone wolf. What you say and do affects other people. What you did affected me."

"How did I telling Marlo and Riddick that I was taking them to court hurt you? They hurt me, not you."

"Rid and I got biz together. . . ." He paused. "You almost jacked that up for me today."

My head began to swim a few seconds after his words traveled through me. "What do you mean you work together?"

"Come on, Angel. This is Georgia. There are some places I still can't go unless I bring someone like Riddick in there with me. This is business. Plain and simple."

Rage bubbled inside me. I held onto one of the storefront's white pillars to keep from throwing something. "Did you tell them to do this to me? Is that why you knew what happened?"

"Angel, do you still have a concussion? Why would you ask me something like that? I've had your back when nobody did. I'm the one that dragged you out of that bar without us getting killed, and I'm the one that told you what went down." His voice grew louder after each sentence. "I'm the one who gave you a job when your own sister shamed you in front of the entire city. I'm the one, some seven years later, who is still scouring these dirty streets looking for the person that killed Bella's father."

"Don't you go there. Don't you dare go there! The only reason I went to the Draft House—to have the side of my head sliced, by the way—was because of a phone call you made to ME!"

"Ang!" He said something under his breath then cleared

his throat. "Before you say something more stupid than the last thing you just said, let's take a break and regroup."

"Yes, let's." I huffed.

Mama stepped outside and stood beside me. "What's going on?"

I shook my head as if to say "nothing" and waved her to meet me at the car with JJ. She pointed at her watch and mouthed two minutes.

"Tiger, I think—"

"You need to go on that vacation I suggested yesterday."

I frowned. "Vacation? What are you talking about?"

"You heard me. I need things to settle down on my end and you're going to take that break—at my expense, of course. Take Bella to Disney World or something."

"The kids are about to begin standardized tests soon. No."

"Oh yeah! Do that PI class. This would be good for you. How long is the class?"

"I don't know, one hundred hours."

"Good, take two weeks. If you need a third week, you've earned it. I can give you that."

A three-week vacation? I frowned. There had to be more going on that he wasn't telling me. However, I knew Tiger wasn't sharing. There was more to this Riddick partnership than met the eye.

"What if I say no?" I asked.

"Grace, you do not understand me," he said, using my middle name, something I hadn't heard since my dad was alive. Yep, something was definitely up. "If you don't, then this break will be your contract termination with BT Trusted Bail Bonds. Our contract ends in a few days and I can't lose Rid over this thing with you."

"What?" I screamed. "I haven't done anything wrong, so why am I being punished?"

"You're not . . ." He sighed. "Come on, Angel Soft. You know you're my girl. I'll take care of Rid in my own time, in my own way. But we have to be smart. Remember, this is Georgia. We're not just dealing with convicts, but old demons."

"Don't do this to me, Tiger."

"It's for your own good. I've left your money with Ava. I threw in some extra for the baby's birthday. So you take this break. Get your hair fixed. Become a certified private investigator. I promise I'll renew your contract at the end of the month." And then he hung up.

I stood on the Douceur de France front walk with my mouth gaping open and stared at the phone.

Someone tapped me on my shoulder. I jumped and turned around. It was Lana.

"So does this mean you will be able to go with us to the ROTB?"

She had to be listening to my phone conversation to have made that assumption. She also had to be eating a box of hot rocks, if she thought I was spending my forced vacation playing Wedding Wars.

"No, I have to go," I said without hesitation and then scurried to Mom's car.

9

Saturday, 8:30 PM
Home, Sugar Hill, Georgia

After a long Saturday morning and even longer sitting under the hood at Halle's, I took a nap before Justus rang my bell. He hadn't told me where we would be going, but he had assured me that it would be unforgettable. However, when he stepped inside my house, I didn't want us to leave the room.

Justus took my breath away. Again he brought more roses, but he was more handsome than them. He had cut his locks. His sugarcane syrup–colored eyes warmed me up more than before. His smile dazzled even brighter, now that the hair was not in the way.

"A birdie told me that I needed to compliment your gorgeous haircut."

"You like it?" I rubbed the back of my neck and blushed.

"I love it." He leaned down and kissed my cheek, then my neck, and then my mouth. "Let's get out of here before I get us into trouble."

I nodded, but I didn't want to leave.

Saturday, 9:30 PM
Holeman & Finch Public House, Atlanta, Georgia

"I've been told that we need to get there early if we want to be in the running for the best burger on the planet," Justus said as we pulled into Holeman & Finch Public House.

I nodded and tried to be calm, although I unbuckled my seat belt as fast as I could. I popped the door open, but Justus caught it before my feet hit the pavement. I couldn't get out of Justus's truck fast enough.

Holeman only served twenty-four burgers every night. Although the burger wasn't on the menu, Atlantans piled into Holeman's with the hopes that they would get the gift of eating one of them. Why? Because these weren't your ordinary cheeseburgers so it took a great deal of time to prepare. Two beef patties placed on fresh out the oven buns with pickles, homemade mustard, and Holeman-made ketchup, then surrounded by a bed of—you guessed it—Holeman-made mouthwatering fries.

But the special burger wasn't the only thing that made Holeman & Finch one of the most beloved spots in the state. The food was stupid good. They made everything taste like it was black-market criminal: fish and chips, braised pork and collard greens, cheese grits, pâté, and bacon caramel popcorn that made you almost lose your religion, and fried apple pie, and that's just a sample of what they offered.

It also had a vibe that was part British, part Greek, part soul food . . .

But what I loved more than anything was the pickled banana peppers. They reminded me of the jarred peppers Aunt Frankie had made every summer when Ava and I were children. I had had to keep myself from drooling through the entire drive into Atlanta. It was a good thing I wore foodie jeans.

Justus widened the door and smirked. "I'm beginning to

wonder whether you agreed to this date because of the burger instead of me."

"A woman is strongly attracted to confidence and charm, just like that texted invitation, not a cheeseburger." I cupped his chiseled jaw with my hands.

His eyes lit up. "Woman, you'll say anything to get into this restaurant."

The way he looked at me melted me. I couldn't turn off my feelings for him if I tried, but I wasn't ready for anything more than that. I didn't want to be in love again. I was still reaping the misfortune of the last great love of my life.

"Not anything." I removed my hands. "Trust and know I'm glad I'm here with you."

"Good, because I've been waiting for this night since I picked you up from Dekalb Medical."

He was referring to the first day we'd officially met. Whitney had asked him to pick me up from the hospital, but apparently I'd picked him up before we got home.

I blushed. "I knew my tattered peach cocktail dress messed you up."

"No, running all over Atlanta with you for the five days afterward messed me up." He opened the gastro pub's door for me.

We laughed and flirted with each other on the way to our table and during appetizers until a chef came from out the kitchen blowing a bullhorn and yelling, "It's burger time!"

When the burgers came, all chatting went out the window. It was nothing but the burger and a few crush-worthy glances. I was having the time of my life.

Our hostess came to our table, but said nothing. I looked up then at Justus. His brow wrinkled.

He wiped his mouth with his napkin and spoke to the young woman. "Is something wrong?"

"I don't mean to disturb you two, but I wanted to let you know that your bill has been paid."

"By whom?" Justus and I asked in unison.

"The gentleman didn't want to disturb your dinner, but he did say that he wanted Miss Crawford to know that he was glad she was feeling better," she said.

"Did this person leave a name?" I asked.

"Yes, Riddick Avery."

"Are you serious? Where is he?" I stood up. "We don't want it. Take it off, please."

"Ma'am, I can't do that. The bill has been paid," she said.

"What's going on?" Justus asked. "Who's Riddick Avery?"

"He's the reason I got this haircut and am on forced vacation," I huffed. "And now he's ruined my night."

Justus reached over and took my hand in his. "Evangeline Crawford, would you please give me tonight?"

I stopped searching Holeman's and looked at him. His eyes were on me. A hot flash ran through me again.

I sat down slowly. "I'm yours."

"No, you're not, not like I want you to be." He grinned.

I lowered my head. "You have got to stop talking to me like that."

"You started it with that haircut."

I shook my head. "It's hard to complete a thought when you're so close to me."

"So what do you do when I offer Communion?"

I gulped. "I pray harder."

He laughed. "That explains so much."

"Well, do you have any more questions? Because I'm giving you tonight to ask away, only under one condition."

"What's that?"

"I want some hot apple pie and crème brûlée for dessert without a sarcastic smirk." I shrugged. "Tonight's my last night of eating whatever before I begin PI training."

"Whatever you want, but I need to let you know that I wasn't going to say anything." He waved the hostess back to the table. "I just want to make you happy."

The hostess returned.

"I would like to order and pay for dessert before another of my date's admirers or enemies beats me to it." Justus pulled out his wallet.

I couldn't help but laugh at that. We enjoyed the crème brûlée, but decided to take our pie and eat it somewhere else. Justus had another surprise.

10

Sunday, midnight
Hartsfield-Jackson Atlanta International Airport, Atlanta,
Georgia

Justus wanted to take a drive to the airport to watch the planes come in. He took us to the roof of the South Parking Garage Deck of Hartsfield-Jackson airport. He paid a parking fee to the attendant and found a place away from the other plane watchers and photographers. He then opened my door and escorted me to the back of his truck. The air up here was cool, but there was little wind. Novembers were always warmer than mid-March for some odd reason. I didn't have to wear my gloves, but I needed my jacket and scarf.

Justus flipped open the back truck door and reached for a large blue plastic bin. I peeked inside. There were two blankets, a thermos, a picnic basket, and a Bible.

I smiled. "Wow. So you planned this?"

"I was hoping." He pulled out one blanket and draped the back floor of the truck. "Did you bring the pie?"

I raised the Holeman & Finch's pastry box up in my hand. "Dessert Part Deux."

We sat down on the truck bed beside each other. He

poured hot chocolate into ceramic mugs out of the picnic basket and draped the other blanket across my legs. I watched him and imagined myself being cared for like this every day. Gabe had been romantic, vibrant, and intelligent, but Justus, he was all that and something I didn't think I'd wanted until now. He was a family man.

"Can I ask you some questions that I've been wanting to ask you since I first learned that you were a bounty hunter?" he asked.

"As long as I get to ask you a few questions I've been dying to ask later on," I said.

"Fair enough." He nodded.

"How did you get into bounty hunting?" Justus asked.

"It's a weird story. Hard to believe, really . . ."

"Let me be the judge of that."

"I was pregnant and distraught and unemployed." I sipped some hot chocolate. "If I had known I was pregnant before I let my big ego call the shots, I wouldn't have resigned from *The Sentinel*."

"Why did you quit in the first place?"

"I became angry after Gabe died. I blamed them for everything that had gone wrong for me at the time."

"You never fully told me how Bella's father died. What happened?"

My stomach churned, but as I observed Justus, I knew that spilling this out would be okay. I could trust him. The only trouble was my heart was still too bruised.

I exhaled. "Justus, what happened is too messy to discuss while watching Delta aircrafts land. I don't want you to think that I am that same person now. Maybe I'll feel up to talking about that later."

"Sure. You can tell me at breakfast," he said.

"Breakfast?" I giggled and noted the time. "You act like there won't be any time for us to see each other again."

"Woman, it took you months to finally go out with me. We'll be married and on our third child before this conversation comes back up."

I spat my cocoa across the truck deck. Some sprayed across his shirt. I gasped.

He looked down at me then.

"I'm sorry." I shrugged. "You caught me off guard."

"You're always on guard, Angel, but I'm not." He wasn't smiling when he said that. He unbuttoned his shirt and revealed a white undershirt. He put the jacket back on, which covered the wife beater. "Tell me what happened. Please . . ."

I gulped. He wasn't going to let this go and he was going to use his gorgeous physique to hypnotize the truth out of my behind. I tried to cover my face with my hands, but couldn't. "Did you have to strip in front of me?"

"That's not what I was trying to do." He touched my arm. "I don't know what I was thinking. I'm sorry. We don't have to go any farther if you don't want to."

Justus's rich honey-colored skin shimmered against the moonlight. I wanted to run my hands along his taut biceps, but he would never know it. I continued as if he had not offended me at all, which he hadn't.

"It was fine, I was visiting Mama D—that's Big Tiger's mother—actually, I was at her place picking up some fried catfish, cheese grits, and hush puppies that would put Holeman & Finch's food to shame. You know she sells soul food on the backside of the BT Trusted Office. The pregnancy made me crave comfort food. . . ." I rambled so fast I couldn't catch myself.

"I was sitting there stuffing my face when Tiger sat down and offered me a job. He had heard from the East Lake grapevine that I was no longer at *The Sentinel*. Said he needed a pregnant woman to hang out with in the lobby of an ob/gyn. Apparently, a nurse was dating some dude who missed his court date. Tiger was hired by another bondsman to bring the guy in. He had learned that the guy always comes through Thursdays to take her to lunch. He offered me $500 to sit inside and let me know when he came in. I did. It was my first job."

"Interesting." Justus chuckled. "So how did you become—"

"The Black Sheep of *The Sentinel* and, if I'm not careful, the Jezebel of Sugar Hill Community Church?"

He caught one of my arms. "Stop it. You're fine. Like a local legend. Is what I meant."

"Oh that . . ." I sat back. He released my arm. I slid my hands into my lap. "Well, I quickly learned that resigning from a job without having another one isn't a great move, especially when you're pregnant and don't know it. I had money saved, but like I said I had a baby to prepare for. The money needed for her well-being I wasn't expecting, nor accounted for, and Gabe was dead."

"But there were other things you could have done besides bounty hunting."

"Of course there were. I could have been a college professor, switched to magazine journalism, public relations, something prettier." I looked around the deck. It seemed like everyone was hanging onto our every word, so I lowered my voice. "I wanted something different. I wanted to sink myself into something that would allow me to live on my own terms while doing it. I didn't want a baby-sitter. I wanted independence."

"Which is ironic since you send people back to jail," Justus reminded me.

"Let me just preface this by saying I'm not a fan of our criminal justice system. We bond criminals out, then pay me to put them back in. It's an oxymoron."

He nodded. "Appears that way."

"But you know what I've learned? Everything was one big oxymoron. Take my job at *The Sentinel*, for instance. As long as I didn't investigate and uncover dirty things about them or their key advertiser, they lauded me. But when I did my job—even if that meant turning the tables on them—I had to resign."

"They made you leave?" he asked.

"No, I left on my own. My conscience wouldn't let me stay there." I smiled, yet felt sad. "I once loved my job. I once thought I was my job, like you think you are."

"It's not the same." He shook his head.

"Yes, it is. You're a minister 24-7. Every decision you make is based on your duty to the church. I did the same thing. Truth and sharing that truth ran through my veins, just like you."

"I see your point, but what happened? What happened that made you change your mind about who you are?"

"They wanted me to turn over my investigation of Big Faith." I sipped some chocolate.

Big Faith was my nickname for Ava's church, Greater Atlanta Faith. Justus didn't care for the nickname, because he thought I was being judgmental of mega churches. Before Devon died I was, but now I championed the church. If I wasn't a member of Sugar Hill, I would have returned to the fold.

"During that time I had contracted Gabe to decode cooked books from a CPA's office that worked for a lot of mega churches. He was very good at that sort of thing. Anyway, Big Faith was one of the churches we were looking into. However, we couldn't find anything on that church."

Elvis Bloom, Devon's murderer, had later confessed that he was siphoning money out of Big Faith's foundation fund. I'm sure Gabe would have found him out, if he wasn't murdered shortly after I killed the story.

"*The Sentinel* thought I was protecting Ava and I was. She and Devon weren't stealing from their church and we couldn't prove who was at the time. Gabe died shortly after that. I felt suspicious about the whole thing and blamed *The Sentinel*. They tried to make me believe that Gabe was a part of some crime ring and deserved what he got. I quit. I needed to clear his name."

Justus picked at his pie. "And how do you plan to do that?"

"I've been poking around things for a few years."

"Is that what this trouble between you and Tiger and this Riddick guy is about?"

"No. That's about being stabbed in the back by your friend." I sighed.

"What? Cat got your tongue?" he asked.

"I don't want you blaming me for what's been going on. Believe me, I blame myself. I can't prove it yet, but I know in my gut that Gabe died protecting me from something bigger than *The Sentinel* and Greater Atlanta. I don't know where to start."

"Can this private investigators class help you with that?"

"I hope so." I nodded. "I'm in the human recovery business. Up until now I've only solved crimes when it affects the people I love."

"Is that why you wouldn't help me last year with my niece? You didn't love me then?"

I grabbed my napkin and placed it over my mouth, then laughed. "Please don't make me spit anything else on you."

"Fair enough. I was expecting you to change the subject anyway."

I blushed. "So what's next?"

"After you admit your feelings for me, then marriage."

I giggled. "No, I mean tonight."

He grinned. His eyes creased in a sultry way that made me swoon. "Breakfast. Or have you forgotten already?"

"No, but I was hoping we'd snuggle together and do some plane spotting for a few."

"Angel, you know we can't do that now." He placed the mugs and linen back into the picnic basket.

"Why not?"

"I can't put you in a position where we both could easily compromise our faith."

My mouth dropped. "Are you kidding me?"

"I'm afraid not." He slid the blanket off my legs.

I shook my head. "You're such a tease."

He stopped. "Beg pardon?"

I hopped off the bed of the truck and landed on something wet. My feet slipped from underneath before I could catch my footing. Justus caught me. He lifted me up in his arms. I gasped. His lips were so close to mine.

"I won't make Gabe's mistake." He panted. His voice was deeper.

I gulped again. "And what was that? To save me?"

He moved closer. I could smell the apple pie from his breath. "Break your heart."

"Can I kiss you now?" My voice was embarrassingly close to a whimper.

Justus smiled, but didn't answer. He carried me to the front passenger door and opened the door with a free hand, which proved to me that he was stronger than I once thought. He lowered me into the truck, fastened my seat belt, then kissed me on my forehead.

I grabbed his face. "One real kiss, please."

"Do you love me or are you still in love with Bella's father?" he asked.

"News flash, Justus. Gabe's dead."

He placed his hand on my heart. "He's not dead in here and I understand that. If you're still mourning him, I need to respect that."

"But—"

He closed my door. The drive back to Sugar Hill was bitter-sweet and loud silence. When he dropped me off, he didn't allow me to linger in his truck. He let me go and I said nothing to stop him. I walked into the kitchen carrying my Holeman & Finch pie container and bag filled with more treats for the house. I popped my box, hoping there was a crumb of pie left, and then I heard a knock on my kitchen window-pane. I didn't jump. I leaped from my stool, unlocked the door, and kissed Justus so hard we both slid onto the floor.

11

Two days after my forced vacation I received a visitor who wasn't Justus or Tiger, or on the agenda my assistant Cathy Blair had made for me. I had just hopped into the shower when I heard three short knocks on the door.

"Who is it?" I leaned out my office shower to see who it could be.

Although I had converted my downstairs guestroom into an office, I spent most of my time in my backyard office. It was a guest cottage nestled in my genealogical garden between Granny's rose garden and the tiny orange tree my Aunt Doe grew for me as a housewarming gift.

From the outside it looked enchanting. However, that was a facade. I used my home office to meet with my non–bail bond clients. It was safe looking. The cottage, not so much. I housed my weapons here. I didn't want Bella to smell them or know that such things existed. Kids smelled Crazy Dangerous faster than adults.

Although the person at the door couldn't see me, I saw them.

"Elaine?" I squinted. "Elaine Turner?!"

"In the flesh," she shouted back, then chuckled. "Put some clothes on and let me in."

I hopped out the shower, gathered myself in my robe, and ran to greet her. I unlocked the door with wet hands, then wiped them on the robe after I realized it.

The Honorable Elaine Turner grabbed my hands and held onto them tightly. I was surprised and ecstatic to see her. It had been six years.

"Evangeline Crawford, look at you." Lana had the same bright blue eyes as her mother. This woman had blazed a trail through Georgia State Court with that stare. "You haven't changed."

"Then you know that I so need you right now." I pulled her into my arms.

We hugged and then I noticed she had not come alone. Her team included her deputy press secretary, another staffer, and a few others, who were more than likely private security detail.

Representatives in Georgia carried their own weapons if they felt threatened, because they didn't want the public to think they were squandering state money on bodyguards. Elaine hated guns. Therefore, she paid out of her own pocket for an executive protective agent to aide her during public events and to ford through her daily death threats.

Last to follow her inside my cottage was her campaign manager, Sean Graham. I paused when he entered and turned to Elaine. Sean was a bull in bear's clothing. If he was in your corner, you were protected. Imagine the opposite of that. One thing I remembered well: If Sean was around, something was about to go down. I respected Sean, but I didn't like him. I especially didn't like his relationship with Riddick Avery.

Elaine and I hugged while the rest of her staff stepped inside.

"Congratulations on the wedding," I whispered.

"Thank you. Lana is elated."

Elaine made her way to my knives display case and observed it. Her eyes were intense. Yet, I couldn't tell if she admired my collection or wondered if I had really fallen off the deep end after I left the *Atlanta Sentinel*.

I stood beside her. "You like?"

"More like I'm perplexed. I wish I wasn't so soft that I couldn't admire the beauty of their craftsmanship. It's the older Southern belle in me I guess." She smiled. "Can't see past the ugliness of violence that these weapons are created for."

"It's not a display case for exhibition, Elaine."

"I know . . ." Her voice trailed off. By the way her mouth was still parted I could tell she had more to say, but only to herself.

She exhaled, then turned toward me. "Please tell me that you haven't taught Bella how to use a machete?"

I chuckled. "Like you, I work hard to make sure my daughter's feet don't trip into danger, including my office and the things that I do in the dark."

She looked at her private security agents. Both were white men who looked like they could moonlight as gladiators if they weren't wearing tailored Brooks Brothers' suits. They were too perfectly all-American for my taste. However, for Ava . . . Any one of these guys could get her out of wearing widow black in a heartbeat.

"You're a good mother, Angel," Elaine said.

"Thanks, but I know you didn't come here to tell me I'm a good mom. You came to ask me for a favor."

She leaned forward. "Is that what your clients call it? A favor?"

I turned my attention to Sean. He didn't say a word, but

his eyes told enough. I hoped Elaine would be more forth-coming.

I looked at her and grinned. "It depends on what that favor is."

I glanced at Sean then rolled my eyes at him. Although he was Elaine's right hand, I wished she would cut him off. He held too many secrets. In the five short years I've been a bail recovery agent for Tiger, Sean's name has come up often as an indemnitor.

Indemnitors, or guarantors, were the people who vouched for the bail. They were our clients. If someone jumped bail, the indemnitor would be responsible for the cost of losing that bail to the courts. The fact that Sean's name kept show-ing up on papers concerned me. Why did he know so many hard-luck people? Why were so many of them skips? And better yet, why was he a friend of Riddick?

I thought about paying Salvador Tinsley a visit to ask him about Sean Graham and my upcoming PI certification class. The Dekalb County detective was with me the day Gabe died, and then almost a year ago, after much reluctance/harassment/warning to put me in jail, he helped me find my brother-in-law Devon's killer. I'm sure he missed me by now. I chuckled to myself. He would be pleased to know I'm on vacation, but salty about the PI class. If I passed this course, that meant I would see more of him. He would be thrilled.

"Lana told me that you'll be attending the wedding and bringing the young man I read about in the papers."

"I hope so," I said.

She clapped softly. Her face beamed with maternal pride. If Lana wasn't her spitting image before, she surely was now.

I squeezed her hand with delight. "I can't believe Lana's old enough to marry!"

"Well, she thinks she is, and to an Atlanta Falcon at that."

Elaine beamed with pride. She was a huge fan of the local NFL franchise. "My girls are women now. Who knows? I may be hearing wedding bells for you in the near future."

My stomach grumbled. I rubbed it and grimaced. "Please don't upset me like that."

"I saw you blush when I mentioned him before. There are more than butterflies fluttering in your heart for him."

I chuckled. "I never kiss and tell."

"You are discreet. I give you that. Speaking of discretion . . ." Elaine cleared her throat. "This is where the favor comes in."

I sat down at my desk. "Okay. Now I'm ready for the ball to drop."

"It's not that serious." She took a seat in the quilted white leather armchair in front of my desk.

"Well, I don't buy that." I smiled.

"Honey, it's true. What I ask of you isn't serious. It's embarrassing, really." She pushed a strand of blond hair from her face to behind her ear, then crossed her legs. "You know my position comes with notoriety. And because of the way the world works nowadays, the media will soon get wind of Lana's wedding, especially since she's marrying a professional athlete."

"I see. You need me to monitor the buzz."

"No, I have Terri, my press secretary, for that." She waved over to the petite redhead with the crisp navy blue suit. Terri waved jazz fingers back.

I nodded at her. "Terri, you're welcome to sit down in the love seat over there."

She nodded, but didn't move. I observed the rest of the lot before I returned my attention to Elaine. My furniture was new, so I didn't know why they wouldn't sit down. I glanced at Sean. His face was buried in his smartphone. Something smelled fishy, but there was no food.

I leaned toward Elaine and whispered. "Why is everyone standing? Is something wrong?"

She sat back and shook her head. "Oh no. They're just doing their jobs. They don't want to get too comfortable. Must stay on their toes."

"I have a workroom in the back. It has tables, chairs, and Wi-Fi. It connects at least six more devices. Maybe your staff would like to work while we chat." I pointed down the hall. "Just don't touch the peach cobbler moonshine. A client pays me with that. . . ."

Elaine crossed her other leg, then made a dry cough. I remembered that cough. It was a sign of disapproval, a tic she tried to hide, but the media had discovered it and had a field day since.

I patted her leg. "My apologies. As you can see, I have all kinds of clients, Elaine, including the ones you don't approve of."

"Of that, I'm sure. And that's exactly why I need you. I need someone who doesn't look like security to keep Lana safe, especially in unsecured public places."

"Like where, exactly?"

"Filene's Basement. You know? The Running of the Brides. It's the last Saturday of this month. Lana and her bridal team are attending. Unfortunately, I can't be there. I have a town hall meeting that day. There are rumors that the governor may hold a special election to fill a state senate seat. I need to talk to my constituents about the implications of this election and to introduce my pick for that slot. The event is too important to postpone."

My back tightened at the words "Filene's Basement." The last time I was there, Gabe had died. Elaine knew this. Why would she put me in this position?

I sat back. "Come on, Elaine. Three weeks' notice?"

"Hear me out. It's not that I put my work before my family. Sometimes the state needs us more." She watched me intently, then changed her gaze toward the framed *Atlanta Sentinel* photo and article about my saving Ava last year. "I know you understand that, and I know that Lana has asked you to join them at Filene's. You said 'no.' I'm asking you to reconsider."

I looked away.

Elaine had been my mentor since undergrad. If it wasn't for her, I never would have gotten my job at the *Atlanta Sentinel*. She introduced me to Gabe. After he died and I quit *The Sentinel,* she invested in my recovery agency when no one understood why I wanted to do this work so badly. She had never refused me. Never. But I wanted to refuse this. I was indeed in a pickle.

"Elaine, your request may be too hard for me. I'm still not over losing him."

She patted my hand. "Oh darling. I know that the location holds bad memories for you, but you can't hide in this house forever and you can't keep finding detours around Filene's or Phipps Plaza. At some point you have to let him go. You've already begun with Justus."

"Don't do that." I slid my hand away from her. "It's not the same, regardless of whomever I'm with. Gabe will always be in my heart."

"Exactly. Don't forget I'm a widow. I see bits and pieces of Chris in Lana every day."

"Yes, I see Gabe in Bella, too."

"We have that great gift of actualizing these great men whenever we need to. That is why you can move on. You can let go of the possibilities you were going to have with him, because you're living the reality of having him always in sweet Bella. Understand?"

There was something about her words that stuck in my chest. I cried.

Elaine stood up and so did I. She outstretched her arms, then wrapped herself around me with the biggest, most sincere hug. I melted until I heard feet shuffling nearby. I looked at our captive audience, to find Sean and Terri peeking through the door. I released Elaine and then wiped my eyes with some hand tissues that sat in a pink eggshell porcelain box on my desk.

"Let me think about it. I'll let you know by the end of the week. Okay?"

Elaine smiled. "That's all I'm asking. Lana would be so pleased."

I eyed Sean. I wanted to speak with him, too. He must have read my mind, because my phone buzzed. I reached for it and read it: STOP BY MY OFFICE NEXT WEDNESDAY REGARDING RIDDICK. I nodded and hoped I hadn't just shaken hands with the devil.

12

Next Monday, 7:30 AM
Home, Sugar Hill, Georgia

"I can't believe I'm saying this, but you've improved in the kitchen," Whitney said between licking her fingers and sopping up honey and the last bits of butter-me-not biscuits on her plate. "You did that, big sis."

Bella giggled.

I smiled at her until I noticed she was missing not just one but her two front teeth.

I gasped. "When did you lose your teeth?"

"At the soiree PJ," Bella said, then hopped up from the table and ran out. She ran back in and slapped a sequined coin purse on the table. "The tooth fairy left me lots of money and a sparkly purse under my pillow. It's to carry my tooth money in."

"It's very pretty, but it's almost time to go. Get your coat," I said with a smile. Deep down, I was pissed off. Why was I just now hearing about this?

"Oh yeah. I forgot to tell you. . . ." Whitney wiped her mouth with her napkin, then whispered. "Her baby teeth are stored in a keepsake box Mom bought. It's in my bedroom."

I rolled my eyes at Whitney. "Are you kidding me?"

"What did I do?" Whitney frowned. "It's not my fault that you didn't notice Bella's snaggle teeth after we came home Sunday."

"You're right. I've been missing a lot of things lately."

"It's a good thing you're on vacation. Now you can catch up on what you've missed."

"True." I checked my watch and thought about my visit to Sean's office tomorrow night. I needed something special to wear and a baby-sitter. "Whitney, I need a favor."

Bella bopped into the room. "I'm ready, Mommy."

"You sure are. . . ." I followed her toward the garage door and opened it.

"Before you leave, what's the favor?" Whitney asked.

After Bella walked past me into the garage, I said, "I need you to keep Bella for me tomorrow night. I won't leave until after Bella's asleep."

She grinned. "Are you and Justus going out again so soon?"

I shook my head. Until then, I hadn't thought to ask him to come, but since he wanted to be a part of my world, this would be a good chance for him to see. "Only if he says yes."

Monday, 8:00 AM
Sugar Hill Elementary, Sugar Hill, Georgia

My first official vacation activity was to spend the day with Bella. Mrs. Dowdy, her kindergarten teacher, had invited me to come and I was looking forward to it, especially to lunch. The food service staff made a mean tomato soup and grilled cheese sandwich. It made me feel warm and fuzzy inside. After Elaine had left my house yesterday, Big Tiger's layoff had begun to unsettle me again, so I needed the soup's yummy goodness to keep my mind off of what I couldn't control.

Sure, I could spend this free time pitching my services to Tiger's competition. They would take me easy, but it wouldn't be right since he was paying me for the time off. Truthfully, I didn't want more work and I didn't think Tiger meant me any harm. Yet I didn't want that sinking, who-do-I-trust-now feeling you get after betrayal reveals itself either. And I hated secrets that held my life at bay. This whole situation reminded me of what had gone down between Ava, Devon, the *Atlanta Sentinel,* and me all over again, except this time I had Bella, Whitney, Ava, Mama, and Justus holding me up. Justus had agreed to come with me tonight.

I smiled about my new blessings when I stood in front of Mrs. Bitter inside the school's front office. I was ready for her mean self today.

"Good Morning, Ms. Crawford. Here's your Volunteer badge."

She handed the name tag to me. It was a standard Hello sticker. I thanked her for it and put it on.

She leaned over her desk. "May I ask you a question?"

I nodded.

"Out of all the good women in Sugar Hill, why did Pastor Justus choose you?"

I stepped back. If Mrs. Dowdy's class wasn't expecting me, I would have run out of there. However, I just smiled at her and silently asked God to keep me from going to my car and getting a weapon that would change the contour of her witchy grin. Like I said, I was ready for her.

At the end of the day I was glad that I hadn't let Mrs. Bitter steal my thunder. It was a great day and the tomato soup was divine. But as I sat in the car-pool lane, waiting for Bella to be released (she didn't want to walk out with me, but with her classmates), her words hit me again. Was I bad for Justus? Should I let him tag along with me tonight?

Someone tapped on my window. I unlocked the door for

Mrs. Dowdy to help Bella climb inside. No one opened the door. Just more tapping. I turned to see what was going on. It was Dale Baker, my new best friend. I sighed and lowered the window.

"Ms. Crawford, I'm so glad I caught you before it was too late."

"What's wrong with Bella?" I unstrapped my seat belt.

"Nothing. She's fine. No need to get out of your car," he said.

I looked around the school parking lot and shrugged at Dale. "So what's the problem?"

"There's no problem. Usually you're at the end of the carpool lane, but today you're early and I wanted to catch you before the kids were released. I need a favor from you."

I squinted and tilted my head. What trouble had Dale gotten into? "What kind of favor?"

"As of an hour ago, we're short a chaperone for the field trip to the state capitol next Monday." There was a hint of panic in his voice. "Mrs. Dowdy said you were on vacation, so I hope you can help us out."

I shook my head. "It's true, but I'm supposed to start a class on Monday—"

"Mommy, please. Could you?" Bella squealed. I couldn't see her because she was shorter than my truck, but that voice could not be duplicated.

"Dale, let me check with my class and see if I can miss one day. I can't guarantee anything just yet, so you may need another pinch hitter until I can confirm."

"Perfect, if you can confirm. Thanks so much, Ms. Crawford."

"Call me Angel, Dale," I reminded him as he walked off with his daughter.

"Mom, I would be so happy if you took us to the capitol," Bella said, as Mrs. Dowdy placed her in her booster seat.

"I know." I smiled with a heavy sigh. How could I be in two places at one time?

Monday, 4:00 PM
Town Square Green, Duluth, Georgia

In order to become a licensed private investigator in the great state of Georgia, I needed to take a one-hundred-hour certification class approved by the secretary of state's office. Georgia Gwinnett College, which was about fifteen minutes from my house and Bella's elementary school, had a fourteen-week class I could enroll in. Ava had agreed to pay for my training and I was beginning to look forward to it. There was a session on white-collar-crime investigation I was very interested in. Gabe had shared so many interesting stories with me I wondered if I could use them to my advantage as a PI/bail recovery agent. That title was too long. I would figure out something catchier later. The only major hangup I had was this school field trip hiccup.

"So you're saying you may not take this class because you have to chaperone Bella's class to the state capitol?" Ava asked and then her eyes narrowed. "Somehow I don't think you are giving me the full story."

We were having a late picnic with the kids in Town Green Square in Duluth's historic Main Street district. As long as Bella and I had lived here, I hadn't taken the time to take her here. Ava brought Lil' D and Taylor to join in on the fun. This vacation afforded some surprising perks.

However, we weren't alone. It was unusually warm for March in Atlanta. The place was of course crowded with kids, stay-at-home parents, nannies, and day-care centers. Ava and I had to huddle together in order to talk without screaming across the blanket at each other.

"You know there's more to it than that," Ava insisted. "You finally found a good excuse to drop out."

"No, I don't want to drop out. I just need to miss the first day, but this is a state-certified course. There's no way I could miss any hours."

Ava nodded. "We'll figure something out. I'm so proud of you."

I sat back and smiled. "Where did that come from?"

"You're making lemonade out of what happened between you and Tiger. I think it's a good thing. You put too much of your faith in him anyway. I'm curious why Justus hasn't mentioned it."

"He did when we were trying to keep you from going to jail." I smirked.

"Touché." She grinned. "But you know what I mean. Tiger had too much space in your life. Now you have more room for Justus, which is fine by me."

I leaned forward. "Do you think it's strange that he likes me so much?"

Ava licked her vanilla ice cream sugar cone, then smiled at me. I wondered if my smile was just as brilliant. "Why does it matter? The man is gorgeous and single *and* so into you that I blush when he looks at you. Don't you see it?"

"What I see is unfathomable. Although I've been fawning after that man since he took over for Brother Allen, I had no clue he was interested in me, too." I shook my head. "It doesn't make sense."

"You don't believe in love at first sight?"

"I did. I don't anymore. Not happening again. I don't." I thought of Gabe. The love we had was a one-of-a-kind thing.

"Are you thinking that allowing yourself to explore a relationship with Justus means you love Gabriel less?" Ava asked.

Then I remembered she was a renowned relationship expert. This time I actually believed it.

I blinked, then shook my head. "I'm afraid of losing a love like that again. Do you have a clue how I feel now?"

Her eyes widened as I referred to losing Devon. She bobbed her head. "I do, but I've been a widow for less than a year, and I had a conversation with Devon years ago before the kids were born. I was pregnant with Taylor at the time."

I leaned back on the quilt and listened.

"We talked about protecting the family. Insurance, wills, that kind of stuff. And then we began talking about who we were as a couple and what would happen if one of us went to God before we wanted to go." She chuckled and looked up toward the sky. "We always had this great belief we would die together holding each other in our medical beds after we had raised great grandchildren."

My hand found hers and I sat quietly while she reminisced.

Then Ava continued. "We knew that this life wasn't perfect and if one of us left the other for heaven, then we believed that person would send the one who was left a companion to help us through our days."

"Really?"

She nodded. "I don't know if I'll ever find a love like Devon's again. I don't know if I want to, but I'm not going to shut myself off to the possibility. Devon wouldn't have wanted that and I know Gabriel wouldn't have wanted that for you. And you have to consider how Bella dotes on Justus. They love each other."

I hadn't considered my own child. Bella and Justus had had a special relationship since before he and I met. He was her vacation bible school teacher last year when he first arrived and taught her lines for the Christmas pageant. Maybe Justus had been waiting patiently for me to see him as not just our pastor but a man who would step in and be the father Bella needed.

Ava stood up from our picnic site and began putting away our picnic supplies.

I caught the leg of one of her pedal pusher pants. "What are you doing? The kids are still playing."

She folded a throw in her basket and wouldn't look up at me. I didn't know what I had said that turned her cold.

"What's wrong, Ava?" I asked again.

"There's nothing wrong. I have a solution and we need to plan properly." She kicked my feet, wanting me to get up off the picnic blanket.

I hopped up and felt confused. "Ava, you're scaring me. What plan?"

"Next Monday I'll be you." She snapped the blanket in the air, to knock any grass off it.

"What?" I chuckled. "I know we're identical twins, but honey, we look nothing alike. I have a haircut now."

"It will be your first day. Your instructor doesn't know what you look like. All that will happen is class housekeeping rules. He won't require me to shoot any gun or kick box. I hope."

I laughed. "You and me both."

13

Wednesday, 9:00 PM
Flappers, Atlantic Station, Atlanta, Georgia

Sean's "office" was a cigar-smoke-hidden booth in the back of Flappers, a secret speakeasy bar that opened only Friday and Saturday nights. It was hidden in the basement of Bottoms Up Brewery and Pub in the Atlantic Station district. In order to get inside, patrons had to enter a phone booth and enter the secret password on the rotary phone inside the booth. However, in order to get the password, you had to either visit Bottoms Up and hope a staffer gave you the phone number and pass code, or have a frenemy like Sean in your back pocket.

There was much truth in keeping enemies closer. I just hoped my renewed dealings with Sean wouldn't bring more danger to my doorstep. Besides, I wasn't a fan of the history of prohibition in Georgia, especially Atlanta's sordid past. Many moonshiners had sold crappy white lightning to blacks who couldn't buy alcohol in the state. Like, for instance, in 1951 Fat Hardy sold bad whiskey to blacks in the Atlanta slums. Thirty-seven people died. One of them was my great uncle Charlie. He was fifteen years old. Fat was later nicknamed the Moonshine Murderer.

Flappers and other 1920-era secret bars had popped up about five years ago in New York, Los Angeles, Chicago, San Fran, and the UK. It finally made its way to Georgia right on the cusp of their downturn. However, this was the South, the land of blackberry moonshine, mint julep corn whiskey, and fig rum. We had never stopped making bathub gin and giving it to our friends, so this wasn't new or trendy.

But this place was more like a boomerang except now it was legit liquor and employed some of the best mixologists in The A. The retro bar was still exclusive, but now pseudo secretive, and the kind of place I never worried about bumping into violent criminal elements or my skips.

It was designed like an old-fashioned speakeasy and included a restricted entrance. Once inside it was a sophisticate's dream. Mahogany tables, hostesses dressed like flappers with pin curls and super-tight fringe dresses, men dressed like Cary Grant. The drinks weren't cheap and you couldn't dress like a dirty South thug or hillbilly to get in. It was a great spot to meet Atlanta's posh, Geek Chic, and a discerning ex-white-collar criminal like Gabe.

As Justus walked around his car to open the door for me before the valet got to it, I wondered whether he would have a problem taking me on a real date to a place like this. It was one thing to meet Sean about Riddick, but another to take Justus deeper into my world. Unlike Gabe, who'd reveled in the rich underbelly of Atlanta, I felt like I was shoveling dirt on Justus's toes, which wasn't my plan.

"Is something wrong, Angel?" Justus asked, because I still hadn't taken his hand to get out of the car. Actually, my jaw was still dropped from the moment he'd picked me up at my house.

Justus wore a forest green cashmere vest, a tailored pin-striped plum and gray button-down shirt with a Windsor collar and monogrammed cuffs. His pants were tailored and he wore black and white wing-tipped Correspondent shoes. I shook my head in delight. He could pass for a boulevardier. Or perhaps he had always been one. I was just too caught up in myself to realize it until now.

"I was itching for a Georgia Peach Martini, but looking at you has satisfied my thirst." I smiled.

He took my hand and lifted me out of the car like I didn't have heavy thighs. I gasped.

"Woman, what did I tell you about giving a man who adores you a compliment?"

I shrugged. "That I would get a kiss."

"Good try, but so wrong." He grinned, then extended his arm for me to slide my arm around his elbow.

He escorted me to what looked like an abandoned men's clothes atelier next to a red British-styled phone booth. Justus released my arm from his hold. Before I could give him Sean's personal code, he walked toward the booth, stepped inside, but didn't call like Sean had instructed to me. Instead he tapped the key pad.

A gentleman dressed in a three-piece brown tweed suit opened the door of the atelier. "Madame and Mr. Morgan, welcome to Flappers."

I waited until Justus slid my arm back under his, then looked up at him. "Should I even ask what you just did and how?"

"Let's just say that I'm more similar to you than you think." He kissed my forehead. "Your hair smells great."

I blushed. "It won't be after the cigar smoke inside adds its special scent."

I touched my head and sighed. Halle had hooked me up this morning with a finger wave. According to her, the retro 1920s style was in and so was this look. It also flattered my vintage navy blue velvet Cabaret cocktail dress. Whitney had bought this for me for Christmas. I had been longing to wear this dress out on the town for a while, but didn't imagine in my wildest dreams I would be wearing it while sharing this night with the pastor I had had a crush on for the past year.

Justus stopped short of the host at the entrance, leaned down, and whispered, "Should I take you home?"

I fumbled with my pearl earrings. "I just didn't think I was going to have such a good time before we stepped foot inside."

He touched my ear and gently secured the jewelry to my ears. His skin was hot, but didn't singe me. It ignited a spark in me, to be alone with him as soon as possible. And the cologne he wore became a catalyst that made every touch from his hand, every word from his lips, and every change on his face pull me in deeper and deeper. I felt myself slipping and falling in love too fast to make good sense, but felt so right despite it all.

"Am I full of surprises?" he asked.

My hand held his jaw, while my legs and stiletto sling backs lifted me toward his lips. When we kissed, when he pulled me into his body, when he moaned my name, I knew that he was telling the truth about his feelings for me and this time I no longer wanted him to take any of his feelings for me back.

The doorman cleared his throat. Justus ended our kiss and looked up. I caught my breath.

"Mhmm . . ." Justus shook his head and sighed. "Let me get you inside before I forget myself and you forget why we're here."

I couldn't respond or remember, because I was still lingering over that kiss.

"We're here to meet Sean Graham."

"Correct, Sir Sidekick." I nodded and caught his arm again.

When we stepped inside, more than the rich cigar aroma

took our breath away. I had forgotten the ambience, the glam and trappings that had drawn me into getting too involved with Gabe.

"How do you know about this place?" I whispered to Justus.

"If Christ could meet prostitutes where they hung, why can't I chill where modern cyber pimps strategize."

I stopped and frowned. "What are you talking about?"

"Cyber prostitution. It's a crisis in Sugar Hill and all of Atlanta, really. I'm surprised you don't know about this."

"Had no idea. Most of our skips' offenses are bad, but not soulless." I paused as Rosary's face came to mind. "When did you have time to get involved in this?"

"While you slept. I'll fill you in on the details later, because your friend is standing behind you." He nodded for me to turn around.

Sean stood dressed to the nines. He wore a beautiful burgundy silk tie to complement his gray Prince of Wales double-breasted flannel suit. I knew men's fashion well, because Gabe was an aficionado. Before he died, he was about to launch an Asian American/African American men's clothing atelier in Johns Creek called Bl.āsi Atelier with his college roommate Khali Knight. That dream also disappeared with our future. Khali left town a few months after Gabe's funeral.

"Sean, thanks for meeting me." I squeezed Justus's hand. "This is my escort, Reverend Doctor Justus Morgan."

"Actually, I'm her man." Justus chuckled.

They exchanged handshakes while I studied Flappers further. It was like I remembered it. Inside, it looked like a high-end cigar club, craft cocktail lounge with a 1920s vintage private club barback vibe. Polished mahogany wood panels, tables, chairs, and the bar; great lighting; and very much a throwback nod to elegance. Gabe and I used to sit in a private section behind the bar. I wondered who now paid the extra bill to have the secrecy.

"We've met before," Sean said.

"You did?" I asked them both.

"Yes, we have." Justus rubbed his chin. "At a fund-raiser for Street Grace, a nonprofit coalition of churches united to bring the abolition of child sex slavery and exploitation in Atlanta."

I turned to Sean. "I can't believe you're involved in something that does not help you in any way."

"We all grow up sometimes, Angel Crawford." He winked, then pointed me toward his standing booth. "Let's have a seat at my office."

Justus ordered a bottled sparkling water for himself and a Georgia Peach Mocktini for me. After listening to Sean and Justus chat about the convergence of social media and charitable giving, I wanted the real deal. Somehow this meeting had become too provincial for both my and Flappers' taste. I rolled my eyes and sipped until the cocktail waiter returned.

"Is there a drink that will make me forget my troubles without getting me drunk?" I asked the waiter.

Justus placed his hand over my hand that rested on the table. "How about a hot chocolate heavy whip?"

The waiter nodded. "We have a great French blend that is decaffeinated for expectant mothers."

I coughed. I looked down at my stomach and adjusted my dress. I wanted to make sure that the fringe wasn't giving off the illusion of a pouch.

"You look wonderful." Justus patted my back. "Don't worry. He's a prophet. He's talking about our future."

Sean chuckled. "I hope you don't mind me saying this, but you two are an adorable couple."

"Thank you, sir," Justus said.

"Sean, I've had my share of small talk." I jumped in before they began their bromance chat again. "I need to know what's the deal with Riddick Avery. Why is he out for me?"

Sean looked at Justus, then at me. "He's just jealous of all the media attention you've been getting lately. Don't take it personal. He's not. He was acting like a total jerk, but this has gotten out of hand. I would be glad to help you guys kiss and make up."

"Sean, I have a haircut because he paid someone to hit me on the head."

He sighed. "Angel, if there was malicious intent, the young woman who was arrested would have had heavier charges. Quit being so stubborn and let's move on."

I shook my head. "Tiger told me that he and Riddick have a business relationship, so I feel I was led there to get hurt. Are you a part of it? Is that why you're giving me the deer-caught-in-headlights treatment?"

Justus cleared his throat and wiggled his collar. I could tell he didn't like this conversation.

"Angel, why are you making me seem like a bad guy in front of Justus?"

"Because you are a bad guy, more like a wolf in sheep's clothing, literally. Get it. Flannel. Sheep's clothing?"

"Yes, that was a funny barb. I had forgotten you had such grit and wit." He rubbed his vest and chuckled. "Angel, there is another reason why I asked you here."

I folded my arms over my chest. "I knew it. I knew there was a catch."

"Before you get all toasted, it's not what you think. I need you to find someone for me." Sean's voice was no longer as light as before. It was a low and fast whisper. "Your home girl, Rosie DiChristina."

"Rosary?" I looked at Justus, then back at Sean. "What's wrong?"

"The list is long when it comes to that girl." Sean reached for his black attaché case, which sat beside him on the bench. He unlocked it with a secret code and pulled out a leather bound notebook, but he wouldn't let me see the contents of it.

I glanced at Justus. His eyes were on me. If I didn't know any better I'd have thought he was reading my mind. *What had Rosary really done and why did Sean think I could find her?*

"How about you start with the bottom of the list then?" I smiled.

"I bailed her out of jail over the weekend and no one has seen her in two days."

I shook my head and leaned farther back into my seat. "Don't worry. She's not gone anywhere. Probably getting her fix. You know her family still runs shine."

He groaned and covered his eyes with his hand. "Please don't tell me that."

Justus nudged me. "What does that mean, 'her family still runs shine'?"

"Moonshine," I said. "Her family brews moonshine and sells it."

Justus chuckled. "But why? Alcohol is legal now."

"True, but making shine goes back generations and some folks don't want to pay the high state tax to buy alcohol."

"Or not be able to buy alcohol on Sunday unless you're in here or in a restaurant," Sean chimed in. "Let's not forget to mention how dangerous some of that lightning is. I heard some of them cut it with bleach instead of water."

My nose turned up at the thought of drinking bleach. "Either way, she's probably upstate helping her family. But she never stays for long and she never misses her court dates."

"A U.S. marshal by the name of Max has been looking for her. He came by Elaine's office to ask me about her. Elaine's?! Can you believe that? It was embarrassing to say the least."

He took a swig from his glass of brandy. "If I don't find this girl, he'll come back and I don't need that kind of bad color tainting Elaine's public image."

I gave Sean the side eye. The only person's image he was concerned about was his, not Elaine's. He had to come up with something better than this to convince me to help him.

"I know what you're thinking." He looked at me, then at Justus, then back at me. "How do my dealings with Rosary DiChristina hurt Elaine?"

"That is the magic question."

He looked around the pub, leaned closer to us, and whispered. "Elaine asked me to bail Rosary out of jail."

"I don't believe you." I scoffed. "Why would she do that? That's not like her."

Justus touched my hand. "Let's just hear him out."

I felt my neck turn in that no-you-didn't sort of way, but caught myself. Crap. I must be in love with Justus Morgan to let him tell me what to do.

"Elaine makes bail for her special constituents. In my opinion, she's too sweet for her own good."

"Is that why your name is on so many bail contracts at Tiger's?" I asked.

Sean grinned. "We couldn't have Elaine's name tied to all that foolery. Now could we?"

"Well, that explains a lot."

"Of course, I didn't expect the kindergarten playground fight between you and Avery when we made bail for her. Now you have me in a pretty pickle."

"How so?"

"Tiger has had Riddick's team and those Big Bad Boys out looking for her for two days and they can't seem to find her. I don't think they ever will, but you can."

"No, I can't either. I'm on vacation with express orders from Tiger to stay out of Riddick's way."

Sean opened the notebook and handed me a small manila folder. I looked inside, counted, and gasped.

I looked up at Sean. "There's $25,000 in cash in here."

"If you bring Rosie to me by next Friday, I'll hand you another twenty-five."

I closed the envelope and gave it back to him. "I'm sorry. I promised Elaine that I would take Lana to the Running of the Brides on Friday."

"Elaine said you would be hard to convince." He reached into the envelope and pulled out another envelope. "There's a $10,000 incentive inside."

"Elaine knows about this?"

"Elaine knows everything." He took another drink. "I know about your problem with Riddick and you know that Riddick is my friend. But you and I both know that friendship and business don't mix."

Sean looked at Justus and grinned. "Except for you two, of course. Y'all have something special."

"Don't go there, Sean," I said.

"Just trying to lighten the mood of the room." He chuckled, then cleared his throat. "Seriously, I need that marshal off my back. I need Rosie. If you bring her to me, Riddick will ride her in."

I scoffed. "No way."

"Hear me out. If Tiger sees that the both of you have kissed and made up, then it's a win-win for everybody. Don't you agree?"

I turned to Justus; his eyes screamed, "Don't go down this dark road again."

"Are you sure Riddick didn't ask that Marlo girl to hit me at Draft House?"

"Angel, let it go." He chuckled.

I sighed. "That won't ever happen, but I will see what I can do about Rosary."

"Fantastic." Sean smiled. His face looked serene, a little too peaceful, if you ask me.

The last time I saw that expression was when Elaine had to participate in a runoff election with Sid Marcus. It was her first campaign and Sid was a shoo-in. He was synonymous with The Georgia Gentlemen's Club, a powerful PAC group whose agenda was to continue to keep Georgia minimum wage lower than the rest of the country and their banks larger than any public library in the state.

There was a lot of old money bankrolling Sid's campaign, unlike Elaine's ragtag army of middle-class, college-educated, Southern women united to change the future of our state to a more progressive and equal one for all. Consequently Sid's campaign contributors could afford to put pressure on the media and threaten to drop future advertisement dollars if they dared mention Elaine's name or her liberal causes.

While the rest of Elaine's interns—myself included—did everything but throw ourselves off roofs, Sean did his secret work and smiled with glee. Two weeks before the election, Sid dropped out the race. Said he decided he needed to devote more time to his family.

Years later, after I had been working at *The Sentinel*, the truth of Sid's forfeiture came out. Sean had learned that Sid had a mistress living in Peach County, Middle Georgia. She was a beautiful Mexican migrant worker who once pulled rotten peaches out the carriers on Sid's brother-in-law's peach orchards near Fort Valley. Now she ran a bed-and-breakfast near Hazelhurst with two teenaged sons, one a dead ringer for a young, tanned Sid on holiday.

How Sean found that information back then I had no

clue. However, now I suspect that the many folks he had bailed out of jail all these years returned the favor to him in the best way they knew how . . . with what they knew.

"Sean, are you sure there isn't more to this than you're letting on?" I observed his face for any more tells.

"After all these years you still don't know me." He smirked, reached into his pocket, and pulled out a cigar.

Justus reached in his breast pocket and pulled out a gold lighter.

I frowned at Justus. "You smoke?"

"No . . ." He flipped a flame and lit Sean's cigar with it. "But I have enough common sense to bring a lighter to a cigarette bar."

Sean inhaled his potion and chuckled. "Y'all are absolutely adorable."

I threw back my mocktini and gulped. "Now I really need a stiff drink." I raised my hand for the waiter to return.

14

Wednesday, 11:00 PM
Flappers, Atlantic Station, Atlanta, Georgia

Justus didn't allow me time to strap myself into the seat belt before he gave me his two, three, and four cents about my meeting with Sean.

"I'm thankful that you let me tag along with you tonight. I hope that this big step forward also includes me being able to share my thoughts about what just happened in there," he said.

"Share away, just as long as you turn the heat on. It's cold in here."

He chuckled, turned the ignition, and drove us out of there. However, he didn't say another word until we were well on I-85 North toward home.

"Although I've only spent about two hours with Sean, I think the guy isn't telling you the entire story. Tiger has more than enough agents searching for your friend."

"I agree."

He coughed. "You do? Then why did you take the money?"

"The money in my purse isn't contingent upon me finding Rosary DiChristina. It's an incentive. Now if I bring her in, then I get another twenty-five thou." I leaned my head back.

"So you have no intention of looking for Rosie?"

"A little. I don't know . . ." I closed my eyes. "I'm curious why the best recovery agents in Atlanta can't find a drunk, dark-haired hoochie with bright blue eyes. She's hard to miss."

"I'm curious that your speakeasy pal wants you to search for a known bootlegger." He chuckled. "I feel like we walked through a wormhole or the fourth dimension tonight."

"Wow. I didn't know you were such a science geek."

"Not really. But don't you think Sean insulted your intelligence? He wants you to believe that finding Rosie helps Elaine when clearly finding her—or her private stash—helps him."

"That's exactly why I kept that money. I might be stupid, but I'm not dumb."

He laughed. "Somehow I understand exactly what you mean."

I chuckled with him until I got this brilliant idea.

"Justus?" I opened my eyes and sat up. "Are you thinking what I'm thinking?"

"Probably not." He glanced at me, then back to the road. "I'm sure I'm not, and batting your eyes at me will not convince me otherwise."

"But it's a good idea."

"No, it's a crazy, you-haven't-learned-the-last-time idea."

"But I can't do this without you," I whined.

"And that's exactly why your idea is a crazy one, because there is no reason why I should be involved."

"Just hear me out." I shifted my body toward him in the seat. "I promised Bella an afternoon movie Friday. No sitter for Saturday, got church on Sunday, school field trip on Monday, and the next two weeks are filled with PI training and pretending to be on vacation. Tonight is my only night to bop over to Amicalola Falls and snatch Rosie out the woods without Tiger being the wiser."

"Snatching someone out the North Georgia Mountains is a clear indicator that you've been out way past your bedtime." He shook his head. "Give it a rest, Angel."

"I'll split the money with you."

"Don't want it. You know better than that."

"Fine." I huffed and plopped back in the passenger seat. "I'll go by myself."

"Angel, don't be foolish," he said while turning into my subdivision.

" 'And wisdom was taken from the prophets and given unto fools.' "

"You can't use the Bible to fit your agenda like that."

"I know, but everybody else does it." I unzipped my purse and located my garage remote.

He pulled into my driveway and didn't say anything for a while. The tension in the car was so thick it made my knees shake.

Justus took my hand and placed it over his heart. "Angel, don't go anywhere else tonight. Stay here, please. I'll do anything, if you just stay."

"Anything?"

"Anything." He nodded.

His new haircut made him look more handsome than before and made it way too hard for me to hide my attraction from him. I ran my hands around his nape. He closed his eyes and groaned. It felt fuzzy and I could run my fingers through it. A sliver of silver peeked just above his temple. It complemented the sparkle his eyes gave off when he was either happy or angry with me. When he opened them again, the glow shimmered, but he wasn't happy. He was dead serious.

"If Rosary doesn't turn up by this Thursday afternoon, will you go with me to get her?"

"And if she's not there? Then what?"

"Then it's over. Deadline missed. Besides, I have Running of the Brides Friday morning."

"Do you mean it?"

"Justus, don't take this the wrong way, but you're right."

He scoffed. "Okay . . ."

"I'm going to hang back and let the dust settle this time. Like Mom often says, 'The truth is like a man caught with his pants down. Eventually the truth will come up.' "

15

Bella's class field trip at the Georgia State Capitol went off without a hitch. The kids oohed and aahed and then cried for their mommies. I thought of Elaine while we were there. I had planned to call her to confirm her knowledge of the $25,000 Sean Graham had given me to find Rosary. But I took the high road and spent the weekend with my daughter, my family, and Justus. Tiger had paid me to rest and I did just that. Shoot. I made Bella take a nap, too.

I had just lowered myself into a warm lavender oil bath when my doorbell rang. If I hadn't just gotten Bella down for a few winks, I would have let it ring until Calgon took me away. I stepped out, threw on my robe, and stomped downstairs.

When I saw Ava standing on my porch wearing a floor-length white fur coat, black sunglasses, and a Jackie O wig, I knew my vacation had taken a turn. She held papers in her hand.

"What happened in my class, Ava, and what are you holding?"

Silence, except for the sound of papers flitting between her hands. Not good.

"Ava, don't make me drop-kick you off my porch."

"You'll get arrested, and tighten your robe."

"I'll get arrested for more than that if you don't answer my question."

Still silence.

"I don't know how to tell you this, but you've been expelled. The instructor is very good, by the way. He knew who I was and that I wasn't you before I warmed your seat."

She lowered her head and sighed.

"Stop. Reverse. What do you mean 'expelled'?"

"I tried my best to speak on your behalf, but this guy wouldn't budge and I can't understand why, since he wasn't your actual instructor. He was a substitute."

I closed my eyes to keep my body from boiling with anger.

"Are you okay?" Ava touched my shoulder.

"I can't believe . . ." I backed away from her and painted on a smile. "Ava, thank you. Give me the notes you have and the name of this substitute. I'll take care of this."

"But I don't think it would be wise for you to go back there. Look, it was my fault. My brilliant scheme backfired, so of course I will pay for another class. I don't want you to take this as an opportunity to quit. The class is perfect for you. I learned some very interesting things about law enforcement, private investigation, and even bail recovery. That's what you do, right?"

"Ava, stop babbling. You and that throwback outfit of yours is making my head hurt. Now come on in. You can help me with dinner and I'll tell you about my date with Justus."

She smiled. Her guilt hadn't completely vanished from her face, but she looked better than she had a few minutes before. I escorted her into the kitchen. I suddenly felt the urge to make pancakes, something we used to eat when we felt bad.

Tuesday, 8:45 AM
Georgia Gwinnett College, Lawrenceville, Georgia

Mr. Deacon West stood outside his office staring at me and chuckling as I walked toward him. I did my best not to let him see me gulp.

He extended his hand. "I'm assuming that yesterday you and your twin were my surveillance faux pas reenactments or a foolish ex-student who thought she could give me the old switcheroo. Which one is it?"

"Not the latter, but I would be lying if I agreed with the first," I said. "The truth is I'm the real Angel Crawford. On short notice, I had to chaperone my daughter's kindergarten class field trip yesterday. My sister tried to help me out by pretending to be me. It didn't work, of course, but I hope you'll reconsider. I need this class."

He scratched his head with his pen. "Are you always this long winded?"

"No, sir. My grandma once told me, 'You can't hear your lesson with your mouth wide open.' " I zipped my lips with my imaginary zipper.

He tilted his head toward the classroom. "Get in there."

I scurried to the only available seat and did what I told Whitney to do her first day in college. Shut up, take notes, and shut up.

The class was wonderful. I could have kicked myself for not having done this kind of continuing education sooner. The only challenge I had was that I didn't have time to thank Deacon West once again for allowing me back into his class.

I had about a half hour left before I picked up Bella and four of her classmates from school car pool. As a part of the city's new conservation plan, our school district created parent car-pool rings for those of us who didn't want to put our children on the bus. My scheduled date to pick up our kids was today. I cringed, because I had forgotten to vacuum the car. The only thing I had time to do was run my handheld vacuum that I kept in the trunk through the backseat before I left the parking lot.

I double-checked my watch, grabbed my backpack, and bumped into a hard chest.

A long-legged, black jeans/black cowboy boots/black Stetson hat–wearing Adonis frowned back at me. "What do you not understand about the word 'expelled'?"

I assumed Hot Cowboy was the substitute. "That's a conversation you had with someone else, not me."

"I'm very aware of that." He stepped closer.

I could smell why Old Spice cologne had made a comeback. I made a mental note to get Justus some of it for his birthday. I hope it's soon.

"Then you should be aware that the real instructor, Mr. West, allowed me a reprieve."

His brown eyes thundered all over me. "Unc, you let this woman back in your class?"

Unc, as in uncle? I gasped.

"Yes, I did, Maxim," Deacon yelled back. "Now leave her alone, else you got a crush."

Maxim cleared his throat, stepped back, and lowered his hat. "My apologies, Angel."

"Do you know me?"

"I'm aware of all annoyances in my jurisdiction, including bounty hunters." He gave a mischievous grin. He knew we didn't like to be called bounty hunters, but I let it go.

"Your jurisdiction?" I observed him more closely until I noticed the Department of Justice's six-point star within a circular ring badge. I threw my hands on my hips and laughed.

"What's so funny?" he asked, the grin now gone.

"I think you're my marshal?"

He looked at me with a deeper frown than before and raised his eyebrow. "What's that supposed to mean?"

"A birdie told me you were looking for a Rosary DiChristina."

He shook his head. "Birdie told you wrong. I never heard of her. Who is she?"

I hadn't been in PI class but one day and had already failed the first lesson. *Ask the right question to get the right answer.*

Sean had lied about a U.S. marshal looking for Rosary. I wondered what else he had lied to me about. Unfortunately, the only person who could help me with the right answer was Rosary. I had made a promise to Justus not to search for her until Thursday. But hunting and paying her a visit were two different things. Weren't they?

16

By the time I reached my car, I was spitting bullets. I couldn't call Sean's office fast enough. Good thing for him he didn't answer; good thing for me I hadn't spent one dime of that money he gave me to bring back Rosary.

I wanted to call Justus, but I already knew how that conversation would go down. *I told you so, Angel,* in a nutshell. I backed out of the parking space and headed for Bella's school.

When I stopped for a red light I told my handheld phone device to dial Tiger, then hung up. I couldn't tell him anything about this because he had paid me and warned me to stay out of predicaments like this. I huffed. *Who could I talk to?*

Tuesday, 4:00 PM
McDonald's, Suwanee, Georgia

"Angel, explain to me why you do everything in your power to ruin the name I gave you," Mom said while we watched Bella play in the indoor playground at McDonald's.

It was too cold and rainy for her to play outside. We preferred this location because it had a nice fireplace and the franchise owner kept fresh flowers on the tables. Mom called this Budget Brunch.

"Mom, I don't know what to do."

She sipped her black coffee from her own ceramic coffee cup. "Simple, return the money today."

"You don't think I should call Elaine?"

"For what? You should have called her when Sean gave you all that money. Too late to involve her now." She leaned forward. "Are you going to Running of the Brides with Whitney?"

I nodded. "Maybe I should take the money to Elaine after ROTB. Sean can explain himself to us both then."

"No, you can't keep that money another day. Who's to say that Riddick character and Sean aren't trying to set you up? That money must go."

"Right." I sighed and shook my head. "I can't take it to Sean's office, because he's out of town with Elaine on a press junket. There's not enough time for me to get downtown and leave it with his secretary."

"Do you know where he lives?"

"Yep, he lives in Gallery Buckhead."

It's a high-rise condo on Peachtree Street not far from Elaine's office and Flappers. Sean lived a very good life.

"Wonderful." Mom clapped her hands.

I frowned and folded my arms over my chest. "And how is that wonderful?"

"After Bella gets her fill of fun we will run over two doors and have Eve at the Suwanee Gift Shop wrap that money in a pretty box with a bright red bow. JJ and I'll take it on our way home. I'll hand-deliver it to the concierge at Gallery. He'll make sure Sean gets his money back."

My face perked up. "That might work."

"Of course it will. You're washing your hands clean of this nonsense and sticking it to him real nice-nasty and lady-like."

"What about Rosie? Should I look for her? Warn her family?"

"If anything happens to that poor girl, you know nothing. You hear me? She should have taken your offer for rehab when she had the chance. Can't save her now and definitely not with Sean's dirty money in your back pocket. Let her own mama fix her situation."

"Yes, ma'am." I nodded. I couldn't argue with the truth.

Before Mom and JJ left us, I gave Mom a hug.

"Thank you for helping me, Mom. I don't know what I would've done without you these past few days," I whispered.

She released me. "You're welcome. However, you might take back your hugs and kisses after you hear my last unsolicited piece of advice."

"Go ahead and hit me with it."

"Tell Justus. He was with you when Sean gave you the money. He'll be curious what came of you and him searching for Rosary in 'Where Black Folks Don't Tread' Georgia this Friday. And he's more than just your boyfriend, baby. . . ." She patted my cheek. "Communication between a man and a woman isn't easy unless you practice. Put the time in. Tell him."

"I'll tell him when I get home. You call me as soon as you drop the package off."

Tuesday, 7:00 PM
Home, Sugar Hill, Georgia

I waited.

Tuesday, 10:00 PM
Home, Sugar Hill, Georgia

And I waited.

Wednesday, 1:00 AM
Home, Sugar Hill, Georgia

Something rang and woke me up. Justus and I had fallen asleep on separate couches in the family room while waiting on Mom to call.

I picked up the phone. "Mom?"

I heard the ringing again. I held the phone in my hand, confused. "What's going on?"

"It's the door, not the phone," Justus grumbled.

His eyes were still closed. I tapped his foot. "Why are you still here?"

"The door." He pointed.

"You're going to get in big trouble being here," I hissed.

The last thing I needed was the neighborhood spreading rumors to the church that Justus had spent the night in my house, although technically he just did. I tried to drum up some excuses for what happened as I stumbled toward the hall.

I peeked through my front door peephole and woke up for real.

"Maxim?"

He stood on the other side of my door wearing a blue tweed jacket, blue jeans, and that black Stetson hat. He looked like a cowboy on a mission to haul my butt to jail.

"Who's at the door?" Justus asked. His voice made me jump.

"Big Trouble." I gulped.

17

"If I knew you were coming over, I would have cleaned my house."

Maxim and I sat in my home office while Justus hung back in the den. Whitney was still out in the streets. I hated to admit that I was glad Justus was still here. The house felt different at night with him in it. It was a good different.

"No problem. This won't take long," Maxim said.

He unbuttoned his jacket, placed his hat on his knee, and relaxed in my black and white damask wingback chair. His marshal badge served double duty as a belt buckle. By his demeanor it looked like he would be here longer and he wasn't arresting me.

"Yesterday you mentioned a Rosary DiChristina to me. In fact, you assumed that I knew the woman."

"Yeah, it was a mistake. My bad. I confused you with another Maxim West." I giggled, but he didn't laugh. "That was a bad joke."

"Right . . ." He smirked. "After you misspoke, I received an e-mail from headquarters concerning this Rosary DiChristina and then I realized something. Either you're psychic, or whoever lied to you to get you off their back knew I was coming. I need two things from you."

"No problem. You need the name of the person who told me about you."

"No, I've got it on good authority that Sean Graham told you."

"How do you know that?" I sat up.

"Have you talked to your mom lately?" He reached in his jacket pocket and pulled out something, then slapped it on my desk.

It was the money envelope Sean had given me, but where was the box? Where was Mom?

My chest tightened. I hopped up from my seat. "Did you arrest my mama?"

"Sit down and stop being melodramatic." He frowned and shook his head. "Your mom gave me the box. Okay? Do you know how respected your stepfather is? The man's a legend."

"I don't know him. She didn't let us know about them until after the wedding. . . . What does this have to do with the box?"

"Your mother shared your predicament with your stepdad. Out of concern for you both he called my office. I have the box. And you're off the hook."

"Off the hook for what?"

"Anything that happens from here on out except for my uncle's class." He stood up and lifted the envelope off the table. "You may need to do some extra credit to catch up in there. Enjoy your night, Ms. Crawford."

He placed the envelope back in his jacket. I followed him to the front door.

I stepped in front of him before I opened the door. "Maxim, can you tell me what's going on with Rosary? Is she in serious trouble?"

"She's not in trouble with us, but she's a person of interest for a federal case. If we don't get to her before the bad guys find her, however, she will be in trouble."

I thought about the warning the correctional officer at the Gwinnett County jail had given to me about Rosary. "Does this have anything to do with that jail hooch? She agreed to go to rehab for that."

He crinkled his nose. "Angel, that's not my jurisdiction. I can tell you that Rosie isn't in trouble with the law. We were the ones who had her charges dropped. She's an informant now."

"What? Informant?" I stepped back. "So no one bailed her out?"

He shook her head. "She was released, then disappeared. Now we're worried."

"Have you questioned Sean?"

He rolled his eyes. "His lawyers will be meeting us Friday afternoon to clear things up."

"Yeah, but that's two days from now."

He rubbed his hat. "Sean didn't come across to me as being the violent type. I don't think he had a clue what he'd gotten himself into or the people he'd involved himself with. He's not the bad guy. He's the dumb, smug, arrogant one who couldn't live a day in general population and he knows it. I think he was trying to fix this problem on his own. But if you've never been dirty, then you don't know how to get clean."

"If you've never participated in criminal activity, then you don't know how to cover your tracks. Amen to that," I said. "Maxim, how many extra credit points will I get if I help you find Rosary?"

"That reminds me of the second thing I need from you." He grinned. "I need you."

Someone coughed. I turned around. Justus stood behind

me near the staircase. His eyes were on me. He wasn't smiling.

I turned back to Maxim. I felt my cheeks burn. "Umm . . . it's too late to have a coherent conversation. Can we talk later?"

"If you want to help with this, more like if you can, call me." Maxim handed me his card and tipped his hat to Justus before he skipped down my steps.

I think he even whistled when he walked.

Justus met me at my threshold. "Before I leave, I'm going to say this. Do you hear me?"

I nodded. "Yes."

"If you follow that man into those woods tonight, I'm not coming after you."

"I can't go if I wanted to. Whitney isn't here."

"Whitney's been here since midnight," he said.

"Wait a minute . . ." I closed the door and followed him back to the den.

He was now folding the comforter I had draped over him earlier. "Angel, I have said all that I am going to say on the subject."

"But I didn't say I was going with him. Maxim didn't say he was going anywhere, as a matter of fact."

Justus threw one finger in the air. "I do have one more thing to say."

"The floor's yours." I folded my arms across my chest.

"His name is ridiculous."

I laughed. "Are you jealous, Justus Morgan?"

"Woman, I told you I loved you earlier. So what do you think my answer is?"

I walked toward him and flung the comforter out of his hand. "You're being ridiculous."

"I love you, Angel." He wrapped his arms around my waist. "That was hard for me to admit to you, not because

I'm too manly to say it, but because I'm scared you're going to walk out that door one day and not come back."

"Crap." I sighed. "I'm sorry."

"I know your job is sometimes dangerous, but do you always have to sprint toward it?"

"No, but if I don't get you out of my house within the next minute, I'm jumping you."

"That means I have about forty-five seconds to do this." He smiled, then kissed me.

His words raced through me as his soft lips almost set me on cloud nine. The reality that I would be calling Maxim as soon as Justus left kept my stubborn feet on solid ground.

18

Wednesday, 2:00 AM
Home, Sugar Hill, Georgia

I waited until Justus was well on his way home before I tip-toed upstairs to gather my things and call Maxim. When I opened my door, however, Whitney was sitting in my bed. She held a stop watch in one hand, a flashlight in the other, and a pamphlet in her lap.

I turned on the lights. "What are you doing?"

"Checking to see if that kiss between you and Justus beat the Guinness Book of World Records." She pointed the flashlight at me. "Next time he comes over, I need to chaperone."

"Stop it," I hissed and nudged her over with my hips so I could sit. "He's going to be in enough trouble for being over here so late."

"He won't get in trouble if you marry the man." She turned off the flashlight. "It's gonna happen, so why delay it?"

"Don't be so sure." I pulled Maxim's card out of my pocket.

"Oooh . . ." Whitney snatched it. "You've only been on one real date with the man and you already creeping on him with Big Hat Hot Body?"

"I'm not sneaking around." I took the card back and sighed. "Well, not what you think."

"I'm up, so I'm all ears," she said. "But hurry up before I get mad that you're treating my pastor bad. You know how we women get about our pastors."

"If you don't stop with the jokes . . ." I texted a message to Maxim on my phone, then continued. "Big Hat Hot Body is a U.S. marshal and one of my PI class instructors. He's going to give me extra credit if I help find Rosary DiChristina. She's in danger, and get this: Sean Graham is involved."

"So why are you getting involved exactly?"

"You sound like Justus." I stood up and went to my closet to retrieve a warm jacket and my steel-toe boots. "Rosie's good people. Her daughter reminds me of Bella. I don't want anything happening to her on my watch."

"But isn't that the point of your vacation? You aren't on anyone's watch," she said. "To be honest, I was hoping this time off would help you see that you don't have to be at Tiger's beck and call anymore. I hoped you would meet other bounty hunters in this class and learn that there are other bail bondsmen you can work with, or lawyers, or journalists. You have more options than you realize."

"Where's all this coming from all of a sudden?" I turned toward her. "I thought you understood why I do what I do."

"Of course I do. You know I got you. I just don't want you to get hurt, helping people who don't want to be helped. You're a bail recovery agent, not a cop."

"And that's exactly why I'm going and I'm sure that's why Maxim wants me to come. I don't have an agenda. I just want to find my friend." I zipped my coat up. "If I'm not back by morning, get Bella to school for me."

"And what about Justus?"

"If it's meant to be, it'll be."

Wednesday, 3:00 AM
Amicalola Falls, Dawsonville, Georgia

Rosary came from a long line of North Georgia Mountain moonshiners. DiChristina was her married and now divorced name. However, Rosary was a Calhoun, seven generations of apple-pie moonshine experts.

We were about forty minutes north of my home in some woods I had never been in. Maxim drove a Ford truck that was modified for mud bogging. The slip differential was lowered to maximize the size of the engine and tire performance, then a snorkel system was installed to raise the air intake, a bigger engine with more horsepower was dropped in, and mud tires were installed. Either Maxim was a bogger or whomever he rented it from just returned from drag racing. Fresh red Georgia clay was splattered all over the windows. I couldn't see a thing.

"Good thing we're not here for a stakeout." I chuckled.

"One of the most important lessons I learned from Uncle Deacon was surveillance. Surveillance isn't just about sitting in a car waiting for a skip to slip up, so you can drag them back to jail, where they should have been in the first place. Nope. Surveillance is an act of perseverance, courage, and patience. . . ."

I rolled my eyes. "Surveillance is also an act of silence. We need to be able to hear the difference between normal and someone stoking the still."

He grinned. "So you did pay attention in class."

I motioned my hands, as if I were zipping my lips.

He chuckled. "I guess you took some miming classes, too."

I tried to hold my tongue, but he was pushing it.

"I fish in Jackson Lake most mornings," he said. "That's why my truck looks like this."

"This is your truck?"

"Yeah." He turned to me. "What, you thought I asked someone for this?"

"I thought you were dressing like a country boy because that was a part of your marshal shtick. I didn't think you actually were one."

He gave a crooked smile. That tickled me more. I looked away from him.

"Why do you think Rosary would be hiding out here?" I asked.

"This isn't hiding it's her home and home is the first place *we* look."

I nodded. "You could be right."

He turned to me. "Why do you say that?"

"Because I hear footsteps. Someone is coming," I whispered.

19

Wednesday, 4:00 AM
Amicalola Falls, Dawsonville, Georgia

"You stay in the car. I'll handle this." Maxim pulled out his gun and quietly stepped out the truck.

I tried to glance toward the sound before he left, but all I saw was the gleam of two flashlights moving toward each other. I noticed the outline of a truck not too far from them. I couldn't make out the number of people out there with Maxim or in that truck. I took note of that plus the size of my small gun and ducked down in the truck. Men in woods carried rifles, so I was outgunned. I decided to wait for five minutes and then crawl out, to see if Maxim needed me. I really hoped that he could handle himself.

During that time every cricket chirp and twig snap made my skin jump. It couldn't be dark enough, the oak leaves couldn't camouflage enough, and the stillness outside wasn't quiet enough, to make me feel safe. I felt like a sitting duck in that mud truck, waiting to be snatched and taught a lesson for being the only African American woman snooping around moonshine stills in one of the most racist places on the planet at dark thirty in the morning.

It was understood that Atlanta wasn't like the rest of

Georgia, especially here. North Georgia moonshiners didn't have the best legacy with my kind and Maxim. Back in the day some of them had teamed up with the KKK to defend themselves against the Internal Revenue Service. As bad as I hated to admit it Tiger was right when he said there were "places we still can't go in Georgia without a little help." Shoot, I thought I'd seen a noose still hanging from a tree on the drive up.

I grew more scared for Maxim by the minute and began to second-guess my decision to save Rosary. I prayed she would show up and save us.

There was a tap on the driver's-side window. I pushed my back against the passenger door. My legs were balled up, but my hands were steady and ready to defend.

The driver's-side door popped open. Without hesitation, I slid my gun from my back, cocked it, and prepared to squeeze.

"Angel, if you shoot me, I'll kill you," Maxim said.

I sighed, while disarming my gun. "What happened out there?"

"An ATF member on my task force tipped me off of this place. That's who I was just talking to. A couple of days ago he and his partners found a still near here rumored to be Calhoun's."

"Did he know anything about Rosary?"

"He knew a lot since Rosie is his informant. The short version is that Rosary isn't here. She was spotted in Atlanta getting a ticket at Greyhound. Thinking she's heading South, I alerted the marshal down there to keep an eye out."

"Heading South where?"

"Georgia. That's all I have for now," he said.

"So we're done here?" I hopped back onto the seat.

"Yep and no. We're not walking down to that still, so you can take those boots off and put on the ballet slippers in your purse. Class is over." He slammed his door shut.

"I'm keeping my boots on." I pouted and clutched my bag to my chest. "And stay out of my purse."

"Zip that thing up, better yet, don't bring a purse, else it's game." There was a hint of aggravation in his voice. "By the way, why were you curled up under my seat like a fraidycat? Is that what they teach you at Bounty Hunter Camp, because I know Unc didn't teach you that."

"And I guess he didn't teach you any manners. You left me parked near the last house on the left underneath hanging trees in the KKK playground. I would be stupid not to hide. I don't like feeling trapped."

"I hope you're not like that with the Reverend." He chuckled as he turned the ignition.

"What is that supposed to mean?"

"You said you didn't like feeling trapped, yet you're dating a man of the cloth. If that's not a trapped situation, I don't know what is."

"Are you married or are you one of those guys who think that marriage is a form of imprisonment?"

"I'm married. Married to my badge for ten good years." He revved the engine. "So that's why you're doing Running of the Brides. You're a First Lady in the making. I get it, but don't get how you were going to help me find Rosary by attending."

"I'm not going for myself. I'm on the congresswoman's daughter's bridal team. After I help her find her gown we were going to meet Elaine at her town hall meeting. Sean, of course, will be there . . . without his lawyers."

"Hmm . . ." He grinned as he drove us away. "So you're a bridesmaid. Now that's a shame. You look like bride material, especially with those steel-toe boots. Very cute. I didn't know they came that small."

I frowned. "You're getting way too personal with me, marshal."

"I'm not getting personal enough."

I huffed and threw my hands in my lap.

"By the way, you couldn't wear those down to the still. It would tip off the shiners that someone was out there snooping around and that would ruin our surveillance operation. That's something they don't teach you at Bounty Hunter Camp. How well do you know Rosary DiChristina?"

"I know her well enough to know that she didn't take a Greyhound to South Georgia."

"Why do you say that?"

"Maxim, skips don't take the slowest thing on the planet to get away from the law." I sighed. "Besides, she's a mom like me. There's no way she would have left her daughter. She would've taken her with her."

"How do you know her daughter's not with her?"

"Who told your guy that Rosary had bought a ticket? Should be two."

He turned to me, then quickly back to the road. "I can check on that. Good work."

I smiled. "Why, thank you."

"If you want to skip class in a few hours, get some rest, spend time with your child, you have my permission. I'm subbing for Unc today. Don't worry. I'll make sure you have your required hours for the certification. This definitely qualifies as extra credit. We'll mail you your certificate. "

"What? Did I do something wrong?"

Maxim didn't say another word to me until he pulled into my driveway.

"Thanks for the tip about Rosary. I agree. She's still here. Probably trying to find a way to get her daughter out of here without being noticed. I'm gonna call WITSEC to help her. I should have called them first."

"Can you tell whether Elaine's in trouble? Is this just about the moonshine?"

"Ms. Crawford, I'm not supposed to divulge any more information than I already have. But I'll tell you that the congresswoman has nothing to do with this. It's a simple case of a few bars trying to shortchange the IRS on the new liquor tax. Rosary's in deep, because it's in her blood. Thank you for being of service."

He opened my door for me and waited until I unlocked the front door and went inside.

"What just happened?" I said to myself as I watched Maxim drive away.

"That's what I want to know," Justus said from behind me.

I spun around. He had his tracksuit on. I checked my watch. Whitney must have let him inside after his usual morning run, but I wasn't here. I was screwed.

I gulped. "Justus, it's not what you think."

20

My home had a wraparound porch on the first level.
When I bought the place, I thought it was the best
thing smoking. I put a bed swing on it so that Bella and I
could take a nap or sleep under the stars in it. Now I'm always concerned some vagrant will break in just to sleep for
the night. As I watched Justus sitting there in the dark, I
thought about a different kind of sleeping together. My cheeks
burned as I walked closer to him.

"Do you know how many times I've waited for you on
this swing, to find you gone on one of your manhunts?" he
asked.

"No, why are you telling me this now?"

"Because you weren't here to hear it before," he said.
"Come sit beside me. I have more to say."

I sat down. As usual, I just stared at him dumbfounded,
marveling over how handsome he looked in that running
suit. Today Justus wore a white velour Sean Jean tracksuit. It
felt cool and soft against my skin. It was quite windy this
March. Every time a wind burst through the porch his jacket
rippled and revealed a T-shirt he wore underneath. I caught a

glimpse of his wife beater, a term used to refer to a ribbed white cotton T-shirt. I wanted to touch his side and see if I still fit there. To make matters worse, I could also see indentations through the shirt. It suggested a six-pack and an impressively massive, snuggle-worthy chest waiting for me.

"Don't just stand there with your tongue wagging; sit beside me, Evangeline," he said.

I sat beside him and ribbed him with my elbow. "My tongue isn't wagging."

"I know. Your eyes are bulging." He chuckled, then wrapped one arm around me while I rested my head on his shoulder.

"What can I say? I have a slight crush on my pastor?"

"I have a deeper crush on your new hair. If heaven smelled like this . . ." I heard him sniff my head, then moan.

I giggled. "How can someone with so much game still be single?"

"I'm not single, just in love with a bounty hunter whose hair smells like strawberries and who, against my better judgment, won't listen to me."

I cringed when he said he loved me again.

"Don't worry. I'm not expecting this woman to tell me that she feels the same way yet," he said.

"But you think she loves you back?"

"Oh, I'm positive, although one would think she doesn't when she spends the night with a man in a big bog truck." He squeezed me. "But I do have some concerns. We have some things to work out before that fuzzy stuff clouds my judgment, and as the head of this relationship I can't let that happen."

I turned my head and looked up at him. "Like what?"

"Woman, we don't do stupid. You left this house after I almost begged you not to."

"I'm sorry," I whispered. "It was just business, class, whatever . . . I'll tell you everything that happened and then you'll see what I mean."

"You haven't told me about your class yet. How was it? Was it worth it?"

I laid my head back down on his shoulder and snuggled closer. "It's been embarrassing. I blame it on the bad notes Ava took Monday."

"Bad notes? That doesn't sound like her."

"She took great class notes, but she didn't tell me anything about my classmates or that my instructor's substitute was my instructor's nephew. A U.S. marshal."

"A real life marshal?"

"In the flesh. . . ." I paused. "That was the guy you didn't want me to run off into the woods with. I should have introduced you two, but I didn't know he would show up on my doorstep and that you would be here most of the night."

"I didn't think I would be here either. It's getting harder to stay away from you."

My heart fluttered. I couldn't say anything, but this was the perfect time for me to share with Justus that he was right—Sean had, in fact, lied. Maxim West and the marshal's office at first didn't know anything about Rosie, and then I had opened my big mouth, which sent us out to a place no black person should tread. But I didn't say a word. I was still tongue tied over the "it's getting harder to stay away from [me]" thing.

"How mad were you when you found out the marshal with the stripper name knew nothing about Rosie?" Justus asked.

I sat up and smacked him lightly across his rib cage. He had more than a six pack down there. "How do you know this?"

"I listen to God." He grinned. "In other words, I peep game. Plus, I heard the whole conversation between you guys from the stairwell."

"So you knew this whole time and let me spill my guts?"

"Confession is good for the soul and for us, Angel." He smiled.

"Okay, I have something else to confess then." I blushed. "I stand outside in the back and watch you through the fence peephole while you run."

He wrinkled his brow. "I knew it. I knew you were stalking my morning runs."

My cheeks burned like walking in six-inch stilettos.

He lowered his head and chuckled. "While you're speechless, I want to tell you why I came back here to see you."

He pulled the jewelry box out of his pocket again.

My eyes widened. I held my breath. *He can't be serious.*

"Promise me you won't faint," he said.

I nodded, while slowly exhaling through my mouth. "I'm cool."

He popped the jewelry box open. My hands shook as I studied the contents. Inside the black velvet box was a pair of diamond stud earrings.

I ran my fingers over them. "These are so pretty. Why did you get these?"

"Remember the first time we officially met? I picked you up from the hospital. You wore one earring just like this one. I assumed the guy who had attacked you knocked the other one out of your other ear."

"I remember." I touched my ear. "But those earrings were fake, Justus. I was in costume. I never wear real jewelry in the field."

His face and neck turned plum red. "Just when I think I've swept you off your feet."

"You did, literally." I pointed to our legs swinging. "I love them. Thank you."

"You're welcome." He kissed my cheek and held me tighter. "I really like this."

"Yeah, this porch can become addictive."

"No, I mean giving you things."

"Stop, you're making me feel guilty."

"Well, good. I hope my killing you with kindness works."

"Well, it has, because as of last night I have a free pass for my last day of class, so I'll spend it with my sisters and prepare for The Running of the Brides."

"I don't believe you."

"Seriously, that's all I'm doing besides Bella duties and play."

He looked past me. "I'm sure the person who just walked up the porch steps will help change those plans for you."

"Who?" I turned around to see who Justus was referring to.

It was Maxim West. He had taken off his hat and was smiling at something.

I stood up, to see what he was looking at. "Do you men know that leaving my house means you have to actually leave it?"

21

Wednesday, 6:30 AM
Home, Sugar Hill, Georgia

"Hello," Maxim said with a smile. "May I speak with your mom?"

Bella peeked around the porch pillar. "Mommy, you told me not to talk to strangers!"

"Good girl." I chuckled. I turned to Justus. "She must have awakened and heard us out here. Where is Whitney?"

"Probably asleep." Justus laughed, too.

He hopped off the swing and then held his hand out to help me up. We walked toward both Bella and Maxim together.

"I'll take her inside if you want," he whispered.

I couldn't respond for watching Maxim. He looked at Bella with so much intent it bothered me.

"Morning, baby." I leaned down and kissed Bella's cheek. She squeezed my neck and hugged me tight.

"Good morning, Isabella." Justus hugged her and whispered something that made her smile wider. "Are you still in your PJs?"

"Yes, it's Pajama Day at school," she said.

"I wish I could wear PJs to work." Justus extended his hand to Maxim. "I'm Justus, the pastor at Sugar Hill and a friend of the family."

"Nice to meet you," West said. "Sorry about breaking your date last night."

My mouth dropped. *No he didn't.*

Bella tugged my jeans and gestured with her hands for me to lean down to listen to her. "Is this Aunt Whitney's new boyfriend? She said he was tall."

Whitney has a boyfriend? That would explain the late nights out.

"No, honey. This is Marshal West. He's my teacher and very, very important. He wouldn't be at our home this early unless it was absolutely necessary."

I looked up at Maxim.

His eyes were on Bella. "Your mom is exactly right, Miss Ma'am. Oh, do you mind if I call you that, because you definitely look like a Miss Ma'am?"

She giggled and nodded. "I like that."

"Good, Miss Ma'am. I just need your mom for a tiny minute."

"That's okay. I have to get ready for school." Bella smiled. "Why don't you join us for breakfast? Brother Morgan just told me that he's cooking his famous pancakes. You will like them so much. They have ears."

"Thank you kindly for the offer, Miss Ma'am, but I can't stay long. Unlike you I didn't listen to my mom last night, and I stayed up way past my bedtime, playing hide-and-seek with friends. You know how that goes."

Maxim looked at me in a way that worried me. It made me shudder.

I stood behind Bella with my hands on her shoulders. Justus stood behind me with his hands on my shoulders. We looked like the portrait of an American family except to the neighbors. They knew the truth. My eyes scanned the streets for any dropped jaws.

"Justus . . ." I nudged him. "Can you take Bella now?"

"I got you," he said.

Bella waved good-bye to us; Maxim waved back. He still had that fuzzy look in his eye.

The screen door shut behind them and I had Maxim follow me back toward the swing. I didn't sit down on it, since my gut told me that what he had to say wouldn't be comfortable.

"Did I leave something in your truck?" I asked.

"No." He took off his hat and looked at me. The sun rose behind his head. "Remember when I gave you a free pass for today?"

I nodded, then sighed. He was here to take back the day pass. "Oh, it's fine. I shouldn't get any special treatment for hanging out with you last night. Matter of fact, I need to be there at all times. I think I'm the worst in the class. After I drop Bella off at school I'll be there."

"Wow. Unc said you were long winded, but wow . . ." He scratched his head. "Angel, you're not going to class. You're coming with me."

I frowned. "Coming with you? What?"

"Your boy Sean wants to talk, and he wants you there when he does it. But he doesn't want to do it at his typical spots."

"Okay. Where does he want to meet then?"

"Your stomping ground, BT Trusted Bail Bonds."

I plopped onto the swing. "You can have your extra credit back. I don't want it."

Wednesday, 9:00 AM
BT Trusted Bail Bonds, Decatur, Georgia

When we entered Tiger's office I remembered that his weekly Safety & FTA Pickup meeting began thirty minutes ago. Tiger stood at the whiteboard charting a hunt that he and the Big Bad Boys were working on without me. I wanted to slide into a chair, pull out my notepad, and take notes, but I couldn't. Maybe Tiger would change his mind about my suspension when he heard what I'd done for the U.S. Department of Justice.

Maxim stepped in front of me. "For the record you could do better than this," he whispered to me.

Tiger stopped talking. I peeked over Maxim's shoulder, to see him staring at us.

My neck felt hot. I touched it lightly. "Who says I want to do better?"

"Angel Soft, is that you?" Tiger asked.

"Your high score in my uncle's class tells me so," Maxim whispered, then spun around on his cowboy heel.

Tiger walked toward us. The Big Bad Boys peeked at us from the War Room.

I whispered, "Does Tiger know I'm coming along?"

Maxim shook his head and smiled. "Of course not."

Oh, boy. My heart raced. *I'm in trouble now.*

When Tiger reached us Maxim stuck out his hand. "Mr. Jones, I believe a friend of yours is waiting for us here."

Tiger looked at Maxim's extended hand, then at me. He frowned. "Us?"

"Yes, us, meaning me and the private investigator the marshal's office just contracted, thanks to you. Angel made it clear that if she wasn't taking a holiday from your great work she wouldn't be able to help us." He looked back at me and winked.

I gasped. Private investigator? Contractor? Hmm. I liked that.

Tiger folded his arms over his chest. "Is that a fact?"

"Yes, it is. You were interviewed on Fox 5 *Good Day Atlanta* morning TV show a few months back singing this woman's praises. There was a quote that stuck out. Let me remember . . ." He placed his index finger under his chin. I had to do my best not to laugh at him. "I remember now. You stated that 'a brilliant woman is the best element of surprise.' "

Tiger smiled. "I did say that."

"Yes, you did." Maxim nodded, then patted him on the back. "Anyway, we convinced her to play a little hooky from her vacation today for the greater common good. You understand."

Tiger nodded. "Ain't nothin' common 'bout my Angel Soft."

My Angel Soft. Is he serious?

"Yes, sir, nothing common at all," Maxim said. "We don't want to take up any more of your time. Has Sean Graham arrived?"

"He's here in Mama's kitchen. Angel knows where it is."

Maxim's phone buzzed. "Let me step out and take this," he said, then walked back outside.

I searched for him through the front window, to make sure he wasn't leaving me to deal with Tiger and Sean on my own.

Tiger tapped my shoulder. "Are you gonna tell me what's going on, Angel Soft?"

"Sean didn't tell you?"

"You and I both know that Sean only tells us what he needs us to know."

I decided to use one of my cognitive interview-taking skill techniques that I'd learned yesterday. They were designed to help the interview subject recall certain information. I had glossed over these tips before in undergrad, but they were nothing like this.

"What did he tell you?" I asked.

"Sean calls me up and asks to use the back room for a few hours for a meeting. He shows up with a lawyer. You show up with a marshal. I thought I told you to lay low."

"This is my way of laying low. What lawyer?"

He gave me the side eye. "Come on, Angel."

"Don't blame me. Blame Sean. Better yet, blame your boy Riddick for bailing Rosary DiChristina out of jail just to spite me."

"So is that why you're hanging with the Black Maverick? Didn't I tell you I would take care of Riddick in my own way? Can you let a man lead for once?"

My jaw dropped. I stepped back. "Pump the breaks. Hit reverse. Now say that again and guard your mouth this time in case I kick your teeth out of it."

He threw his hands up. "Hold on, Angel. I didn't mean it like that and you know it."

"Who's the lawyer?"

"Roger Willis. Who else? Angel, you know we always swim in shallow ponds. So don't start trippin'."

"Trippin' . . ." I rubbed my neck.

Now my neck was on fire, more than likely because of lack of sleep and stress. Although Roger Willis had represented Ava during that ordeal regarding Devon's murder, he wasn't my favorite attorney. In fact, he had tried to convince her to accept the charges against her. Again, I don't like him. In my opinion, dealing with Roger Willis meant the shit had hit the fan. I wondered what crap Sean had gotten himself into.

22

Sean Graham and Roger Willis sat in two of three chairs around Mama's pie-baking table. It was an old, white wooden table that stuck out from the stainless steel fixtures and furnishings in the refurbished professional kitchen. Sean and Roger looked just as out of place as the table. Sean smiled shyly at me; Roger nodded. Roger's long neck made him look like a turkey when he bobbed his head. I waved back at them.

There were two other men in the room. They stood near Roger. I had never met them before, but I could smell law enforcement in the air. I assumed they were either more marshals, or ATF, or GBI. My body tingled with excitement over the not knowing.

Maxim walked to where the two sat. "Let's skip the salutations and get down to it."

"I like the sound of that," Roger said.

I didn't. I wanted to know all the people in the room.

Maxim pulled a notepad and pen from inside his right jacket pocket, but didn't sit down. "Have a seat, Angel."

I sat in the chair beside where he stood, feeling a little confused. Maxim turned on his emotions like a kitchen sink faucet, hot and cold in an instant. He was cold now.

"Mr. Willis, I assume you're client has had a change of heart about our offer to have him as a participant informant," Maxim said.

A participant informant was someone who was a go between or middle man for a criminal ring. In this case Sean had decided to cooperate with Maxim or risk being arrested for the illegal sale of alcohol.

"Yes, he has, marshal, and I'll be speaking for him from here on out," Roger said.

"So will you be telling me why Sean asked me to come here?" I asked.

Roger raised a brow at me. "Oh, that's simple. We need you to pretend to be Rosary."

I gasped. "Say what?"

"Since your sister tried to okey-doke me and failed, and you've been doing so well in class, I deduced that you must be the twin who has the talent in deception. That's an important prerequisite to being a good private investigator," Maxim said.

I folded my arms over my chest. "You deduced? Are you sipping on bad gnac?"

He grinned, but ignored me. "Sean has been giving up the location of a nip joint that houses the largest supplier of white lightning in this area."

Sean raised his hand. "Actually, it's a blue-light-type thingy and there's nothing nippy about it. These people have lots of money. Ghetto, perhaps, but a nice spot for good people who have a passion for aged whiskey."

"Sounds like white code for black folk hosting rent parties with cheap liquor."

Sean smirked. "It didn't come from my mouth; those were Rosie's words, mind you."

"So hold on . . . how do you know that these 'aged whiskey connoisseurs' are selling illegal shine, if you're so innocent?"

"That's what I discovered after I bailed your friend out of jail and then she run off to God knows where."

"And before you paid me to bring her back. You do know that being a pompous prick and dumb as dirt don't mix, Sean. How much of this have you involved Elaine in?"

"She doesn't know anything about this. This is my private enterprise. My mistake only."

I frowned. "But you told me when you gave me the money that she knew about Rosary."

"Darling, you didn't hear me correctly. I said that Elaine said if I wanted to get your attention I was going to have to do something big, ergo the $25,000."

"You son-of—" I marched toward him and swung.

Maxim caught my arm. "Angel, I can't afford to arrest you, so calm down."

I huffed. "I'm taking you down, Sean. I don't care what deal Roger has made with the Feds. When this is over you're mine."

"Get in line." Sean straightened his jacket.

"Fool, I'm breaking the line," I shouted.

Maxim grabbed me in his arms and looked to Roger. "Willis, what happened to you speaking for your client? Muzzle that mutt."

"Calm down or I won't let you go," Maxim said to me. There was a glint of joy in his eye as he held me.

I didn't care, because I was so mad I could spit. I had to take a few breaths to calm down.

"Get on with it, Maxim," I said between breaths.

He released his hold of me, but his eyes hadn't let me go. "Angel, the owners of the nip joint will host a party tomorrow. Details are sent via text and in order to enter you have to bring your phone with the text showing."

"My phone?" I asked.

"No, we have Sean's phone. The phone is to ensure that the text recipient hasn't shared the information with someone like us, and to identify the person on the guest list," one of the guys in the corner said. "Very intelligent system."

I looked at him, but he still hadn't looked at me. His eyes were on Sean. I assumed he was standing in Sean's whooping line, too.

"Sean received the text early this morning and is cooperating with your team to clear him from any wrongdoing," Roger said.

"And what about Rosary? If Sean got a text, did she get a text?"

"She had to, because they're expecting Rosary to buy ten gallons of distill at the party for Flappers, but she's MIA," Maxim said.

"We thought about having a female undercover ATF agent join us, but none of our teammates look the part," the mystery guy spoke again. This time he looked at me and smiled.

"Same for Dekalb County," the other said. "You do have a look about you, Angel."

Now I knew who they were. What their names were was another mystery.

I threw my hands up. "Hold up. You do realize Rosary and I look nothing alike. We're not even the same race."

"Regardless of race, you and she share the same coloring and the place will be blue lit. Besides, once they see those pretty brown eyes it won't matter," Maxim said.

The room grew immediately quiet.

He looked up and frowned. "What?"

No one said anything. I was still too in shock to respond. I have pretty brown eyes, but look like a white woman. I didn't know what to do with that information.

I cleared my throat. "And why, exactly, is Rosary buying the hooch and not Sean?"

Everyone turned to Sean.

"I assume you want the mutt to speak now. Very well . . ." Sean rolled his eyes. "Rosary was our distill procurement specialist at Flappers."

"Are you kidding me?" I asked. "You hired a habitual DUI, alcoholic, whose family is mountain moonshiners, to purchase spirits for Flappers? Please tell me you're not the one who knocked her off the wagon, Sean."

"For the record I hired Ms. DiChristina to procure legit artisan liqueur distill. She came highly recommended and I believe— just like you do—in giving people second chances," he said. "You cannot blame me if she couldn't control her environment."

"Sean, there is no such thing as legit corn likker or whatever you want to call it to make it sound pretty. You hired Rosary to buy shine. That's what she did and that's why she's missing. Roger, please school your boy." I turned to Maxim. "Are we going to look for her?"

"The deputy marshal in South Georgia is on the lookout for her. We'll find her."

"Good." I sighed. "She has a young daughter who needs her here, clean and sober."

"Duly noted," Maxim said, then cleared his throat. "Now, you're to meet the host before the party begins. His name is Luxe. From what we've learned Luxe's throwing a party for some baller's twenty-fifth birthday. So there will probably be some jailbait there trying to get in."

"We need to make sure that alcohol doesn't get into the wrong hands," the ATF guy said.

"Like teens? What kind of party is this?" I looked around. "There's a big difference."

"Birthday party, baller party. Teen, blue light. Same difference," Maxim said.

I laughed. He said that like it was true. However, there was a big difference when teens were involved. Teenage house parties were more dangerous than a strip joint off

Metropolitan Road. In the past few months three kids had been shot and one gutted at these parties. Maxim must have lost the last bit of his mind if he thought I was batting my pretty browns up in there.

I pursed my lips. "Um, Maxim . . . not for nothing, but were you joking when you told Tiger that y'all were contracting me for this?"

"No, I wasn't joking. You'll be compensated as a private investigator."

"How much is this compensation, by the way?"

He frowned. "The going rate. Why? What's the problem?"

"My rates just went up." I snapped my fingers. "Way up."

He huffed. "Do explain."

"I'll have to spend all of tomorrow morning at Halle-Do-Ya Salon & Spa to wash the thirties and the twenties off my face, then I need a quick Yoga class to limber up. And the clothes. I have to dress baller chic to go up in there. And I need a smaller stun gun. My old one is cracked."

"You're there to buy, not become a baller's baby mama or tase anyone," Maxim growled. "Anyway, those young girls look just as dried-up nowadays, so . . ."

"Are you calling me dried-up now?" I reached into my pocket, pulled out my phone, and found the calculator feature. "Let's add an extra $250 for a microderm abrasion peel. Shall we?"

"Angel, stop. You know you look dang good. You look younger than your own twin. Wear that dress you wore to Flappers the other night. It was hot."

I stopped play-calculating. "You were there?"

He nodded. "We were there."

"Get a room," someone mumbled.

I blushed. "I think someone can help with the wardrobe, if you can help with the gun, because I'm gonna need that for real."

23

I couldn't meet with Maxim before the party because he was already there in surveillance mode somewhere between the trees and hopefully not in that bog truck. However, he did manage to text me three times on Sean's cell phone that he would be waiting for me as soon as I brought Luxe outside. That gave me little consolation.

Those words reminded me of the many times Tiger left me hanging in the back alley of some club. He, too, was supposed to be waiting for me when I brought someone out, but he was often late. I rubbed the bruise Cade Taylor had left on my shoulder when he dragged me through Underground Atlanta last year. It still felt tender. The betrayal was always there. . . .

To top it off, my gut wasn't satisfied with Sean Graham. He wasn't telling us everything. Like Tiger said, Sean only told us what he wanted us to know. I hoped that whatever he withheld didn't put me or anyone else in danger.

Mom had agreed to stay over and take Bella to school in the morning so that Whitney could get Lana a good spot at Filene's Basement. I would join the bridal team later after I did my job here and recovered some of yesterday's sleep. Therefore, I needed to get in here and get out with no hiccups and surprises. I would be a fool to not prepare for the hiccups just in case.

Sean's phone rang; I answered.

"Why didn't you wear that dress that I suggested?" Maxim asked. There was a hint of pissedoffness in his voice.

I squinted at the phone. "Can you see what I have on?" I asked.

"Of course I can and I don't like it. Well, I do like it. But I don't like it for this. That's not what I asked you to wear. This is going to be a problem . . . for me," he stammered.

"Are you okay, boss?" Ty chuckled.

I gasped and hit Ty, the ATF guy, in the back of the head. He was my chauffeur for the night and enjoying every minute of it so far. Unlike moonshine runners back in the day, these retro renegades today didn't use pickup trucks and Bedford vans to drive shine across county lines. Instead, they put pretty girls in limos and paraded them around celebrity parties and red carpet affairs. All the attention was on the girl, while the chauffeur handled the real business—the moonshine delivery and transportation—in the parking garage. It was very intelligent on their part, indeed.

"Turn the camera off," I whispered, more like spat out. "I don't want him looking up my legs."

"Too late," Maxim said.

"Can't. Government property." Ty chuckled. "Honestly, I like the dress. It makes your skin pop. We men like skin."

I bit my lip and returned to Maxim's call. "Did you hear Ty? Men like skin. So what's wrong with what I'm wearing?"

"The other dress you wore on your date with Brother Boyfriend was pretty and subdued. You looked innocent and safe. You fit in, but didn't sparkle. That's what I needed. Low key and definitely not that high up your hip. You definitely can't sit down in front of Luxe with that on. He may forget his train of thought and have us out here in this cold all night."

"I can sit down in this dress. I'm sitting down now."

"Yes, I know." He huffed. "I think we should call him and tell them we have a delay while you change. We're not that far from your sister's house. I'm sure she can give you something more than just that fur coat. By the way, you look like a pimp's daughter with that thing."

"When Ava wears it she looks like an angel, but when I wear it I look like the child of a pimp? How insulting."

"You know that's not what I meant. We just don't have a margin for error and I can't fail this because of a shiny, too-short dress."

"Chill out. No pun intended." I crossed my legs. "This is a posh party and that's what I look like. You can't tell me that I can't lead Luxe away from the party with this on."

"More like lead him on, the way you're dressed, and you better hope no one recognizes you in there, because all eyes will be on you the moment you step out of the car."

"They won't recognize me, because I'm white tonight. Remember? Your words."

"You got jokes." He scoffed. "Just don't get yourself killed. A stun gun can't beat a Glock in a gun fight."

"Who said I wasn't packing heat?" I asked.

"Packing where? You don't have on any clothes." He scoffed. "Now that was funny."

"That's for me to know and you to never find out." I rolled my neck.

"Is this how you talk to your boyfriend?" Maxim asked.

I frowned and took a deep breath. "Hey, you've been out of line since we began this conversation. You keep talking to me like that and we can end this conversation and call this a night."

"You're right and we're out of time. See you on the other side. . . . I'm sorry." He hung up.

"We're here?" I hung up the phone and pulled out my compact.

"In about ten minutes," Ty said. "I can see the security gates up the road."

I double-checked my makeup and added more lip gloss to my lips and cheeks. The more the glow the better.

"You know he didn't mean it the way it came out," Ty said. "He's not a jerk."

"Well, he's doing a good job at being a first-class jerk. I could have been home in my bed asleep or preparing for my class tomorrow."

"Do you like the training?"

"I like his uncle, not so much him. He's a stickler for the rules, even if the rules are stupid."

"Are you sure you're mad not at him but what he represents? I know you bail recovery agent types tend to live close to the edge."

"The people we deal with are close to the edge. I'm pretty sure they're standing on the edge in ATF."

"Nope, most bad guys aren't that bad. Most of the time they're trying to take care of their family the best way they know how, regardless of what the law says about it."

"I agree."

"We're here," he said.

I looked ahead and my heart almost jumped out of my chest. Luxe's home was a luxurious, Italian-style mansion that resembled a castle tucked behind miles of magnolia, Georgia pine, and a massive brick wall. At night under the lawn lights it shimmered golden.

"This is amazing." I oohed and aahed.

"Keep your garter belt tight, Angel. We have work to do," Ty said.

"I know, but if you guys seize this property tonight, I want first dibs on the auction." I giggled.

Ty chuckled. "I'm pulling you up to the black carpet. You have sixty minutes to get him out before we have to arrest every NBA player and shot caller in Atlanta tonight. Got it?"

"That shouldn't be hard with my short dress on." I nodded, then checked the time. I'd be home before I knew it.

As I stepped out of the limo, I heard the cold night air laughing at me. Whitney had styled me tonight like usual, but she'd taken it up a notch. Her words. I wore an ice blue, beaded cocktail dress with a high v-neckline. It was short enough to keep the attention on my legs and not the Kahr gun strapped to my blue garter belt. I held a white faux fur coat in my hand that was on loan from Ava. My only fear was someone spilling red wine on it. Then I would have to fight.

Ty wrapped me in the coat after he closed my door and whispered, "Maxim had a few more words for you."

"And what is that?" I grumbled.

"Keep that coat on or else." He snickered.

I didn't know where Maxim was, but I knew his eyes were still on me. I sauntered up the stairs toward the publicist standing at the door and handed her my phone. She nodded to the guards at the door for them to welcome me inside. But before I went in I slid my coat off slow and dropped it in front of the guards. Then I took my dear time wiggling myself down, in order to get it off the ground without showing my money maker. Maxim couldn't text me back because the publicist still had Sean's phone in her hand, but I knew he wanted to. I'm sure the text would have been filled with expletives and words I'd never heard before, if that phone was in my hand.

"Ms. DiChristina, I can help you with that." One of the guys whisked my coat off the floor, then caught my arm. "Luxe had express orders for me to bring you to him as soon as you got here."

"Then please do." I smiled and batted my eyes. "I can't wait to see what he's done for the party tonight."

From the outside I knew Luxe was loaded, but I didn't know how rich he truly was until I walked inside. Twenty-five rooms, was what my escort told me. Each room was different and had a different theme: casino, tiki, disco, Parisian, Alice in Wonderland. . . . I spotted a speakeasy-style bar in another room and soon realized Luxe was a genius. Whatever fantasy you had in mind, he had a room for it. How kinky you wanted the party to go, Luxe would supply it. I didn't know what kind of parties they had in here before, but I could tell it was definitely worth the money.

I followed my escort to a corner room between the restrooms. He unlocked a plain door in the hall and welcomed me inside. The room was small and painted black. There was an antique gold pie table placed in front of the wall. A black and vintage French porcelain and gold rotary phone sat on top of it. There was an etching of a naked woman framed in a gold Italian frame above it. Luxe sure had taste.

My escort quietly shut the door and smiled. "Don't freak out, ma'am, but you remind me of my pastor."

I looked down, then frowned. "I thought this dress made me look hot, not holy."

"No. You look fine, very fine . . ." He rubbed his hands together and licked his lips. "Too fine."

I didn't know what stupid woman gave this guy the impression that looking at her as if she was a fresh-out-the-oven batch of fried chicken was cute, but if I found her, I would slap her. Because that look wasn't sexy at all.

"It's just you look a little like her," he said.

"What's her name?"

"Pastor Ava McArthur of Greater Atlanta Faith Church."

I almost dry heaved the cashews I'd eaten on the ride over here and then I collected myself. "But isn't she African American?"

He nodded. "Yep, my bad. I don't know what I was thinking. The more I look at you, you don't look like her at all."

"It's all right. I heard she's very pretty." I rolled my eyes and thanked the room for being dimly lit.

"She's not as pretty as you are." He blushed.

How cute? I giggled. "I like you. I hope Luxe is paying you well for buttering me up."

"Pedro, leave Rosie alone. She's a very busy business-woman," someone said from behind us. "I don't want her man on my bad side. That wouldn't be good for us at all."

I hadn't been aware that there was another door. I turned around. Another man stood in front of me now.

I extended my hand toward him. "Luxe, I assume."

He smiled. Luxe wasn't as pretty as his name, but there was a glint of charm in his hazel eyes. His skin was lighter than caramel, but darker than tan. The light brown fuzz around his lip and chin did a bad job of hiding how boyish this man looked to be in his forties. The rich tone in his voice and the laugh lines around his eyes and mouth gave his age away. He was skinny, but not bone skinny. If he ate peanut butter and banana sandwiches for breakfast for six months straight he would chisel-up easy. The more I looked at him, the better he looked. Something about that discovery made me smile.

"Sean didn't tell me you were stunning," he said. His eyes followed every move I made.

"I have a business policy not to blush on the job." I blushed. "You're getting me into trouble."

His eyes danced. "Well, let's get business out the way then. Shall we? I want to see what you can do when you're off the clock."

Bingo. I nodded, pulled a roll of cash out of my coat, and handed it to him. "Let's do this then."

The sting operation happened fast and fabulous, thirty minutes fast. Luxe sat in the back of Maxim's Crown Victoria threatening my life, while Ty and the sheriff seized: 100 gallons of white lightning, 20 firearms, ammo, 500 pounds of marijuana, and a white tiger. Thank goodness I didn't see that thing or I would have never left the car. Who in the world would bring a white tiger to a party?

I sat in the limo next to Maxim. He wanted to talk to me before he took Luxe in.

He laid the coat across my lap. "Job well done."

I looked down at my covered legs and chuckled. "Does that mean I graduate?"

"Uncle Deke will determine that, but I will give him my extra credit grade for you."

"And what grade would that be?" I batted my eyes and cheesed.

"Whatever you need to pass with flying colors." He grinned. "And your eyes and legs had nothing to do with it. You earned it."

"Thank you." I chuckled and shook my head. "So are we done here? Am I free to leave?"

"Indeed you are. Ty won't be driving you home, of course. Neither will I."

"So do I get to drive the limo home?"

"You're licensed to drive one of those?" he asked.

"Yes, I have a hack license. Don't ask why."

He chuckled and waved his hands in the air. "Well, it

doesn't have to be turned in until close of day tomorrow. That's plenty of time to take the bridal posse to Filene's Basement in it."

I sat up and straightened my dress. "Are you serious? I can have this for the rest of the day?!"

"Call it a perk for taking illegal alcohol, drugs, and firearms off the streets. I think you beat a record or something. That went down fast." He scratched his head.

I hopped over and hugged him. "Thank you. Thank you. Thank you."

He patted my back and lifted me back to the other side of the limo. He cleared his throat. "It's okay. You need to get a move on if you want to surprise the girls before they head downtown."

"You're right, but I need to get out of the backseat if I'm driving this puppy." I handed him his coat back and let him help me step out of the limo. "I'm curious. What will happen to the partygoers and Luxe's staff?"

"If they're innocent, then they're innocent. We have our ways of knowing. Don't worry about that. Now go."

"And Rosary? Luxe is pretty pissed at me, actually her. We haven't found her yet. What if Luxe sends someone after her? Is she in any more danger?"

"Luxe, better known as Lucas Dumas, isn't a concern. The person who supplied him the shine is, however."

"The distiller?"

Maxim nodded. "We need to find the supplier. Hopefully, Luxe can give us that information."

"I don't know if he can. It's a pretty secretive enterprise. What will happen to Rosary if he doesn't know anything?"

He squinted at me, then touched my arm. "We'll find Rosary before any real trouble starts."

I wanted to believe him, but my gut wouldn't let me.

Thursday, 11:45 PM
Home, Sugar Hill, Georgia

When I reached home Justus was waiting for me in the driveway. I motioned for him to back out so I could pull the limo in. I hoped it didn't stick out into the road.

"If we keep this up, I'll have to get you a key." I stepped out of the limo.

He gave me a half smile. "Angel, is this what you wore tonight?"

I twirled around in it. "Yeah, Whitney picked it out, and that girl knows how to dress me. I owe her big."

"Did the task force specifically tell you to wear that dress?"

"Of course not, but that's beside the point."

"No, you're missing the point." He wasn't smiling now.

"What does that mean?"

"Angel, you're the investigator. You pick out your own disguise. Why did you choose this dress? What were you really after?"

"Someone Bad." I huffed. "Look. Bad people don't act like you. They're greedy. They want what they can't have and the way I look—this fantasy—is something they cannot have, but they will do their best to try and get it, even if that means going to jail for it."

"And then what does that make you?"

I waved one hand in the air. "Now you sound like Maxim."

His eyebrow rose. "And what did Maxim say?"

"Same thing you are insinuating. But you're both wrong. I came out in one piece and I'm back here in record time, something that wouldn't have happened if this dress didn't play. The dress played well."

"Is this a game to you? Is this limo the prize? Because you're worth more than that."

"Justus, where is this coming from? When you met me I wore something just as provocative. You didn't mind then."

"Back then I didn't think that there would be a possibility that you would be mine."

Justus had a way of saying things so final that you couldn't respond. You had to act.

I reached into the limo and put Ava's coat back on. I wrapped myself into it tightly. "You won't see that dress again. Now I have to help a bride fight for a dress in the morning."

He touched my hand. "Did we just make it through our first argument?"

"If that's your idea of an argument, then yes. Can I have my good-night kiss now?"

"Uh huh. I can't kiss you like I want to when you're dressed like that, though. How about a date tomorrow night?" He chuckled, then gave me a kiss so hot it melted the cold bad girl in me away.

24

Usually at this early in the morning you would find me trolling through Decatur dive-ins or peeking into Winder hole-in-the-walls to find FTAs (failure to appears), deadbeat dads, guerrilla pimps, or my daughter's supposedly dead father. But today this bail recovery agent and pseudo-graduated private investigator was on the hunt for something most hunters ran away from: a size eight, ivory, silk taffeta, strapless Amsale gown from the Blue Label collection.

Don't get too excited. The gown wasn't for me. It was for Lana.

Sure. Justus had a way with me (last night's kiss), but getting engaged after knowing him for such a short time wasn't one of them.

"Congratulations on your big bust," Tiger repeated for the third time over my phone.

"Are you saying it because you mean it, or is this a backdoor way for you to fire me?"

"You're fine, Angel Soft. I'll be your huckleberry forever, and to show you that I mean it I'll talk to Sean today about Rosie for you. There's no need for him to tell the Feds, but he'll tell me, if he knows what's good for him. That way you can relax, finish out your vacation, and help Lana find a dress that Congresswoman Turner would love you for life for," Tiger said with his deep raspy voice.

Tiger had promised me he had stopped smoking, but it didn't sound like it. I could taste the smoke rings through my earpiece.

"The best thing you have working for you is having Turner in your back pocket. Rosie's gon' need her help once we bring her back and I wring Sean's neck," Tiger added.

He was right. "Elaine could help me, but Sean might throw Rosary under the bus, if he hadn't clearly come clean to Maxim."

"I'll kill him before I let that happen."

"You will do no such thing. . . ." I chuckled, but I understood his sentiment.

I wanted to talk privately with Elaine about the events that had happened the past few days, but there was no time. She was overbooked and too overcommitted to take her own daughter bridal-dress fighting today, let alone chat with me about her right-hand man. So Elaine was about a half hour away hosting a town hall meeting with Sean that snake.

Knowing Tiger would be hanging around made me feel a little better. I was glad to have my old friend back. I wondered what new information Maxim had discovered from Luxe.

"It would make my day to get enough information on Sean Graham to get him fired."

"Now, that could work," Tiger said. "His little show in my office scared off some of my best customers. You know convicts can't deal with that much fuzz around."

I laughed. "Ironic, but yeah. I got you."

"I was surprised to see you there, but I had it coming for not having your back with Riddick, Angel Soft."

"Water under the bridge. Where's Riddick, by the way?"

"Don't know. Haven't heard from him since that day you threatened to sue him."

"Hmm, that's weird."

"Nope, that's Riddick. He's like a ghost. It's a good trait to have in our line of work."

Someone patted my shoulder. I looked up. It was Whitney. "I gotta go."

"Have fun, Angel." He ended the call.

"You hungry?" Whitney asked.

"Is there food here?" I asked.

She pointed to our right. "Over there."

I squinted past the crowd until I spotted the Incredible Flying Soup Mobile food truck. It was stationed in the Phipps Plaza parking lot.

My mouth watered. "Yummy."

"They brought a special morning batch of Italian Wedding Soup to warm up the brides."

Brides began moving around us. Noise swelled toward the host radio station kiosk. I'm not sure if Filene's Basement was about to open, but there was a lot of clamor in its direction.

I stood up. "I think we may be missing breakfast."

"Aw, sookie sookie now. It's about to be on. I'm going to get the girls." Whitney squealed and ran off toward the limo where the girls were.

I'm thankful Maxim lent me the limo. Lana was a giddy mess when we picked her up last night. Despite her mom's political obligations Lana had more pressing concerns. In two months she would wed Atlanta Falcons new star wide receiver Kenny Harvey. The wedding would take place at a barrier island off the affluent end of the Georgia Coast.

Although Harvey had local celeb status, Lana didn't have baller-wives' bank, yet. Lana had just passed the bar and would not begin her first gig as a peds attorney consult at Children's Healthcare until after the honeymoon. So her money was funny. However, we needed a highline dress with Elaine's constituency-approved price points and very little time for error. Therefore this jaunt to Filene's Basement Atlanta Department Store's annual Running of the Brides was paramount for Lana and, of course, stressing her out.

To make matters worse, Lana's maid of honor and self-appointed publicist, Stacy Albright, had been reminding Lana all night that being here was also great PR for Elaine and Kenny. I didn't like her. To me, she was a fame seeker and dumb as a pack of synthetic Yaki. I'm sure Sean would spit her out of the loop the second her big mouth placed Elaine's candidacy in jeopardy.

My phone rang. I pulled it from my pocket. It was Mom.

"Hey, Mom. How's Bella?" I asked before she spoke.

"She's fine. But I have a question for you. Will you be snatching a dress for yourself or will you do with Justus what you do best, throw away another golden opportunity?" Mama asked.

"What are you talking about?" I noticed the bridal team— Lana, Whitney, Stacy, and Lark —coming toward me.

"I saw you guys last night. The whole neighborhood saw you last night. If you don't marry this man, I'm going to have a light stroke and you know my face isn't built for medical challenges. Now Beth Morgan across the street, that woman's face can withstand a tornado. She's withstood a stroke; a broken jaw from that weasel of a dead husband of hers, Carl; the scar on her eye when she went splat into her garage the day she brought her bike home from the store; and then—"

"Ugh, Mom!" I shook my head and searched for the Q100 FM Radio's complimentary coffee kiosk. "Justus and I aren't talking about marriage or anything remotely close to that, so stop eyeballing me, texting me, and please don't even start putting the cart before the horse. No wedding dress. Just dating."

"What's that supposed to mean? 'No wedding dress. Just dating'?" she mumbled. "That kind of man doesn't date. If you're not seriously considering being a pastor's wife—"

"Mama, stop. I'm concentrating. I need to keep my mind clear." I spotted the kiosk and began walking toward it.

"Justus isn't an ordinary man."

"I know that, Mom. Is Bella ready for school?" I hoped she would catch the hint and get off the phone.

"Don't change the subject. I said that Justus is not an ordinary man. Darlin', you . . . well, you're a piece of work, and for a man of the cloth to even consider taking your mess on is a miracle. If I were—"

"Mama, please stop insulting me, else I'm going to break it off."

"Stop acting simple and stop interrupting me when I'm talking. I just want you to consider your future with a man who obviously has contemplated one with you."

"I'll think about it while you get Bella ready for school."

Whitney and the girls had finally joined me. Lana was still farther up chatting with another bridal team.

"Fabulous. I'll make sure Whitney pulls some dresses for you while you're there. We need another wedding in this family and right now you're my only hope."

Mama had a knack for sounding borderline rude and downright overbearing. Yet after what went down a few months ago with Ava, the Atlanta PD, and my murdered brother-in-law, I knew she spoke to me only in love. Plus she knew that getting under my skin was the best catalyst to kick me into the right gear. I did need to think about my future with Justus.

"Do that, Mom." I nodded back, although I knew she couldn't see me.

"Ladies, we'll be opening the doors in one hour for our ROTB contest winner only," Jenn Mobley, one of the radio personalities of Q100's *The Three Jenns Show* and host of the Atlanta's Running of the Brides event, spoke to the crowd. "She'll get five minutes of alone time in Filene's, then y'all can go for what you know."

Some women clapped. The women around us sighed about the wait and joked about their hope that the winner didn't choose their gown during her spree. It didn't bother me.

I had a good idea where Lana's dress was or at least on which rack. What self-respecting bounty hunter wouldn't? Everyone knew VR3 wireless cameras shared the same four frequencies as basic baby monitors and are, thus, accidentally compatible to them. The shared frequency made it super easy to listen in on and watch what went down on the other side of those thick department store walls. I knew the fastest way to retrieve it, and I also knew that Courtney Miller, the bridal spree winner, was about four sizes too big for Lana's dress. *We have this in the bag,* I smirked to myself.

I turned around and surveyed the line of women watching us or pretending to sleep through our foolishness and then my nose twitched. The hairs on the back of my neck stood up.

I gasped. "You gotta be kidding me."

I spotted through the crowd, at about five teams behind us in line, a team so huge they could only be described as a football team. Ten men and ten women dressed in pink and black. The men wore the pink shirts with blond ponytail wigs and fake handlebar mustaches; the girls wore the black shirts and were—no surprise there—blond. But what made the hairs on the back of my neck stand was the content of their WeddingWire posters.

WeddingWire, a sponsor of the Running of the Brides, provided large posters bridal teams used to share with the other contestants the type of dress they were searching for and the dress size. These posters proved helpful after the run when brides traded the dresses they yanked for the dress they really wanted.

Lana wanted a size eight, strapless Amsale. The bride of the pink and black super team wanted the same dress. Unfreaking-believable.

"I hope the groom isn't in that bunch," Stacy Albright said. "Any self respecting man wouldn't be caught dead playing a woman's sport unless he was on the down low."

"I agree, but now I wish we would have forced the groomsmen to join us."

Whitney squeezed my shoulder. "It's too late to convince me that you're afraid of a few divos."

"Nope, I'm not, but I promised Elaine I would be good today."

"So all this time all I had to do was ask?" Stacy smirked.

I gave her the side eye.

I giggled. "Would you be mad if I told you the truth?"

Whitney softly popped me on the back of my head with her hand. "Be nice."

"Ow." I rubbed my head. "I was going to say that I would be mad if we let those bridal cheaters steal Lana's dress."

The girls began cheering. I scanned the crowd again until I laser focused on an old, familiar, unfriendly face.

"Whitney, do me a favor. Take the girls back up to our spot with Lana. There's someone I need to speak to who could be the answer we need."

"Why?" she whispered. "What are you about to get us into?"

"Nothing. Go prepare the girls for the run. I'm coming and that's all you need to know."

She huffed and stomped off. I could hear her mumbles, although her body had disappeared from my view.

Tara Tina Ramirez was the name I knew her by, but according to Tiger's great jackets she had plenty more. Her longtime boyfriend, Cesar Cruz, was an old headache at BT Bail Bonds. Rosary was supposed to be helping me locate him, but she was missing and Riddick had probably paid her not to tell me anything either. Tara Tina, affectionately nicknamed "TT," was also Cesar's indemnitor, the person who signed Cesar's release on the bond and my reluctant source. She had disappeared with him, too, until today.

Before my vacation I had had every intention of bringing his sorry butt in and getting that five grand bounty. Now I wanted to enjoy the rest of my vacation, plus I didn't want to chase anyone at the Running of the Brides. That wouldn't make good sense.

Tara walked toward me in line with a team of three Latina women who were also recognizable to me. They all wore candy red tees, painted-on skinny jeans, and smirks that let everyone know that they didn't mind getting gully about a wedding dress. Only Tara wore an additional baseball cap with BRIDE etched in white crystals across the brim.

Bad disguise. I shook my head and smiled. I wondered whether my boy Cesar was the groom.

I saw them making their way up the line, but they didn't see me. I knew this, because if TT had, she would have scattered fast like a lost WeddingWire poster in March's whipping wind.

When she got within earshot of me I shouted her name. "Tara Tina Ramirez. Why am I surprised to see you here?"

She stopped, then lifted her brim from over her eyes. When she saw me her jaw dropped. Her knees bent. Her friends stepped back into a stance. I hoped those chica divas didn't try anything crazy, because I had no problem going straight loco on their behinds.

Someone pushed me from the back. My heart raced. I glanced behind me, then hissed.

"Whitney!" I frowned. "What are you doing back here?"

"Wondering what's taking you so long. We need to get ready."

I ignored her and returned to the ladies. I needed to keep my position and my eyes locked on TT and her girls.

"Hola, Angel. It's been a long time," TT said. She now stood in front of me, but not too close.

"It has. You look good." I ribbed Whitney with my elbow, but she wouldn't get the hint.

TT looked past my shoulders and smiled. "Is this your sister?"

I slid my hand past my gun, resting behind my sweatshirt, nestled between the small of my back and my jeans. I didn't want to hurt anyone, but I would shoot anyone who messed with my baby sister.

"Hi," Whitney said in that sweet and soft voice she reserved for talking to her boyfriend on her cell phone.

"Whitney, call the police." I whispered between my teeth.

She said nothing.

"It has been a very long time, TT." I nodded. "Congratulations on the engagement, by the way. You'll be a beautiful blushing bride on your wedding day and I assume these ladies are your bridesmaids?"

Her girlfriends didn't flinch or smile.

TT shrugged. "Something like that."

"Something like that, huh?" I checked my watch and glanced at Jinn.

She was talking to the crowd at the Q100 Radio tent. I could read her lips even through the crowd. ROTB would begin in sixty seconds.

"So, who's the groom, Tina? Because it can't be Cesar. See, he's already engaged to a two-year stint in DeKalb for a VOP and then a possible five-year commitment with the state pen in Valdosta, Georgia, and you know what that's for."

Tina backed up. I noticed tears falling from her face. She pointed at me. "Leave me alone, you b—"

The Running of the Brides participants gasped, pulling out cell phones and pointing.

"Everybody relax . . ." I pulled my bounty hunter's badge from underneath my shirt. I kept it on a gold chain now instead of my belt. "I'm—"

"It's the lady bounty hunter!" someone shouted.

I tried to shush the woman, but it was too late. Others saw me and either screamed or cheered. Filene's bell chimed and scared me. I ducked. TT and her crew took off. I watched her sprint and disappear into the wild crowd.

I threw my hands over my hips and huffed. Really?! "I just wanted y'all to help me get a girl a dress."

No one heard me. Everyone was too busy running past me or running from me.

Whitney grabbed me. "Come on!"

I pulled my grab gloves out of my pockets and slid them onto my hands. "It's not like I have anything else to do."

25

Screaming girls fell around me like geese out of formation in an October sky. I lunged over them and kept running. Squealing moms and older women wielded pompons and WeddingWire posters toward the Q100 FM radio personalities who had amused them most of the morning. I couldn't help but laugh, while dodging and zipping past them until a plastic dress cover smacked my nose.

Ow. I huffed and blinked at the same time. The hit surprised me. Yet I continued running and got slapped again . . . this time with a very large dress containing ridiculous amounts of ribbon that would have tripped me had I not been accustomed to running with unstrung athletic shoes and Bella's toys strewn on the floor.

I then realized I was being ambushed. I flung the dress off my head and saw TT's ride-or-die chicks tossing more taffeta, lace, and silk at me. These girls had to have a softball pitching background, because they hurled those balled-up dresses so fast and hard I almost gave up the chase. Almost.

Despite their efforts they never blinded my view of those

pink blond boys racing up the escalator. Those boys weren't getting Lana's dress, so I would not yield. It was on.

My legs and arms pumped harder; my badge pounded and clapped against my chest. It felt great and greatly missed. I zipped and bounded after her toward the top floor.

"Whitney!" I shouted through my earpiece. "These girls are attacking me. I may need a little help, because I'm about to black this chick out and her goon squad, too."

"It's a madhouse up here, too. But Lark and I can handle these boys in ponytails. Don't do anything that could get us kicked out of here. Lana isn't tough like us. Maybe you should let this thing go with TT."

I was almost at the top of the escalator.

"If only . . ." I grunted. "I'm coming up."

TT saw me approaching her and toppled a petite brunette wearing a child's princess tiara at the top of the escalator. I caught my breath. The woman's arms flailed. She began falling backward toward me. I gasped and prayed. I had to reach her before she tumbled down—or worse, injured her anxious-to-be-getting-married flushed face.

I hopped over the terrified woman's crown and caught her. My backside hit the floor and I almost saw stars, but got the bride in time.

I rubbed my butt with my hand. This was getting too dangerous and I had yet to grab one of those pink and black defensive tackles.

The crownless bride hugged me. "You saved my life, Angel."

I double looked at her. "You know my name?"

"Everyone does."

I harrumphed and looked a few paces forward. TT was standing still, looking at me. I tried to hop up, but forgot I was pinned.

"Miss, I need you to let me go," I said to the woman.

"Oops." She rolled off me, got up, and resumed her quest for the perfect dress.

I watched her run off and buzzed Whitney. "We got any dresses for Lana yet?"

"Why don't you look up and see for yourself," she grumbled.

I raised my head and saw Whitney waving her hands in the air. I waved back and then I saw something weird. She stood in a corner near the south left wall. Lark and Stacy weren't moving. They were watching something. I followed in the direction of their gaze. TT's friends stood in front of a dress rack, clutching Lana by her chignon.

My heart dropped to my shoes, while my anger flew up to my chest. *Elaine's going to kill me.*

"Put one of them on the phone," I growled. "Actually, put the ugly chick staring at my backside on the phone. I've wanted to give her a piece of my mind for a while now."

By now most of the crowd was upstairs trading dresses, so the noise had died down.

Since TT and I were still not where the commotion was, I didn't have to shout to her.

I motioned for TT to come over. "Look. I'm not here to bring your boyfriend in. Get over here. I need your help."

She didn't budge.

"Angel Crawford?" Someone with a Colombian accent spoke through Whitney's phone.

I answered. "Hold on for a minute. I'm talking to your cousin."

I lowered the phone. "TT, I have your cousin on the phone. Get over here, please."

TT slowly walked closer. I could tell in her eyes she was one wrong word from sprinting again. But I didn't need that. My plan had gone haywire and I hoped that I hadn't ruined things for Lana.

Once she got close enough to hear my conversation with her cousin, I returned to the call.

"Look, I didn't want your cousin. I wanted you guys to help me get my friend a dress in exchange for my silence that you were in here."

"What?!" they both asked me.

"Yes, that's what I was trying to tell you before you bolted and yanked my friend."

"Oh, my bad," the cousin said.

Tina smiled and raised her hands. "Sorry, Angel. My cousin overreacted."

"I can see that." I looked up. She had released Lana, who popped her with a plastic bag. I tried not to chuckle.

"Well, what dress did you need?"

I searched the room until I found the Black and Pink Ponytail Mustache Squad. "I need the dress that gang in the black and pink has in their hands."

"You don't care how we get it?" she asked.

"No violence, just a fair trade," I said. "Give them something nice."

Tina now stood at my side. I guess she thought we were friends now.

"What is it about these dang wedding dresses?" I asked her.

She shrugged. "Every girl dreams of a princess wedding. You know?"

"Not really, but my sisters seem to." I sighed. "Yet I'm curious. Why would you come here with all these TV cameras around to get a wedding dress? Does Cesar know you're here?"

"He dropped me off," she said matter of factly.

I nodded and tried to ease my nose itch. My objective right now was to make sure the girls were safe and to get Lana through the checkout line with that dress. But soon after all was well, I was going to take those chica divas down. The only problem I had was trying to contact Tiger. He still wasn't the best about showing up on time, although he'd just promised me he would do better. Maybe I should just give them to the police. That way I'd keep my word about not taking her in.

"So when were you two tying the knot?" I asked.

"Next week."

"How? You can't get married without a license. Cesar has a few warrants out for his arrest."

"We got the license in Atlanta before he had any warrants there. Doesn't matter, though. They're too backlogged to search for Cesar. Besides, the jail is overcrowded and they had budget cuts on the police force."

"Seems like y'all have become pros at being outlaws."

"Well, Cesar never had a green card, so . . ."

Are they kidding me right now? I looked around me, to see if I was really standing here listening to this crap.

Whitney whispered through my earpiece, "We're coming down with the dress."

"Okay," I said, as I saw them gliding down the escalator.

I felt for my handcuffs. I still couldn't determine which one would get arrested, TT or the cousin. Then I saw one of the guys from the Black and Pink Ponytail Mustache Gang. He had a black eye.

I shook my head. "TT, I told your cousin no violence."

She turned around. "I told you my cousin overreacts."

I spotted the crazy cousin and marched toward her. She was carrying the Amsale dress, I assumed for collateral. "Why did you hit that man?"

"He didn't want to give up the dress."

"That's not what I told you to do."

"Don't worry about it. He's okay." She waved me off.

"It's not okay and that was not our agreement."

She frowned. "So what? Are you going to take it back now, because of that?"

"Nope. My word is my bond. I said I would not take TT in." I slid my phone out my pocket and dialed the Atlanta police.

"Then what's the problem?"

I motioned for her to hold on until I placed my call. "Yes, this is Angel Crawford reporting a 240 at the ROTB Filene's Basement."

"No, you didn't." The girl lunged at me.

I bobbed out of her reach.

Tina pushed me. I slid the phone back into my pocket.

She shouted, "You said you were letting me go."

"I'm letting *you* go, but your cousin . . . She pissed me off by dragging my girlfriends into this foolishness."

"You should have never brought them along on your stakeout."

"Trick, we're shopping for wedding dresses!" I shouted. "Who in their right mind would come here to look for FTAs. Are you stupid? You gotta be out of your freakin' mind!"

"Look," the cousin said. "We got you what you wanted. Just let us go."

"But you had your hands in my little play sister's head instead."

My temper bubbled up at the thought of those girls roughhousing Lana. I snatched the girl and threw her on the floor. Whitney and the girls got into the fray. I think I heard someone scream.

Filene's security guard ran over to me and pulled me off the cousin.

I yanked the dress out of her hand. "Do you know how long I have staked out this place for that dress in your quick-to-fight hands? Do you know how much money your dumb-as-dirt cousin owes my boss?"

"Ma'am, let the woman and the dress go," one of the guards said to me. They were plain clothed, but revealed tasers on their waists just like mine.

I raised my badge toward them. "It's fine, gentlemen. I already called APD. This woman assaulted one of your patrons and the other is wanted for aiding a convicted criminal. I'm licensed in the county to bring her in; believe me, I'm doing you a big favor. Besides, boys, I can take a tase."

"Perhaps, ma'am. But according to our dispatch, you didn't alert us to the fact that you were about to make an arrest," some man said from behind me.

I turned around. Two of Atlanta's Finest stared back at me.

"It's about time you got here," I huffed.

"Don't look too happy. Looks like we're going to have to take you in, too. You know the law."

In Fulton County bail recovery agents had to alert the county sheriff's office when we were about to apprehend a failure to appear (FTA). However, I hadn't intended to take in TT. I'd just wanted her to help me roughhouse those guys into getting that Amsale gown. Somehow my plan didn't quite jell, but I wasn't going to jail for it.

I couldn't tell which one had just spoken to me, so I addressed them both. "I didn't know a jumper would be here shopping for a wedding dress. Come on, guys. That's not fair."

"Do you think it was fair to cause pandemonium in here? You almost started a riot," the younger one said.

I squinted at his badge. His name was Floyd, Officer Floyd. He looked like a Floyd, too, thin, long neck, red haired, freckle faced, and a button nose to complement his rosy cheeks. He was adorable, if you were into snarky Buckhead cops. Real talk. I used to be, ten years back. Now . . . huh uh.

"Pandemonium? For real? You just said that?" I chuckled, while one of the guards came toward me with handcuffs. "I asked Jane over there to call you, but as usual you guys are late. So what was I supposed to do, let the felon waltz out of here with a dress? Really?"

"Disruption of property, Miss Crawford." Officer Floyd gritted his teeth. "Your pandemonium equates to disruption of property in this county."

"Disruption of property?" I looked around us. Pompons and fake flowers were strung all over the place, taffeta and lace still falling from the ceiling. "Officer, which part of The Running of the Brides frenzy are you going to pin on me?"

Floyd grunted. "Don't start—"

"Excuse me?" I heard a woman's soft voice surface above my conversation with Officers Jacobson and Floyd. "May I chime in?"

"Ma'am, this is police business. Please go on about your way," Officer Jacobson said.

I knew his name was Jacobson because we had met before. I hoped he remembered.

"Angel shouldn't be arrested," the woman said. "She saved me from being thrown off the escalator by that woman." She pointed at Tara Tina. "Who knows what that woman would have done next? And she's not alone. Her friends terrorized Angel's family. She had a right to protect them."

Other women who were hovering around nodded in agreement. Some applauded.

Officer Jacobson waved his hands. "Ladies, please let us do our job."

"Let Angel go." They began to chant. "Let. Angel. Go."

Their voices grew louder. This shouting went on for about thirty seconds until the store manager, who was being questioned by another officer during my interrogation, walked over to where we were.

"Actually, gentlemen, we don't want to press charges. Nothing was damaged. We just need to clean this up fast. Brides are still arriving to purchase gowns. Your police cars and presence may scare them off."

"That's fine," Officer Jacobson said. "But unfortunately, Angel, you'll have to come with us."

My chest tightened. "What did you say?"

"Captain's orders," he said.

A scream pierced the air. We all looked in the direction of the wailing. It was Stacy Albright. She was on the ground holding her leg. Whitney was consoling her.

Stacy looked up at me. "It's broke, thanks to you."

I frowned and threw my hands on my hips. "It's not broke, it's sprained; and you're welcome."

26

Friday, 10:00 AM
Filene's Basement, Lenox Mall, Atlanta, Georgia

Stacy sat in an EMT van pissing me off with her melodramatic screams, while the police officers escorted me toward the squad car. They didn't cuff me or seat me in the back. Instead they surrounded me, folded their arms over their chest, and chuckled. I then realized I wasn't going to jail. They wanted to shoot the bull and rib me.

"What in the world, guys?" I scoffed. "You made me think you were taking me to jail."

Officer Jacobson laughed. "We couldn't laugh about this inside Filene's. We'd get written up, or worse, those bridesmaids would make us look bad on television. They were about to start a wedding riot in there, if we didn't let you go."

"Actually, the folks at Filene's were very sweet to me about this mess I caused. I'm thinking since it was already going to be a mess inside, no one would be the wiser."

"Then you're both wrong," Officer Floyd said. "Some of the brides have been taking photos of the Bounty Hunter Bridal Brawl and uploading them to the Internet for at least an hour."

"Angel, you're Internet famous now!" Jacobson bent over and slapped his knees. "Internet famous."

"It's not funny. I did my job. And you would have done the same." I wiped my brow. "There's no way I would let a wanted felon's fiancée be in here trying on wedding dresses."

"But did you find Cesar under all those dresses?" Officer Jacobson joked some more.

"I don't have time for this." I rolled my eyes. "If all you wanted to do was poke fun at me, then you've been duly noted. I have somewhere I must be."

"And where's that? The Big Dog BBQs Big Groom Throwdown?" He laughed.

"No, I have Congresswoman Elaine Turner's daughter with me. I need to take her to her mom, to show her the gown we found for her."

The ribbing stopped. Elaine's name had a way of changing these guys' perspective. Lana's father was a fallen Atlanta police officer, who died on duty while foiling a bank robbery.

The guys looked at themselves and nodded. "Sorry."

"We were just cutting the monkey with you, Angel. Honestly, coming here was the most exciting thing we've done all week."

"With the furloughs and the constant threats to cut staff some more, it's a miracle we can keep good morale," the other officer said.

"I understand, but I can't be standing around here playing with y'all."

"How about we escort you guys to the interstate to speed up your time?" Officer Jacobson said.

Office Floyd nodded. "We'll have the EMT's take the maid of honor and the other one to Dekalb Medical, so she can have that sprain wrapped."

"That's great, but I don't need an escort. I need to get this limo back to the car rental and Lana needs to get to her mom. She wants to surprise her with her dress. Actually . . . could you get her there? The congresswoman is at a town hall meeting at Garden Ridge."

"Sure thing." Officer Jacobson handed me his card. "It was good to see you. If you're ever looking for a part-time heavy, I need to have another income egg in my basket."

"For sure." I smiled. "I may be calling you sooner than you think."

I walked toward the limo. "Ladies, it's been real. I have to go. The police will escort you to Elaine's, so come on." I gathered my purse and the gown I'd decided I couldn't part with. "You can get to Elaine before she leaves and I can get y'all out of this limo. I gotta hot date with a good man tonight."

Justus had "opened my nose" as Granny had often said when she'd teased Ava and me about our high school crushes. Life smelled sweet again. I had possibilities and wonder, a future designed just for me. Moms, especially the hard-working, will-kill-for-her-kids lioness kind, needed teenaged whimsy to wake them from tedium. This date tonight felt like God breathing life into my inner Eve.

"Angel, wait." Lana caught my arm.

I gasped. "What's wrong?"

She looked up at me. "Stacy needs her car."

"But she can't drive." I looked over to the EMT van. She sat on the cot eyeballing me.

"She's upset. Lana didn't want to go with her to the emergency room," Whitney said. "While you were chatting with the cops, they got into an argument."

Lana tried to speak between sobs. "She's hurt, but what can I do? I'm not a nurse. She said something that made me really, really mad. I lost my temper. She backed out of being my maid of honor. She says she can't take care of all the things that need to be done on a bum leg."

"It's my fault, so I could escort her around, in order to get things done. I'm still on my vacation for the next few weeks."

"Angel, she doesn't want to be anywhere near you." Lana sniffed.

"But it's for a good cause." I reached into my purse for a hankie and handed it to her. "We can put on our big-girl panties to get you down that altar."

"I wish Stacy thought the same thing." Lark pursed her lips. "She's pissed and doesn't want to be a part of the wedding at all now."

"So you're short a bridesmaid because of me." I pouted. "I'm so sorry, Lana."

"No, don't be. Mom says that disappointments are opportunities to see the silver lining. I think I see it now." She smiled and grabbed my hand.

I smiled back, but shook my head at Whitney. Whitney shrugged. Neither one of us knew what she was talking about.

"Whitney, will you be my new maid of honor and Angel, will you be my bridesmaid? You're the same size as Stacy. It's perfect."

The girls squealed in excitement. I'm pretty sure I didn't accept the invitation.

Lana stopped jumping. "Angel, you didn't say yes."

I cringed.

Garden Ridge was set off Beaver Ruin Road I-85 exit in Norcross. It was definitely on my way home with a small ten-minute drop and ride differential. So I could do it and have plenty of time to love on Bella before I got ready for my date. But I wasn't sure I would get this limo back on time. I texted Maxim my issue with the limo and he texted me back that he would meet me at Garden Ridge with Ty. I guess it was a go. Now as for the bridesmaid thing . . .

I turned to Lana. "I think it would only be fair if I inform your mom about what happened today before she reads it in the paper. And I don't need you worrying and getting forehead wrinkles before the wedding over this bridesmaids' thing so . . . I'll do it."

Lana jumped forward and hugged me too tight to hug her back. "Thank you, thank you, thank you for everything, Angel."

I nodded while removing her bony arms from around my neck. For a petite, quiet thing she was strong just like her mom.

Friday Noon
Garden Ridge Retail Store, Norcross, Georgia

Saturdays at Garden Ridge were no picnic, especially on cold days in March. Soccer moms, soccer mom's moms, schoolteachers, and the oh so crafty traveled the four corners of Atlanta to get their decor on at this do-it-yourself home interiors retailer. I used to come here often during my last trimester of pregnancy, to try out all the nice rocking chairs and buy an excessive amount of terry cloth baby blankets. I couldn't find one of those blankets now.

We parked at the back end of the store near the lawn care department. Lark had to stay behind to drive Stacy's car to DeKalb Medical and make sure she was okay. I asked her to talk Stacy back into her bridesmaid's duties so I could back out graciously.

According to Lana, the congresswoman's meeting would be set up in the lawn and garden department. I thought it was clever, because they didn't need to set out any chairs and tables. They were already out there. The kudzu camouflaged the interstate guards, supposedly creating great sound barriers from the highway noise, but it didn't help a whole lot, in my opinion. It was still loud out here. However, knowing Congresswoman Turner, she would have made some lemonade out of the acoustics nightmare here, else she wouldn't be doing it.

The Honorable Elaine Tempest Turner was a blond spitfire hidden underneath Southern charm and a legal mind that couldn't be matched by most Supreme Court Justices. She held these town meetings all over her district as a way to stay in touch with her constituents and gain some good PR. However, I wondered for her safety sometimes. Of course, she didn't.

Yet her bravery and spunk weren't the things that made her exceptional. It was the way she'd raised Lana. That girl was dang near perfect. I welcomed her advisement on parenting Bella more than I did Mom's.

As we rounded the back wall where we'd heard her voice, I heard a sound from somewhere near the clay planters.

I stopped. "Oh, sh . . .!"

I caught both Whitney and Lana's shirt tails. Clipped us all to the ground. The girls landed first; me on top of them. Splat. Cupped their mouths with my hands and listened.

The sound was the high-pitched, feathered whistle of a shell flying through the air. Someone was shooting at us with a rifle.

It wasn't a sound you felt or could anticipate. If you got the chance to hear it once, you never forgot it. You'd better not.

I knew this sound from years of shadowing dad on his deer hunts. I was the closest thing to a son he had. Ava, of course, hated dirt. He'd pitch me in his deer stand, a wooden shack he built and set high, camouflaged among Georgia pine. All I could do was eat sandwiches and sip cold, flat beer and listen. One day I was munching and minding my own business when it flew past me. There I became frenemies with that whistle.

"Sh . . ." I squeezed the girls tighter and prayed. *God, who do I have to kill to save us?*

27

Friday, Noonish
Garden Ridge Retail Store, Norcross, Georgia

"Stay down and behind the lawn umbrellas." I slid off the girls.

"What do we do?" Whitney screamed.

I whispered, "Don't move, Lana. Whitney, call the police and stay here."

I pulled my Kahr from out of my holster and scanned the perimeter. People were screaming to the east of us. People ran from the west, north, and south. More shots rang out. I ducked, but began running toward the sound of bullets.

Whitney mumbled. "You brought a gun to the Running of the Brides?"

"Shut up before you get us killed," I said in a drier tone like I did the first time the Big Bad Boys let me join a seize and capture. "I have to see what's going on."

I studied Lana's wide eyes and quivering lips. I knew she was concerned about her mom, but I couldn't say anything reassuring to her. I didn't know anything until I found Elaine.

"Gonna find your mother. Okay?"

She whimpered softly and nodded. I patted her head.

"Call the police, Whit, and don't leave this spot," I said

again before I disappeared between wicker lawn chairs and florals.

I ran east, where the screams were loudest, but no one was coming out of the store.

My heart raced. I had no plan but to find Elaine. And I meant to find her fast.

Footsteps approached from somewhere around the corner we had just come from. I stopped and stepped back into a Weaver stance. My legs were bent, both hands on the gun. It wasn't the best shooting position, but my mind wasn't in the best position either. Nonetheless, whoever was coming from the other side better not be squeezing a stick, else they're getting popped.

An unarmed man flew around the wall and fell. He scrambled up. Panting.

"Hey," I whispered. "What's going on?"

He looked at me, then at my gun, and stumbled back.

"No, no, no. I'm not the shooter." I caught him, almost pinned him up against the wall, and reached for my Georgia bail recovery agent identification card.

In Georgia bounty hunters have to carry identification cards. It notes the bondsmen who contracted us and our physical appearance. Big Tiger's ridiculously oversized T was scribbled over my chin on the ID photo.

"I'm here to take down the shooter," I said while placing the gun back into my holster.

He trembled and began to sob in my arms. He was a frail man. Korean descent. Late thirties. Dressed in khakis, a plain white tee, and a blue jean jacket cuffed around his neck.

"What's your name?" I asked.

"Jason Song," he said.

"Jason, I need to help the other people." I patted his back and tried to quiet him down.

"Don't leave," he pleaded.

"But I have to go see."

"He's shooting everyone. He's coming." Jason's hands shook. "I have nowhere to hide."

"Trust me." I placed my hands over his. "I'm coming to get him first."

I reached for my walkie-talkie to call Whitney, then reconsidered. "Quiet is kept" was the best plan so far. I lowered my phone back into my pocket and turned the corner.

Unlike the scene at Filene's Basement, the crowd ran toward me with nothing in their hands, but a whole lot of fear in their eyes.

A man with strong hands grabbed my arm.

I was in shock. I grunted. "Sir, let go."

"No." He continued to run, dragging me with him.

I planted my feet on the ground, which forced him to stop. "Let me go."

He frowned, then looked over my head, then back at me. "Woman, are you crazy?"

"Is the shooter a man?" I yanked myself away from his hold.

"Lady, I'm not letting you die."

I pointed at the gun attached to my hip. "Does it look like I want to die?"

"Who are you, lady?"

"Not again . . ." I huffed and ran past him.

By the time I reached the east entrance, Garden Ridge looked like a scene from an urban zombie movie. One of those Top 40 pop songs—that you couldn't remember the title or the artist, but knew the words by heart—played in the background. However, it didn't muffle the sound of people in agony and the soft crunch of steel-toe work boots coming toward my left.

I slid out the gun again, took a breath, and crouched behind the nearest cash register station.

A tall, white man with a dark buzz haircut, long bowed legs, and blood splattered across his T-shirt walked past the linen aisle toward the entrance. He carried a sawed-off shotgun. I assumed he was either leaving or going out to shoot anyone still outside.

My heart raced. Whitney and Lana were out there. I couldn't let Rifle Man go out there. But then there was Elaine. Where was Elaine? What had he done to Elaine? Until I found her I couldn't let the shooter stay in here either.

I looked behind me and assessed my options. The police hadn't arrived, which meant Rifle Man and I were the only ones armed. I was at a disadvantage, which didn't look good.

The last time I'd been in this predicament I'd gotten a concussion fighting off Cade Taylor, a skip who thought he could drag me through Underground Atlanta. Before I passed out I made sure the police dragged his butt back to jail.

I thought I heard a police siren. I hoped that is what I heard, because I couldn't wait any longer.

His footsteps came closer. I braced my gun with both hands and slowly stood up.

"Sir, put the gun down."

His eyes widened. He stumbled back and began firing. I dropped to my knees and focused on his knee cap. But before I squeezed the trigger and made him a cripple I noticed something peculiar. He wore a Garden Ridge badge around his belt strap. I looked around me. All his bullets had dropped on the floor, but nowhere near where I stood. I don't think the man knew how to shoot a gun.

"Look. The police are on their way and you can't shoot worth a spit. So if you're not the crazy shooter on the loose, put that gun down. If you are"—I lowered my voice—"then put the gun down, because I can blow your head back easy."

He dropped the gun and slumped to the floor. "I'm not who you're looking for. I work here."

I looked around us. "Where is he?"

"I don't know." His shoulders jerked. He threw his hands over his face and began crying. "Lord, help me. I don't know."

I loosened my hold of the gun and ran over to him. "What does he look like?"

"Normal." He quaked.

I held his hands until I heard the police sirens.

"Sir, I have to find my friend before the police arrive. Have you seen the congresswoman? Where is she?"

His eyes widened, then his face crumpled some more. "You don't want to go where she is."

I felt my knees buckle. "I'm afraid I do."

He pointed with trembling hands toward the pottery area near the back of the building, the place I'd been heading toward from the outside before the shooting happened. I begged him to call me after he spoke to the police, gave him my card, then patted his back.

I ran with lead feet toward the pottery area.

If my worst fears were answered and Elaine was dead, I had to check the crime scene before the cops pulled me out of here. Technically I had no jurisdiction here, because the shooter to my knowledge didn't have a skipped bond. But I couldn't. I wouldn't leave Elaine back here to be looked over with pity. She deserved more than that. She deserved my kind of justice.

I tiptoed down the aisle until I saw Terri, Elaine's mousy press secretary, crumpled on the floor. Dead. I gulped and continued on my tiptoes. I was superstitious about being noisy around the newly dead and dying. I felt that the silence was being respectful.

And then I gasped. "Sean!"

My brother-in-law Devon had been butchered by his assistant with a chef's knife and I had watched him bleed out in

Ava's arms. I'd thought it was the cruelest, most cowardly way to kill someone, but as I watched Sean's frozen-in-time lifeless body I changed my mind. This was the cruelest way to kill someone.

He sat in an iron lawn chair with a digital tablet in his lap. His head had fallen back over the chair's backrest. His sandy brown hair dripped with blood and brain matter. His blue left eye appeared to study the detail of the green ceramic garden angel staring back at me. We both knew Sean was dead. His right eye was gone and so was my faith in decorum.

28

Friday, After Noonish
Garden Ridge Retail Store, Norcross, Georgia

Istood frozen, watching Sean's dead body. Prayers came out
of my mouth, but the prayers were more for me. I didn't
know what to do. I needed help; a clue. I observed his head
injury. From a distance it looked like a gunshot wound, but
something was off. The entry wound didn't look like the ef-
fects of a bullet. It reminded me of something else, but I
couldn't think of it, because I was still searching the place for
Elaine.

"Angel." I heard someone whisper my name from behind me.

I spun around. My heart beat so fast. My hands had auto-
matically drawn the gun out of my holster. I pointed the gun
at the air. I saw no one.

"Am I going crazy?" I lowered the gun and dropped my
head.

"No, but whoever did this must be," the invisible spoke
again.

I knelt down and squinted. "Elaine?!"

She was crouched inside a ceramic pot on the bottom shelf
in the back row. "Is he gone?"

"Thank God you're alive." I caught my chest and breathed

a sigh of relief. "Stay where you are. You're probably the safest person in the building."

She gave me a thumbs-up. I checked around for other signs of life.

I tiptoed around Sean and looked on the ground to my right. His wallet had fallen out of his tweed trousers. Yet, I didn't see any blood dripping on the floor. If I hadn't smelled a weird metal-like burned odor coming from near his collar I would have thought he was just unconscious or asleep. Was the bullet stuck in his bone? That didn't make sense, but I wasn't going to move him to make sure, because I didn't want to further contaminate the crime scene.

However, I did kick his wallet away from him so that his blood, which had oozed a bit from his head, didn't stain its leather. Sean prided his things, and in honor of his memory I thought I should at least preserve his wallet. It looked expensive. Yet, I had enough knowledge of crime scene investigation to know not to put my hands on it. I probably shouldn't have kicked it either, because when I did, the wallet turned over and fell open. I gasped at what I saw.

"Angel, it's Maxim. Gwinnett County sheriffs are here with me. Tell me where you are."

"Maxim, we're back here. Congresswoman Turner is back here with me alive, but Sean is dead." I looked down at Sean's wallet again and began to tremble. "Get here quickly; I need to show you something."

I reached for a linen hankie in my pocket. I collected them at estate sales all over Atlanta. They are small, inexpensive, and something I can visualize passing on to Bella. I scooped up Sean's wallet with it, then took a picture of his ID with my phone camera. I then scanned some receipts and his grocery super saver cards in my scanner phone app. You can gather a great deal of personal data from a grocery discount card: home address, e-mail, shopping preferences, prescriptions, and the name of family members who can also use the card. I rubbed the wallet down with the hankie, then placed it back on the floor where I'd seen it and kicked it into the blood.

"Angel, where are you?" Maxim shouted again.

"We're in aisle 9 wicker!" Elaine shouted. She now stood on the other side of Sean's dead body. "Angel, where is my daughter?"

"Max, her daughter Lana is outside with Whitney. Someone secure them, please."

Whitney accompanied Lana and Elaine to Gwinnett Medical via the Gwinnett County Sheriff's department. I hung back to talk with Maxim, Gwinnett County Police, and the Gwinnett CSI on this case. Actually, they made me stay.

We were still at the crime scene. Terri, Sean, and two others were covered in sheets. One was a constituent who was in line to receive autographs of Elaine's latest book, *The New Southern Woman: A Political Perspective,* and the other was her bodyguard. From what I'd learned so far six others were injured from either being trampled on or from ricochet pistol bullet wounds. All the local media were still instructed to wait across the street, including *The Sentinel.*

Maxim chatted with the CSI team and the medical examiner (ME). I snuck a peak at my photos of Sean's wallet again. I had to share my theory with Maxim or I was going to explode.

"You need to put that phone away before they see you," Maxim said as he walked over to me. "Considering your journalism background, they may confiscate it."

"Good looking out." I slid my phone inside my pocket. "Do you know what happened?"

"Obviously, it's an assassination. I just shared some specifics about Sean's involvement in last night's nip-joint sting with the detective." He placed his hands on his hips and sighed. "If Rosary wasn't dead before, she's probably dead now."

"Not if you get to her first," I said.

"Angel, what are you talking about?"

I pulled my phone out and showed him one of the photos. "Remember when you received a bad tip that Rosary had taken a Greyhound to her family?"

He nodded. "And?"

"Do you also remember when I told you that Sean bails out Elaine's constituents, so that probing eyes aren't on her?"

"Come on with it, Angel."

"Like you told me before, I didn't ask the right questions. We didn't think to ask Greyhound whether any tickets were bought in Sean's name." I pointed at the picture of the Greyhound receipt in Sean's wallet. "Two tickets: one child, one adult. Destination: Brunswick, Georgia. Has to be Rosary and her baby. I bet she's headed to her family in St. Marys."

Maxim looked at me. His mouth was slightly opened. His eyes sparkled.

"We have to go now." He took my arm.

"We can't go." I yanked my arm away from him. "You, Ty, and your posse can go and get her. I'm going home."

"Rosary needs you, Angel."

"No, Rosary needs to be protected before whoever just killed Sean finds her. I need to get home, hug my daughter, finish out my vacation, and prepare to be a bridesmaid in a wedding."

"And don't forget you have a date with Brother Boyfriend tonight."

I ribbed him. "Stop with the surveillance, Maxim, and leave my man alone."

"I'm sorry about that. But to be honest, I need you to

leave all your loved ones for a few days." He took off his hat and looked me in my eye. "Angel Crawford, I need you now."

"I'm on vacation. . . ." I shook my head. "Please don't do this to me."

"I'm not trying to do this to you. It's the truth, as bad as I hate to admit it." He grinned. "You've been right all along and I believe you're the only one who can find Rosary. We don't have a lot of time to discuss this further. We need to get to the Georgia Coast."

"What about the deputy marshal guy? Can't he take it from here?"

"She'll try, but she'll succeed if you're there, because you know the area and you know the shine community there."

I squinted in surprise and shook my head. "What do you think you know about me?"

"I know about your Uncle Pete, Granny's, apple pie shine . . . your dad."

I turned away from him and closed my eyes for a few seconds to keep from trembling. "Uncle Pete can't be a part of this plan, Marshal."

He cleared his throat. "Maxim. I prefer Maxim."

"Nope, I didn't make a mistake." I turned back toward him. "Marshal, while you were investigating me, you should have dug a little further, because then you would know that there was no way in hell I was going to talk to that man."

"You don't curse, Angel."

"You don't know me, yet you curse me by bringing his name up."

"Come on, Angel. Part of being a good investigator is using what you know to get what you need. We need to stop this guy and you can. Break the curse by saving someone you can save. In fact, you would be saving two: Rosary and Lucia

DiChristina. Isn't this what you've wanted since I pulled you into this task force? To save Rosary and Lucia?"

A young woman with shoulder-length brunette hair that fell in ringlets walked toward us. She wore officer blues like the rest of the guys walking around, latex gloves, and disposable polyethylene overshoes. She carried two pairs in her hands, I assumed for me and Maxim.

Maxim handed me the overshoes. "Are you in or out?"

I snatched the overshoes out of his hands. "You make me sick."

29

Friday, 2:00 PM
Garden Ridge Retail Store, Norcross, Georgia

"Thank you. Now, hide that phone and those pictures of Sean's wallet," Maxim whispered, then turned toward the detective and grinned.

My chest tightened. I slid the phone back into my pocket.

"Angel, this is Officer Ramona Page. She's the Gwinnett County Police Homicide Detective handling this case. She needs to ask you a few questions about what the scene was like when you arrived."

Ramona stepped toward me and extended her free hand. "You're the infamous Angel Crawford."

"Oh, I hope not." I shook her hand, while slipping on those overshoes with the other.

Detective Page had an accent more Southern than mine. A bit Appalachian unlike Amicalola Falls, but on the other side of the Chattahoochee Forest, more like Blue Ridge. She had a normal build and height, but possessed green eyes that pierced the sun. Sean would have fallen madly in love with her, if he could see her. I looked back at the hole in his face and sighed.

She handed me a pair of latex gloves and then smiled in a

way that seemed heartfelt. "Ms. Crawford, my condolences regarding your friend. I know this is a troubling time for you and I appreciate so much that you have chosen to stick around. I know this isn't exactly where you want to be."

I placed the gloves on my hands while chiding myself for not having them on a few minutes before when I'd gone through Sean's wallet, and I also prayed that my handkerchief rubbing had removed my fingerprints from the wallet." Sean was more like a frenemy type, but he didn't deserve to be killed. If there's anything I can do to help, I'm your girl."

She nodded. "Good, because I need to ask you a few questions."

"Can I ask you a question first?" I cleaned my hands on my pants, then shook her hands. "Is Congresswoman Turner okay?"

Detective Page nodded. "She's pretty shaken up. Whoever this guy is he killed most of her team. We're looking at possible suspects who may have it out for the congresswoman."

"But this shooting had nothing to do with Elaine."

Page folded her arms over her chest and frowned. "Why don't you think so?"

"Because the congresswoman's right-hand man was my informant," Maxim said. "We raided a nip joint last night because of him."

Page's frown softened into a curious smile. "You as in Angel and you?"

He chuckled darkly. "Ms. Crawford is a part of my task force, Ramona. She's a private investigator. Her story is long, but will give you the answers you need, and since it's going to take you a long minute to process this building, perhaps Angel can give you the highlights. But don't take too long. We're going on a manhunt directly."

Maxim's cowboy shtick had returned, which meant he

was getting into his element. I needed to get into mine, but I needed to talk with my family first.

I leaned over to him and whispered, "Maxim, I need to go home first."

"Then don't be long winded." He smiled at Detective Page. "Ladies, I need to make a few calls, gather the boys together, and take care of some things. Don't worry. Detective Page is nicer than I am. You'll like her. I'll be outside where I need to be, so they can tag this place up."

After I told Detective Page everything I wanted her to know she stopped her digital recorder and closed up her notepad. "You've been very helpful, Ms. Crawford."

"So I'm free to leave? I need to see about my family."

"You are. Thank you."

Then she caught my jacket sleeve before I stepped away. "One thing. I hope I'm not being rude in asking, but what's the deal between you and Marshal West?"

"Nothing." I squinted at her and noticed a familiar twinkle in her eye. "You gotta crush?"

She blushed. "Who doesn't?"

"For the record, I don't." I patted her shoulders. "I'll put in a good word for you."

"Please do." She smiled.

Someone spoke into her walkie-talkie.

"Um . . . Angel. Actually, you can't go home just yet. There's been a development."

My stomach thudded. They must have found my print on Sean. I gulped.

"Am I in trouble?"

She patted my shoulder. "You're not in trouble. As you know Marshal West is the senior inspector for the Southeast Regional Fugitive Task Force. They are the first call in this state for a major fugitive investigation. Just about every law enforcement branch in the state is a part of it."

He is? "Of course, that's why I need to get home. We have state stuff to do. We have to hunt down the shooter, whoever he is."

"But according to the statement you just gave, you actually met the shooter."

I frowned. "Can't be. I only spoke to three people before you guys got here: a Korean gentleman, some guy who tried to keep me from coming in, and the bad-shot security guard."

"Who?" She cocked her head. "Because the fourth victim covered up over there is the security guard."

She pointed at another dead person hidden under a sheet. He wore black rubber sole shoes. My head began to throb.

"Who was I speaking with near the checkout counter?" I asked.

Detective Page shrugged. She looked at me in that way a veterinarian looked at you before she told you that your dog had to be put down. "Angel . . ."

"Do you mean to tell me that I had the shooter and I let him go?"

She nodded. "I'm afraid so." Her face appeared as full of regret as I felt.

I felt light headed. I stumbled into her arms. "I need to get out of here."

Detective Page escorted me out of the CSI technicians' way, while they prepared the scene and to meet the rest of the U.S. marshal team in charge of this special fugitive recovery case. During our walk through the store she shared that Deacon West, my instructor and Maxim's uncle, was one of the first African American U.S. marshals in Georgia. U.S. Marshal Services was the second oldest federal law enforcement agency in the country. They had wide boundaries and swept over many jurisdictions, apparently. Maxim was a bigger dog than he'd let on and I felt embarrassed for not being impressed by him earlier.

When we stepped outside the building I gasped.

Police presence at a crime scene always surprises me. Gwinnett Police had surrounded Garden Ridge. The parking lot was filled with white crime-scene-unit vans and white Ford Mustang cruisers. The officers on the scene wore crisp periwinkle cotton shirts and gray pants. Yellow crime scene tape had been put down. A few officers demanded that the press, yet again, move across the street where the old Shoney's Restaurant and Inn used to be. I squinted when I thought I saw a familiar face over there, but it was too far to see.

Maxim ran over to me. "Are you okay?"

"A little woozy, but don't worry; I'm not pregnant." I chuckled. "I think I'm hungry."

"I think you need to be checked out. You have had a very stressful day." Maxim walked away and whispered something to Detective Page. I tried to read their lips, but couldn't. My mind raced with all the surprises that had happened today: Tara Tina Ramirez showing up at Filene's, Sean's murder, and now this crap. I could picture Tiger waving his hand and telling me that he'd told me to stay home.

Maxim touched my shoulder. "I want the EMTs to take a look at you before we go. Is that okay?"

I looked up at him. "Can I take back what I said before about going with you? I don't want to do this anymore."

30

Friday, 3:00 PM
Garden Ridge Retail Store, Norcross, Georgia

The only good thing about being here this long was that Garden Ridge had cushy pillows and nice tables to use as a sort of lounge/work station underneath the canopy. I sat on a bench next to a sketchpad artist and a technician with an electronic tablet that housed current and past felons in a database. We were hidden from plain view by outdoor canopies. Apparently, the crowd made it hard for us to leave.

"When the shootings were happening I ran inside to stop the shooter, but bumped into this guy wearing a Garden Ridge Security Uniform," I repeated to a CSI technician, who now videotaped my interview.

"Is this really necessary?" I asked.

"Yes, ma'am. It'll keep us from asking you to come down to headquarters for more questioning." Detective Page smiled at Maxim instead of me. "Also, these tech toys will help us track down the shooter faster. Is that okay with you?"

"Very." I bit my lip and leaned over to get a better glance of the tablet. "I need to get one of those."

"You should." Detective Page smiled again. "Angel, by any chance, do you remember what the shooter looked like?"

"Yes." I checked my watch.

We had been sitting here for at least an hour and I had been on this scene for maybe three. I'd called Mom and told her what was going on and spoke to Bella. It had calmed me down for a little while, but this was going on way too long.

Because of the economy, low staff numbers, and higher crime rate it took longer to process crime scenes. Murder scenes, of course, took longer: twelve to fifteen hours long. This was worse than staking out a rap artist carrying a duffle bag full of ones into a strip club. Maybe being a bail recovery agent had more perks than I realized.

"Now would be a good time to share his description with us." Maxim nudged. "It'll help us, too, and we have to get a move on."

"Well, he wasn't as pretty as you, Maxim." I gave him the side eye.

He didn't smile, but continued walking toward me. He wore blue jeans well, too.

"Was he black?"

I shook my head. "White."

He coughed. "Was he my build? My height?"

"Your height, but you have a better build. I mean, you have larger muscles. Oh, I'm exhausted." I covered my eyes with my hands. I sounded like an idiot.

Ty had arrived a few minutes earlier. He sat on the other side of me and patted my back. "You're doing good, kid."

I peeked at him. "No, I'm not."

"Yes, you are," Maxim said. "Clear your mind and use what Uncle Deke and I have taught you. Tell me about the Knocker."

He now stood in front of me, yet I saw him in a different way. This was his show. It was his arena and he looked good in it. I gulped. Either the turkey sandwich he gave me a few hours ago hadn't hit the spot or I was missing Justus. Whatever it was it definitely wasn't a growing attraction to Maxim. I was sleep deprived.

I looked to Ty and Detective Page in confusion. "Knocker? What is that?"

This time Detective Page wasn't smiling or nodding. There was a tremble in her fingers. "The Knocker is a person, Angel. A very, very bad person."

"He's back." Ty cursed. "This guy is crazy. He uses a captive bolt pistol on his marks."

"That's why I thought about a horse ranch when I saw Sean," I said. "My family uses that to put their horses and cattle down."

Ty grinned. "You're a country girl?"

"Not really. Ava and I are from South Georgia, but Mom moved us here to Atlanta when she remarried. We were kids then. We only returned during the summers to help out until I was sixteen." A chill ran up my spine.

Maxim pulled a folding chair from the other side of the table, placed it in front of me, and sat down on it. "Is this too much for you?"

"Yeah." I chuckled nervously. "I need to use who I am to get what I want. I can do this."

"We're going to leave in a few minutes and get you out of this space," he said. His arms were on my leg, but I knew he wasn't being flirty, just concerned.

"Angel, your description of him, the large bolt that popped Sean's eye out of his socket, looks textbook Knocker," Ty said.

"So who is this guy?" I asked.

"His real name is Biloxi James. He's a hitman by trade. Has roots in Mississippi, Louisiana, and Tennessee, but word on the street is that he's been living in Georgia for a while now near Kingsland and St. Mary's."

"Bootleggers?" I turned to Maxim. "They have hitmen?"

Maxim touched my shoulder. "Not like what we think. Not like the movies. They're not the mafia."

"Not too far from it, either." Ty smirked. "Moonshine, even in GA, is a multimillion dollar business. Outside of Atlanta, package stores aren't a dime a dozen. Everyone doesn't care for champagne, wine, and wine coolers like you can get in the grocery store. They want whiskey. They want white lightning and they don't want the federal regulated kind."

"So people are hired to protect the illegal kind, the people who make it, and the moonshine way of life."

I gasped.

"What's wrong?" Maxim frowned.

I turned to Maxim. "Sounds like something Rosary would say. Is this a coincidence or a sick joke? Why would he come up here if she's down there?"

Maxim sat back. "I don't think he was coming for Rosary. Someone tipped him off about Sean's involvement. This was a hit to shut his mouth."

Ty huffed. "Do you think Rosary told?"

"No. She's a snitch, for sure, but I have a gut feeling she's devoted to Sean." I sighed, then looked at Maxim. "And if The Knocker saw what *we* saw, then she's definitely next."

"Right. If he's returning to the swamps, then it's made our mission to retrieve Rosary even more difficult," Maxim said. "He'll be even harder to find, if he's down there."

Ty chimed in. "He's probably getting help from the moonshine community, too."

"Uncle Pete . . ." I sucked my teeth and shook my head. "If there are people helping him hide, then it's harder for you to find him. We have skips who've been on the run for years. I'm sure it's because these people make sure they don't hurt for anything."

Ty shook his head. "This reminds me of the Centennial Olympic Park bombing."

Maxim nodded. "It sure does."

In 1996 Eric Rudolph, a terrorist under contract with a mysterious anti-abortion collective, bombed Centennial Olympic Park the night of the Atlanta Olympics opening ceremony using a military-made weapon that contained three pipe bombs nailed under the base of a concert sound tower. Two people died and one hundred eleven were injured. The bomb was the largest pipe bomb in U.S. history.

"Covering this bombing helped me move up at *The Sentinel*," I said.

"The Rudolph search got me interested in law enforcement." Detective Page rejoined the conversation. "The FBI searched for him around my childhood home."

I lingered on Detective Page's words. I knew she was from up in those North Georgia woods. As I watched the three law enforcement officers reminisce over a sad and scary time in Atlanta history, I realized that, in a sick way, tragedy had advanced all our careers, including Elaine's, who was a part of the prosecution team of Rudolph's case.

"If we're dealing with another psycho like Rudolph, then how are we going to get him? That guy hung in the Appalachian mountains for months."

"It's okay. We know where he's heading. We'll get him with your help," Maxim reassured me.

"We'll see." My stomach began to churn in knots.

I wasn't skilled like these people. I was just a bail recovery agent who could use some of my old journalism skills to find someone who was very easy to find. Finding a needle in a haystack was what I was hoping to learn from Maxim and Deacon. But I wasn't expecting this kind of in the field training. I don't know what this man was thinking.

Then I remembered that I'd given this Knocker person my card when I ran further inside to find Elaine.

"Oh my God!" I jumped up, almost knocking Gwinnett PD's laptop off the bench.

"What's wrong?" Maxim shouted.

"My baby." I panted and hopped up. "I gave that man my business card. He knows who I am! He knows how to find me and my family, if he wants to. I have to get out of here."

"Hold on, Angel. We'll get protection to your family, but you can't go. Definitely not now."

"But I want to go home. I need to go home." I could hear my voice shaking.

"Darling, I need you to come with me." Maxim placed his hand around my waist. "Please. I promise I won't let anything happen to Bella and your family."

Friday, 4:00 PM
Gwinnett Norcross Police Station, Norcross, Georgia

I was escorted to the Gwinnett Police Department Norcross precinct to get away from the scene and to regroup the team. Distraught. Detective Page continued her work at Garden Ridge. Ty had gone to ATF headquarters to talk with his crew. According to a text from Whitney, Lana's fiancé, Kenny, was with her and Elaine. Stacy and Lark were fine, but concerned for me. Weird. Mom had taken Whitney and Bella with her to her new home with El Capitan, and Justus was holding a prayer vigil at church. Expected. Everyone seemed to be taken care of, as best as could be. I thought about Sean again and wondered what family members would be coming to take care of his final arrangements.

I tried to relax, but I couldn't get Sean's death out of my head.

"I remember reading a story about the meatpacking industry a few years back. They called the guy who shot the cattle with a captive bolt stunner the Knocker. Not because the stunner knocked the cattle brain dead, but because of the sound it made. It sound like a pinch. A knock."

"Imagine that done to humans," Maxim said.

A chill ran down my spine. Almost every week for five years I've listened to Tiger talk about the skips we had to locate, but they were never this chilling. The people we hunted had issues, but this guy was an issue.

"If you brought me here to calm my nerves, don't. I work best when afraid. Let's go."

31

Friday, 6:00 PM
U.S. Marshal Southeast Division Headquarters, Atlanta,
Georgia

I called Mom and Justus again on the drive downtown. I
told them I wasn't coming home for a few days and to kiss
Bella for me. I wanted to hear my daughter's voice, but if I
did that, I knew I would have backed out of this thing. Detective Page said she would plant a marked car in my driveway while I was away. However, I knew that wouldn't scare
someone like The Knocker from my doorstep. Most criminals spot an empty squad car a mile away. I needed to call
Tiger.

There was a brunette marshal in the room with me. Her
name was Lieutenant Sanchez. She had tawny skin, so I
couldn't tell whether she was South American, Welsh, black,
or just tan. She wore dark jeans, a matching jean jacket, and
a blue tank. She used her badge as a belt buckle similar to
Maxim's. I liked her style better.

"Welcome, guys. We've been waiting for you in the boardroom to my right," she said.

"Cool, but I need to make a call and there's no service in
this room," I said to her.

"It's out in the entire building. GSA has been working on restoring cell phone coverage since this morning. It'll be up before court begins Monday, so in the meantime, you have to use the landline." She pointed at a black IP digital phone that sat in a cubicle across from the boardroom she'd referred to previously.

She and Maxim went into the boardroom; I went to make my call.

There was a swivel chair inside the cubicle. I sat on it and took a quick visual sweep of the floor before I made my call. It was busy, but bare, not like the sleek offices I saw in movies. It wasn't as high tech either. The only area that looked highline was the receptionist desk and the lobby area. I had spotted a polished red rotary phone in the lobby when we passed it and thought of Elaine. She had a similar phone in her office. Sean had used it often. I pulled my phone out and saw the picture of Sean's wallet contents again. What had he and Rosary gotten themselves into?

As soon as I dialed Tiger, I knew he wouldn't pick up. He didn't fear law enforcement, but the Fed, especially the IRS, gave him the heebie-jeebies. I left a message instead.

"Angel, we need you in the boardroom," Sanchez said.

There were five people in the room: Sanchez, me, Maxim, and two people I didn't know. They smiled at me and waited for me to sit down. Then their faces turned harder than guerrilla-snot hair gel. The night had just doubled in length.

"Have a seat," Maxim said.

I shook my head. "If everyone else is standing, then so should I."

He grinned. "Have a seat, darlin'. You'll need your legs later."

"What does that mean?"

He picked up a letter off the table and waved it in the air.

"We've received a warrant for Biloxi's arrest and a confirmation from an informant that he's hiding in Charlton County."

My heart raced. "Do you think Rosary's there, too?"

"I hope not—well, not with him anyway—but this does close the gap on finding the both of them. We could kill two birds with one stone," Ty said.

Kill? I hoped The Knocker hadn't killed Lucia and Rosary and had just come up here to finish the job with Sean.

"She looks pale, West," Ty said.

"Angel, are you okay?"

"I'm all right." I looked up. "I'm going to be hunting him in the swamps?"

He nodded. "Don't worry. You can rest up on the drive down."

"Are we going to Folkston now?"

He shook his head and paused. "No, we're stopping in Lake Park first. Remember?"

"Uncle Pete?" I felt my lip quiver and then I said a quick prayer. "I need to say good-bye to my family first."

Friday, 9:00 PM
The McArthur Estate, Stone Mountain, Georgia

We arrived at Ava's McMansion just short of midnight. Mom had rounded everyone up and had them say good-bye to me there. As tired as I was, I was pumped to see my little baby. If it wasn't dangerous and Sanchez wasn't hanging on my every move closer than my shadow, I would've smuggled Bella in a U.S. marshal's duffle bag and brought her with me. I didn't want to leave and I definitely didn't want to leave her here another night without me. I just wasn't a fan of the place.

While Sanchez parked the Trailblazer I unbuckled my seat belt and noted the grounds. Since Devon's death much of it hadn't changed. However, the Mission Possible gate was gone and replaced with a dude in uniform, a large stone gate, and security cameras everywhere but where they should be. I stared at the new gate and asked God to place protective angels over it and the guard.

We made our way up the front walk. The magnolia trees still lined the front facade, although the flowers hadn't bloomed yet, because it was still too early. The marble, cherub water fountain still illuminated the path toward the front doors the same way it did when I had dropped Bella off yesterday morning. Yet even the light drip of water lapping the fountain pool and the soft chirps of the nocturnal whippoorwills that sang all night around the gazebo—none of it ever stopped me from dreading my walk to the those brick red double doors. Devon was murdered here and although I didn't see the difference of his absence, I felt it. I felt the guilt.

And I was also haunted by it. Why was I spared?

When we stepped into Ava's pristine house I heard my Bella screaming my name. She raced toward me as fast as her little legs could carry her. I bent down, scooped her up, and changed my mind about what I'd just thought. I regretted agreeing to go on the manhunt with Maxim and Justus.

Ava, Mama, and Whitney weren't too far behind Bella. I introduced Officer Sanchez to them and, after Bella returned upstairs with her cousins, I shared my plan to join the manhunt, but didn't give them any particulars, and surely didn't mention my visit with Uncle Pete. We moved into Ava's sitting room to get more comfortable.

"I don't have a good feeling about this." Mom held a teacup in her hand. She couldn't carry a conversation without holding something indulgent.

"I agree." Ava paced between us. "This manhunt idea doesn't sit well with me either."

"Do you think I raised my hand and asked to join? Maxim—"

"Maxim?" Ava stopped pacing. "I'm getting tired of hearing his name. I think he's going to be a problem if you don't check that, Evangeline."

"He's the U.S. marshal in charge of the fugitive recovery of Biloxi James," Sanchez said.

"He's cute?" Whitney finally spoke.

She had been holding my hand since we sat down. I squeezed it when she made that joke. We hadn't talked much since after the Garden Ridge incident. I could tell she was out of sorts: I could tell she needed Big Sister love.

Unfortunately, Ava wasn't her source for that. She was just as shaken. Elaine had been her poli-sci adviser in undergrad. We'd both thought the worst when I went inside after the shooting. I'm thankful Elaine is alive, but terrified about how close she came to death.

"He's all right." I leaned closer to her and winked at Sanchez. "How are you feeling? How's Lana?"

Whitney looked at me. Her eyes were both sunken and swollen. The sprite spirit that had once glowed from those eyes was buried behind a darkness that I had met six years ago. I had seen so much violence in the past six years I knew how to compartmentalize my life, prioritize my actions, and tuck my feelings away. But as I watched Whitney still shaken from Sean's killing, I wasn't sure if I could continue to keep it together.

She lowered her head onto my shoulder, then clutched my shirt and cried. I held her until she released me; she needed to get it out.

Sanchez checked her watch, cleared her throat, and tapped the watch with her fingers. I knew what she meant. We didn't have much time.

I kissed Whitney's head. "Hon, I have to go."

Whit sat up. "I want to come with you. I want to hunt that fool down."

"I know you do, but you can't come. I need you here." I eyed Mama and Ava, who had worried looks on their faces.

I turned to Sanchez. "I'm ready."

We stood up.

Whitney grabbed my shirt. "No!" she shouted.

I caught her arm and tried to remove it. Her grasp on my shirt was strong.

"You're taking me with you," she said.

"No." I shook my head. "I'm not."

She jerked. "Yes, you are!"

"Look. I don't have time for this. Important people are expecting me back. I can't." I looked for Mom.

She nodded and hopped up to comfort Whitney.

"Stop treating me like a child!" Whitney scooted away from Mom. "I'm grown and I'm going. You don't understand."

"Sit down." I stepped in front of Whitney. "Don't make me stain Ava's white carpet and couch. Don't make me."

Whitney's lower lip quivered. She glared at me as if she were a wild bobcat ready to pounce.

I looked down at her, then sat back down beside her. "I know what you're doing and you don't want it to stick."

"I want my happiness back." She puffed, as tears brought some light back to her eyes.

Mom whimpered. Ava prayed. I asked them both to go upstairs. Sanchez sat on the other side of Whitney. I was beginning to like this woman.

I pulled a hankie out of my bag and made a note to myself that I might need to pay another visit to the antique shops to find more, then handed it to Whitney. "Honey, I need you here. I can't concentrate on what I have to do, if I don't know you are all safe."

"But if I'm with you, you would know that I was safe, because I would be with you."

I looked past Whitney to Officer Sanchez. She held the same blank stare as I thought in my head. Whit was exhausted, needed sleep, and some understanding, but I didn't have that kind of time to give it to her.

"I hear what you're saying, but I'm not the chief inspector of this task force. He'd already made up his mind about who he wanted on the team before he asked me. And you're not licensed to walk a dog, let alone go with us. Study for the bar. Okay?"

"I have to do something." Her voice shook. "I can't look Lana in the eye unless I do something."

I remembered Sean's missing right eye and shuddered. "At least you can still talk with your friend."

"Sorry. I wasn't thinking." She whimpered.

"No, that's totally fine. I know you're hurt." I stood up. "But you're staying with Ava and Mama and that's final."

She jerked her hand away from me. Whitney wiped tears from her eyes, stood up, and ran upstairs. I watched her and wondered if I should run after her. Maybe I should call Tiger and ask him to check in on her, too.

Friday, Midnight
Uncle Pete's, Lake Park, Georgia

Uncle Pete, unlike the many men in my life, was actually family, except for times like these I wished that he wasn't. He lived in the backwoods between Ocean Pond and Lake Park Cemetery in an all-brick, coffee stain–looking ranch on the corner set back far from the road, hidden behind mossy oak trees and old auto parts rusting in the front yard.

We were four hours south of Atlanta.

I knew the property well, because I'd taken him into custody at least twelve times since I began as a bail recovery agent. Uncle Pete went to jail for mostly petty crimes: DUI, driving without a license, bootlegging, driving without insurance, beating Aunt Mary, and some other things I cringed to admit, else I might go down for accessory after the fact. Nevertheless I worked for free for every bondsman Aunt Mary had a bond with. She never knew it, but I made sure Uncle Pete knew.

He kept a few chacha brandy stills in Waycross and Statenville, near the edge of the Okefenokee Swamp. Chacha or "Georgia vodka" was a clear fruit distillate made out of either grapes, mulberries, figs, or whatever fruit a Georgia farmer had on his property. Uncle Pete's favorite was muscadine chacha. He was infamous for it.

If there was anyone who could write the book on moonshine living it was Uncle Pete. Most days I wanted to beat him with said book, but not tonight—unless he had hurt my aunt again.

Sanchez and I pulled into his driveway while the guys hung back in a Navigator parked across the street near Roadway Trucking Company. There was an empty space in his carport. Aunt Mary's car was missing. I didn't know what to assume. I hoped for his sake she was at midnight prayer meeting.

He cracked his screen door with hesitation, but let us in after he saw me mouth "*Open the dayum door.*" Once inside he welcomed us into his man cave, a back room behind the kitchen, hidden from normal view by the water heater and a tacky, bone-stringed-beads curtain Ava and I had made for them at Girl Scout camp way back when.

The tar-stained, wood-paneled walls were covered in maps and multicolored markers, to pin the places he could pull in on his CB radio transistor. I noticed marijuana plants growing in a closet by the CB. Sanchez gave me a look that I could only return with a shamed pout.

To make matters worse, he wouldn't take his eyes off Sanchez. If he licked his lips at her one more time, I would have to stun him with my taser. Under normal circumstances I wouldn't mind if she shot the pervert, but I needed his help before we left for Kingsland.

I kicked him in the leg. He jumped. "What the—"

"Uncle Pete, if I wanted to disappear in South Georgia tonight, how could I? Make it quick."

"I can't make it quick if I'm in pain."

"You haven't felt pain, yet. Now tell me what I need to know."

He lifted his head. His wild eyes were filled with confusion. "You want my help?"

I looked at Sanchez, then back to Uncle Pete. "Yes, sir."

He laughed. His voice was dry and liquored up. "I thought you were coming here to drag me to jail. Bringing that hot Federal up in here like that. You almost gave this old fool a heart attack. Your aunt told you I'm on them blue pills now? Gotta keep her happy."

I slapped him upside his head. "You disgust me. You know that?"

"Not disgusted enough for you to not show your face here." He chuckled. "Your mammy's too good to take the four-hour drive from Atlanta to come see me, but she will see me one way or another."

"Uncle Pete, I'm not playing." I lowered my head and sighed. "I'm trying not to gut somebody who deserves a bullet in the head."

"Well, I know how that feels." He limped toward his leather recliner and plopped onto it. "What do you need from me?"

"I'm heading down toward the coast to bring in a fellow, but I'm going with the marshals and I don't want to stick out like a sore thumb."

"That's easy. Don't go."

"Not gonna happen. I meant, I don't want any of us to stick out like a sore thumb."

"Then lose the Trailblazers. You need some mud-bogging trucks." I'm pretty sure Maxim patted himself on the back in the van after overhearing that.

"Where can we get some of those down here?" I asked.

"I know a fellow, but I won't tell you in front of her." He tilted his head at Sanchez. "When you plan on leaving?"

"Tonight, if possible."

"The Federals got you doing their work for them now?" He sneered, then spit into a rusty coffee can. By the stench of the room I assumed he was chewing tobacco. I did everything I could to keep from tossing my cookies.

"It's not like that," I said.

"Yeah, it is." He leaned back in his recliner until his footstool flung out. It clanked when he dropped his dirty boots onto it. "And they send a hot tamale with you because she favors them migrant workers in the cotton fields down there. Both of y'all are stupid."

I hit him so hard in the jaw I hoped I squeezed the last drip of tobacco juice out his mouth. Then I grabbed him up, opened the marijuana growing closet, and dunked his face into the soil. "You don't want to mess with me tonight, old man. I will burn this house up and take Aunt Mary to Mama's. Kill you, and Sanchez wouldn't open her mouth about it."

"Why you gotta be so mean, Angel?!" He screamed, then coughed. I'm sure the dirt was choking him.

I yanked him out of there and slung him against the maps. "I need you to get me some mud-bogging trucks, have them waiting for me in Howell 'fore day in the morning, or it'll be 'Night Night, Uncle Pete.' You got me?" *Now I sound like Tiger and Uncle Pete.*

He bobbed his head. "That's all?"

"Tell me, how can someone live in the state without an identity? How can they hide, travel, and no one knows a thing? Better yet, how can someone just disappear without leaving the state?"

"There are illegal aliens, bail jumpers, child support stiffs, honest folk who think taxes are criminal, who live among us every day without needing an ID, but to disappear. . . ." He rubbed his chin. "To disappear means never having to show your face again, living in forests, deserts, places where the popo won't tread because the county doesn't pay them enough."

"What about swamps? You think someone could hide out in a swamp?"

"Filled with gators, moccasins, wild hogs, and skeeters with stingers so long it'll pierce you through and through?" His yellow eyes widened. "Yep. You could live there."

Uncle Pete had a knack for making everything that came out of his mouth the most interesting thing imaginable. I used to love listening to him all day when I was a child. But then I learned the truth about him and Aunt Mary. I now swallowed a twinge of bitterness down my throat when I caught myself lingering on his words.

"Outside of the Okefenokee, where else could he hide?" I asked.

"The only swamp large enough to hide and live in for long periods of time is Okefenokee."

"Which part?" I asked. "It's a lot to cover."

"Not too far from Folkston. But if a man really wants to disappear, all he has to do is live with a hardworking, churchgoing woman. She'll hide him good fashion, so the other ladies won't snatch him up."

"I bet she would." He nauseated me. "If I were to go to Folkston, where could I get a track phone, some bait, and a bloodhound without standing out?"

"Are you asking me about where the crackers shop?"

Okefenokee crackers—or swamp people—was what we used to call them before we stopped believing in urban legends and knew better. They lived around the edge of the swamp. They had their own culture and way of doing things. Rosary's father's family was a part of that culture. They didn't like paying taxes, because the government didn't benefit their lives, so the way they shopped was also different.

"There's a house off State Road 40 in Kingsland where you can get what you need. I'll write the woman's name and number down. She only takes cash, so you better get your cash before you get down there. The banks down there aren't as sophisticated as they are here. May not have an ATM."

"There's an ATM everywhere." Sanchez smirked.

"She don't know what she talking 'bout. That one gon' get you kilt, Angie."

"Thanks, Uncle Pete, and have Aunt Mary call me when she gets home."

"Why?"

"I need her to talk me out of hauling your butt into jail for turning Granny's house into a ganja farm."

Sanchez coughed. "Angel, we have to go."

I turned to Uncle Pete. "Where's Aunt Mary?"

"She ain't dead, Angie. She just done gave up on me."

I chuckled. "Have her call me. I won't believe it until I hear it from her mouth, and if you don't have what I asked for in the morning, you may need to disappear right along with her."

When I hopped back into the marshal's black Navigator with Sanchez, Maxim called. I answered but only heard cackling on the other end of the phone.

"What's so funny?" I asked.

"Angel Crawford, you are indeed a chameleon. Who knew you, a sophisticated journalist turned bail recovery agent turned private dickette, was a good ole country girl?" He continued laughing.

I hung up the phone and drove off, leaving them where they parked. I hoped it would take them an extra hour to find their way back to the main drag.

Friday, 1:30 AM
Travel Lodge, Lake Park, Georgia

It was too late for me to call Ava or Mom after we checked into a hotel for the night. However, there was someone I knew would be up waiting for my call. Justus.

He picked up on the first ring.

"I was calling because I needed to hear a familiar voice to help me go to sleep."

32

Saturday, 6:00 AM
Folkston, South Georgia

I had prided myself on being a GRITS—"girl raised in the south"—but I hadn't reveled in the South until now. Deep, twisty gray moss dangled from oak trees like canopies and nets. I wanted to climb onto them and hang there for a while or swing. I wanted to hide in a gigantic hole at the base of an old towering oak tree that we passed a mile back up the road. There was something lazy and sexy about this place. It made me think of Justus and that wedding dress I'd found at Filene's Basement.

We pulled into a gas station that from the outside looked just as modern as anything in Atlanta, but once inside the people and the dusty pork and bean cans that lined the shelves soon made me realize that I had stepped into a new dimension that deserved my undivided attention—at least until I found Rosary or The Knocker, hopefully Rosary, alive, first.

Maxim stepped outside, rounded the corner of our grimy Ford pickup, thanks to Uncle Pete, and let me out. Ty, Sanchez, and our other teammate, affectionately known as

"Jack Daniels Johnson, the ATF guy," pulled up beside us. If I hadn't been standing next to Maxim we would've stuck out like a sore thumb. He was dressed like the next Marlboro Man and I was still dressed like Bridesmaids Gone Wild, more like pink and yellow clumsy roller derby/cheerleaders.

I waved them over. "Look, we need gas and I need to ask someone to direct us to a decent truck stop or shopping center. I have to get out of these clothes."

"Yeah, we don't want to bring any unwanted attention to ourselves." Ty snickered.

"Sanchez, you don't have any clothes Angel could wear?" Maxim asked. "She looks like a retired high school cheerleader who relives her glory days every Friday night at her son's middle-school basketball game."

I jabbed him in the ribs with my elbow. "If you're not the pot calling the kettle outdated, you throwback Maverick."

Everyone giggled for a few minutes. It felt good to take the pressure off our assignment.

"Let's get inside before someone hurts my feelings," I said to Maxim. "Maybe they can direct me to a place to pick up some clothes."

He handed me some cash. "It's my fault that I didn't take you home. Things were moving so fast I didn't stop to think that you still had on your getup from The Running of the Brides."

I handed him his cash back and smiled. "Thanks, but I'd rather invoice you instead."

"Good Lord, woman. If I see a pair of hundred-dollar jeans on your receipt I'm hauling you in for a white-collar crime that'll stick." He laughed.

I turned back and looked down at his designer duds and smirked. "Pot calling kettle . . ."

Saturday, 10:00 AM
Dollar General, Folkston, Georgia

Since we arrived early, Sanchez went with me to Folkston's Dollar General to help me find something to wear until we got to St. Marys. This big box retailer had become the local general store for many rural towns like Folkston. There was so much cool stuff in here I could shop for hours.

Before we headed to the checkout line with my buggy filled with jeans, v-neck tees, and enough toiletries to open a spa, Sanchez stopped me.

"What's going on with you and Marshal West?" she asked.

"Honey, I have a boyfriend." I waved her off.

"Oh . . ." She perked up. "I was concerned there for a minute."

"Wait." I looked at her. "Don't tell me you have a crush on him, too. Girl, he's a ladies' man, can't you tell?"

"I know." She smiled. "But he's different with you, so be careful."

I giggled nervously. "How differently, exactly?"

"We're not camping out with them when we get closer to where Biloxi is reported to be. West has express orders to keep you protected at some bed-and-breakfast on the other side of town. That's my job, to protect you."

I frowned. "Are you kidding me?"

She shook her head. "No, I'm not. Honestly, I thought you knew about this until I saw you with your uncle last night. I realized you were tough enough to hang, but as I watched West with you this morning . . ."

Sanchez was still talking, but I didn't hear another word she said. My blood boiled. I was embarrassed. What was I doing here, if I wasn't bringing Rosary home?

I walked away from my buggy and stormed out. I heard Sanchez shouting after me.

I turned around and shouted back at her. "Are you coming or what?"

By the time we returned to where the guys were I was a brand-new shade of pissed. I slammed the truck door and marched toward where Maxim stood.

He looked at me and frowned. "You too good for Dollar General?"

I grabbed his arms and dragged him away from Ty and the boys. I heard snickers, but didn't care. I was embarrassed enough.

Maxim caught my arm, lifted me a little. "This isn't the time for your theatrics, Angel."

"What do you mean by having me perch in some B&B while you guys go get the bad guy?" I hissed.

His eyes lit up. He looked over at the crowd and pushed his Stetson farther past his brow. "Come with me."

He walked to the backside of the gas station where the restrooms were. Worst place in the world, in my opinion.

"Look, I know you get off talking to Big Tiger and your boyfriend any kind of way, but this ain't that kind of show. Whatever decisions I make you have to deal with it."

"But it's stupid. Why did you drag me here, if I'm not going to be with you guys?" I shouted.

He grabbed me by the arms. "Hush."

I looked down at his hands. "Let go of me."

He sighed. "If Rosary didn't tell whoever contracted The Knocker about Sean's plans, then someone in my crew did."

I gasped. "I never thought of that."

"Exactly . . ." He pulled me closer toward him. "Sean's death is on my hands. I can't let Rosary, Lucia, and you be on them, as well."

"So having Sanchez baby-sit me will do what exactly?"

"For one, if he shows up where you are, then I know it's Sanchez. If he eludes us in the park, then . . ."

"You can't think it's sweet Ty?"

"I hope it's not either one of them." He let go of me and took off his hat. "But you seem to think that your friend wouldn't dime you out and I think that my friends wouldn't dime me out."

"So we're in a pickle," I said.

"No, you and I are at odds." He dusted his pants with his hat. "The fair thing to do is to test your theory. If I'm right, then Rosary becomes a wanted woman. If you're wrong, then Rosary still becomes a wanted woman, but this time the U. S. Marshal's Department will do our best to save her. Fair enough?"

"Fine." I nodded. "And how will the crew not suspect that something is going on between us, because I had to convince Sanchez that you and I aren't hitting the sheets every time we're away from the crew."

"I'll think of something to give off the vibe that I don't like you. Now get away from me. You smell like cotton candy."

"It's my body cream." I swooped away from him. "I didn't know you hated cotton candy."

"I don't. I'm infatuated with it." He put his hat back on and walked away. "Go get some clothes on. Will you?"

33

"I can't believe we're back here. She obviously didn't want the clothes." Sanchez adjusted her shades and looked down at me.

"Stop acting like a spoiled brat," Maxim said. "There are plenty of knickknacks and paddywhacks inside for you."

"Whatever . . ." She rolled her eyes. "There are a few food spots nearby. Are we eating soon? I'm starved."

"Might as well, because once we meet up with the Charlton County Sheriff's Department there won't be time to enjoy a hot meal, except for Angel," Maxim said.

"And you, too, Sanchez, since you'll be with her. Our budget will pay for you to eat scraps from Angel's table." Ty chuckled.

"Oh, that's right." She smirked. "I'll bring you a doggy bag, then."

Everyone laughed, but I kept my mouth closed, although I felt all eyes were on me. I looked at Sanchez, Ty, and JD and hoped that one of them was the mole. Yet in the short time we'd been together I wasn't so sure. Could Rosary be sending us all into a trap? I didn't know what to believe.

We decided to eat at Michael's Deli, a sandwich pub franchise. It had a few locations in Atlanta. There was one in Suwanee, not far from Discover Mills, where I liked to shop. Here it was across the street from Dollar General and I was snug now in a men's plaid hunting jacket and a pair of Dickies work pants. Maxim's task force felt comfortable eating at someplace we knew, plus they had a discount for law enforcement officers. Of course, I technically didn't qualify for the LE discount, but when you're hanging with these guys, no one noticed.

Then it hit me. We couldn't use the discount. What if Biloxi's supporters work here? I stepped in front of Maxim. "I'll take care of lunch. My treat."

"Thank you, but men don't eat off a woman's dime." He leaned down toward me, looked me in the eye, and whispered, "Don't worry about it. I'm not stupid enough to use the LE discount. Glad to see you're on your toes, though."

Even though it was March, it suddenly felt July hot. I nodded and walked away to find a table where we could all eat together. Real talk. I needed to remove myself from Maxim's hotness.

My plan backfired. Maxim sat beside me after he paid the tab. Ty sat to my left, Sanchez across from him, and JD was flirting with our server at the counter.

"How much of that jacket on The Knocker do we need to share with the authorities?" I asked Maxim.

"A good bit of it came from them. Why do you ask?"

"If we're going by the information they have gathered and sat on for years, why should we expect to get the same results?"

"Good question." He paused, while the server brought us our food. "Do you want to know how I got you approved to run with us?"

"It wasn't because of my relationship with Rosary or my knowledge of moonshine stills."

Ty chuckled. "Angel, JD and I are ATF agents. There isn't much we don't know about moonshine."

I folded my arms over my chest. "Hmm . . . I thought it was my skimpy blue dress that won you guys over."

Ty chuckled; Sanchez scoffed.

"I always miss the good stuff," JD mumbled.

"You wish." Maxim grinned. "My boss and my boss's boss think that I brought you down here as bait to lure Biloxi out. Remember, he saw you and let you go. They tend to think he let you go because he needed you to verify his presence there, so he could claim the killing. But I think it's more than that."

My heart fluttered and raced at the same time. I was scared. I gulped. "Like what?"

"He has something to say and he wants you to have the exclusive."

I frowned. "But I'm not a journalist anymore."

"No, you're better. You're an outcast and a hunter like he is now."

"I'm nothing like him, and I don't appreciate you keep bringing this up here. My mom and dad made sure we didn't associate with those people."

"Except Uncle Pete."

"No, I associate with Aunt Mary. Uncle Pete is a handicap."

"But you put money on Rosary's commissary. Her family are moonshiners, too."

"Because I empathize with her. I could have been her."

"Why is that?"

"Let it go, Maxim."

"When I learned that you were taking Unc's course I did a minor background on his class, a Google search really. Since

I would be pinch-teaching for his class, I wanted to know who I was dealing with."

I folded my arms over my chest. "And what did you think you learned about me?"

"I understand why you and your twin are so different."

"Return Uncle Pete's trucks when you're done, because I'm out." I stood up. "I can catch the Greyhound home. They're quite familiar with me."

"Angel, I'm not begging you to stay or sit down. Like I said before—this isn't that kind of show. If you want to find your friend and help us bring in a killer before he kills again, then swallow your pride and put your big girl panties on."

Maxim had pissed me off, but he had a point. However, I made a promise to never go back to that life and I'm not going back now, even for Rosary. I plopped back down and huffed. "If you want me to help you, then you take me and my family out of the equation."

"Unfortunately, that's exactly why I added you to my team. Angel, I didn't bring you here to be a sitting duck or to scoop up a missing informant. You're here because I need you to use that beautiful brain of yours and hunt him just like he wants you to."

I sucked my teeth. "You sound as crazy as this Knocker guy is."

"Crazy recognizes crazy." He grinned.

"Then you know what I can do."

He put his hands on my shoulders and stared at me intensely. "That's what I want you to do."

"I know what you want, but that doesn't mean that I will."

"I believe you will," he said. "Just remember to keep it on the hush until I figure out whether the leak is coming from either you or me."

"Rosary isn't a snitch."

Maxim knitted his brows at me.

"I'll prove you wrong," I said.

"And if I'm right?"

"I'll tell you about me and Ava."

He snickered. "As if that were a prize. . . ."

"It is to a riddle solver like you."

He didn't respond.

I nodded my head. "Like I thought. . . ."

After we ate our lunch—mine was a potato soup and a half turkey club sandwich—Maxim wanted to run by the plan again. We would meet the sheriffs in fifteen minutes.

"And what about ground cover?" Sanchez looked around us. "How many men will be joining us when we fan out?"

"From what I've been told we have about twenty brave men and women at our disposal to go into Okefenokee with us this weekend. I don't want any of them harmed, so we need to find the fugitive and get him out of here before he does any more damage."

Any more damage? My heart raced.

"What about the fires?" JD asked.

Since spring there had been three forest fires slowly scorching through the swamps: Honey Prairie Fire, Sweat Farm Again Fire, and Racepond Fire. Two had been contained, but the oldest, Honey Prairie, was as stubborn as an aged dog lying in front of the front door. We could smell the smoke all the way back to Valdosta and all the way back to Adel.

"There will be a few rangers with us because of the fires, and I've ordered plenty of water to keep us hydrated," Ty said. Since our time together with the Luxe sting, I felt very comfortable with his logistical skills. I hoped he wasn't a mole. "Oh yeah, and some volunteer firemen, too."

I began to choke on my cola. "Did you say volunteer firemen?"

He nodded and patted my back. "You have to be careful drinking those things."

I nodded, then tugged Sanchez's arm. "Can I use your phone to make a call?"

"Sure, but I don't know if my service is any better than yours."

"I'm pretty sure GSA BlackBerries have greater reach."

"True." She handed me her phone. "By the way, why did you cough when Ty mentioned volunteer firemen? I know you're not sick."

"It was nothing. Just sick thinking on my part."

"What were you thinking?"

"Wouldn't it be crazy if our distiller was a fireman? He would always know when rangers, ATF, or any law enforcement were near his stills. He could camouflage the mash burn with a fire." I shook the thought off with my hand. "I apologize. It's years of searching for angles when I worked at *The Sentinel*. Most of the time they're so farfetched it gets me into trouble. Ask my sister Ava. Hope I didn't offend anyone."

"You only shared your theory with me, so you're good. No one pays attention to me anyway." Sanchez smirked. "Don't take long with my phone."

While they talked strategy, I stepped on the other side of the ATV to make my calls. I chatted with Mom about how pretty it still was here, said nothing to her about Uncle Pete, and said countless love yous to Bella. She asked me if I could bring her an alligator. I told her I would. Then I called Justus. No answer, just voice mail.

"Angel, we have to go now." Maxim's voice made me jump again.

"Justus, I love you," I spat out and closed the phone. Then I cringed. *Did I mean to say that?*

34

We introduced ourselves to members of the U.S. Marshal's Southeast Regional Fugitive Task Force (SERFTF), the Charlton County Sheriff's Department, and the other local law enforcement officers in the area who could lend us help around two in the afternoon. Since the sheriff's department had the legal jurisdiction over the operation, Maxim, who led the manhunt, had to run his plan by them and with SERFTF. The longer they chatted, the more nervous I became. Eyes were on me; I stood out like a red rose in the snow.

While we waited the county staff gave us an empty board room near the front entrance. Apparently, one of our assignments was to set up and monitor the crime stopper anonymous tips hotline. A few citizens had volunteered to run calls, but Sanchez wasn't having it until they were vetted. I admired how she didn't want to be the weakest link on the task force. At the same time I didn't want to spend my days down here stuck inside, waiting for phone calls.

Unlike Atlanta, Folkston didn't have the infrastructure to facilitate high tech toys and Wi-Fi. It was a small town that didn't need or welcome big city interruptions. I remember seeing a water tower, some power lines, and a few phone towers. That was it.

From my short stint with Maxim and his crew they didn't rely on local reserves anyway. They brought their own games to play: a Super Wi-Fi hub, walkie talkies, digital tablets, surveillance equipment, and the kinds of guns you saw in action movies.

I also saw some good old fashioned police work among the sheriffs: initiating traffic check points, pounding the pavement, and looking into every possible lead that was called in. It reminded me of my time at the *Atlanta Sentinel*. There was a lot of butt-in-chair work, definitely not as exciting as chasing down a gambler near the Greyhound Station. Being a bail recovery agent wasn't the most prestigious job, but it's version of dull was a ray of sunshine down from where I sat.

One of the deputy sheriffs walked into our task force headquarters, stopped in the middle of the room, and scratched his head. "Why would a wanted fugitive hang around a small town with so much law enforcement checking under the beds? This place is too small to hide."

Ty was double checking his firearms on the long table to my right. Maxim was out in the main office talking with the sheriffs and other law enforcement. I didn't know why this guy wasn't with him or whether Maxim had sent him back because he had gotten on his nerves. Whatever the reason, he shouldn't have come back here without Maxim. Ty, JD, and Sanchez weren't charming like Maxim and didn't care to be.

"The city is small, but the land is vast. Best thing to do is not confuse the two." Ty looked up and returned to what he was doing.

The sheriff scratched his head. "You didn't really answer my question."

I stepped forward and smiled to him. "Ty means that although this area is comprised of small towns, it's still a huge area to cover, a lot of places to hide. And we're also creatures of habit. If this place is home to our convict, then this is where he'll be or eventually will return to. The challenge is whether or not we will be in place when he returns."

"If not, we'll be here to catch him." The sheriff chuckled.

"Sounds like a plan, Sheriff."

Sanchez walked behind me and whispered. "You're not PR for us. Walk away from this guy and get to work."

I shrugged her off, but she had a point. I thanked her and moved on.

JD sat at one desk, talking on the phone to his sources and local farming suppliers about any current captive bolt and firearm sales. I could have told him that no one in their right mind would buy their ammo from the same place they laid their head. My Uncle Pete was a disgrace to the family, but he wasn't an idiot.

"JD, why don't you check the local post office for any shipments from a gaming supplier. If that doesn't turn up anything, check a marina service. Fernandina Beach and St. Marys aren't far. Savannah . . . if it were me, I would take a short boat to Jacksonville to get a stunner."

JD took the phone receiver away from his head. "Angel, no offense, little lady, but I got this. This is what I do."

I shrugged. "Just trying to help."

Sanchez sat at the desk closer to mine. I wanted to bounce off her my theories about the Knocker's mode of operation (MO), but she was busy interviewing a few locals about known moonshine stills. Besides, she still hadn't warmed up to me.

I decided to work on a hunch. For Uncle Pete's freedom he had given us the proper vehicles to drive into the swamps and maps of where he thought a rival moonshiner kept stills. One still was about thirty miles from here near Kingsland. I wondered if the volunteer firemen assigned to help us would know anything about that. More than likely not. The moonshine distribution and sales system was very intricate and existed on an elaborate system of secrets.

We called it the double blind system, whereby the moonshiner and the moonshine client didn't know each other. They worked through a middle man, so if they were caught by law enforcement, neither could rat out the other, because neither knew who the other party was. The middle man was the prize. That middle man was Sean and from the little information Detective Page had gathered from his house and offices, he kept everything in his head or with Rosary. The more I thought of how deep Rosary and Sean were into this foolishness, the sicker I felt. I understood why Rosary would be caught up in this, but Sean . . . ? If I could solve that riddle we would find The Knocker, Rosary, the leak, and then some.

My leg began to twitch. I decided to take a walk around the office.

Maxim stood in the front board room at the whiteboard speaking with the sheriffs and another woman, who I assumed was the district chief for this region. I read his lips about his plan of attack through the swamps to find The Knocker and his decision to assign me and Sanchez to stick around here to continue interviewing locals. I cringed when I saw the words fall from his lips.

I understood his logic, but it still didn't feel right. Sanchez and I were tough enough to fight the swamps. Shoot, I was the only one around here who hadn't gotten attacked by the mosquitoes from Hell. But I also felt that singling her out would backfire. He should have separated the ATF guys, not his deputy marshal.

He must have seen the worried look on my face, because a few minutes after his discussion with the task force he found me. I was outside on the back-end side of headquarters, watching the sea gulls hunting for earthworms on the side of the dirt road a few yards ahead. He carried a bitten apple in his hand; I tried to hide my iced honey bun in my lap.

"What's with that look on your face?" Maxim asked.

"I'm missing my daughter."

"Of course, you are." He handed his phone to me. "You'll get better reception with this."

I thanked him and dialed. To my surprise Mom picked up the phone.

"Are you done? Did you catch him already?" she asked.

"No, ma'am. We just got here about an hour ago."

"An hour ago? But you left last night."

"Yeah, well . . . we stayed over in Valdosta first, actually Lake Park."

Mom sighed; I cringed again. "I hope your trip there meant you put my brother-in-law under the jail."

"No, ma'am. He loaned us some equipment to help speed things along."

"Are you calling me to tell me that you have forgiven that maniac?" Her voice grew louder.

"No, ma'am. That's not why I called. I called to let you know I was fine and to speak to Bella."

She huffed. "She's not here. She's at Girl Scouts or had you forgotten?"

"No, ma'am. I didn't know if you would take her today."

"I didn't. Justus did. He drove all the way here to pick her up. He thought it would be good if we kept her world as normal as possible while you're gone. At first I didn't agree, but she looked so happy when I told her she could go. However, I told her we were not sleeping at your house if you didn't get back here by Monday when she has to return to school. I think you may need to hire an au pair if you plan to take up with the Marshals again."

"Wait a minute. I thought you were supportive of this."

"I am," she said. "I just didn't realize how far away you three live from us."

"Well, I guess before Bella wasn't in school and you and I weren't as close."

"Right," she said. "Whitney's an adult. She comes and goes. See her when I see her, but the baby . . . you know when Ava gifted you the PI training it was for you to have more options, mainly options that would give you more stability, not more danger and definitely not to be down there with that snake." Mom referred to Uncle Pete.

"Uncle Pete will get what's coming to him. Trust," I said.

"A good butt whooping would do for the time being. Make sure you make that happen before you leave from down there."

"That's a done dollar." I chuckled.

"I know you can't stay long, but before you go let me remind you that Justus is a good man."

I frowned. "Where is that coming from?"

"I saw your teacher/boss Marshal West on the television this morning. He looks like the type you gravitate toward."

"What kind of type is that?" I laughed.

"The dangerous type."

"Mom, don't go there."

"You know your Uncle Pete. You see what your Aunt Mary has to go through. Y'all are cut from the same cloth. That doesn't mean you have to wear her dress."

I looked at Maxim then turned my head and whispered. "Mom, he's a Marshal for goodness sake."

"And what does that have to do with the price of milk? Men with badges get a license to be bad. You know that."

I shook my head. "Yes, Ma'am. I do."

"So be careful. I know you'll return to us safe. It's the

sound part that concerns me. I love you, baby," she said, then hung up.

I handed the phone back to Maxim.

"I hope your mom's warning about me sinks in," he said.

I shook my head. "I don't know what you mean."

"Oh, yeah. I forgot you lie for a living. Keep that up. It'll be helpful here."

We ate again. This time one of the sheriff's brought in some pit barbecue that was good enough to make you sugar tipsy. I suspected beer in the sauce.

After dinner Maxim handed me Uncle Pete's keys. "Ladies, get yourselves checked in somewhere then join us at the sheriff's office bright and early in the morning. If you need more time than that, wake up earlier."

I gulped and then nodded. Sanchez didn't say anything. I hoped her silence was an indicator that she wasn't the leak that spilled the beans about Sean and the Luxe sting, because I needed someone to talk to. These guys were too tight-lipped for me. I missed Tiger and Mom's wisecracks. I missed having fun on a hunt.

"We need a place to stay off the beaten path." I pulled out the wrinkled paper Uncle Pete had shoved in my jean pocket last night and handed it to Sanchez. "There's a B&B not too far from here and that house shop Uncle Pete talked about is in the area."

Sanchez glanced at the map and passed it back to me. She grinned. "You're beginning to earn your keep."

"Don't know if you'll think the same after you hear me snore." I smiled.

35

Georgia Moon B&B looked like a show house in a *South-ern Living* magazine catalog. It was a light blue bunga-low trimmed in white and surrounded by palm trees, Georgia pine, and white sand from the Georgia coast. It was charming.

Claudine Morgan, the proprietor, showed me to a room that was pink, luscious, and filled with magnolias. I giggled at the thought of Sanchez gagging once she saw her room. She didn't look like the Southern lady type. Mom often said that most Atlantans were far removed from the elegant re-sponsibility of being Georgian. As I sat on my bed and rubbed my hands across the lace and silk duvet, I wondered if there was a ring of truth in there. Just like the heritage and prestige of creating your own family chacha or mountain dew, places like these were luxuries now that most people no longer cared for.

There was a white, porcelain claw-foot tub in the bath-room and it made me sad. I should have taken my vacation seriously and booked this place as my weekend retreat. Bella would have loved the warmer weather and the chance to wiggle her tiny toes in the sand. Lana's wedding would be a few minutes up the road in a few weeks. Perhaps I should surrender to that bridesmaids' gift. It would be a great excuse for me to ask Tiger for more time off. I could use some of the money Maxim would pay me for finding Sean's killer to spend a few extra days here with my baby, maybe convince Justus to book a room down the hall—not as frilly as the room Sanchez had, but something nearby. It would be our first test as a family together and alone from our own professional and family responsibilities.

As soon as Ms. Claudine dropped my room keys into my hands, I wiggled out of my clothes and pretended I was the lady in the Calgon bubble bath commercials.

When my phone rang I assumed it was Sanchez calling to remind me of our schedule. I wiped the bubbles off my hand, reached for the phone, and answered.

"Angel, it's Rosary. Did I just see you on the local news?"

I sat up straight. Water splashed everywhere, including on my clothes.

I pulled the phone back from my ear, to make sure I hadn't dozed off. "Rosary, is that really you? Are you in Folkston?"

I whispered. I didn't want Sanchez to hear for fear she was the mole and might tip off Biloxi's contractor.

"I'm in Statenville at my auntie's house. Lucia is with me."

Statenville. I knew it. "You know we've been searching for you."

"I know I skipped my bail, but folks don't care about that as much down here. I got a job, because my boss is in the same Sunday School as my auntie. When I get my money right I'll contact the courts and pay whatever the cost is to clear the warrant. So please don't look for me, Angel. I can't go back up there."

"Do you mean you can't go back to jail or back to Atlanta?"

"Both." She paused. "I can't give you the details, but right now, until things die down, it's the right thing to do."

I cringed when she said "die down."

I rubbed the back of my neck. "It's not that easy, Rosary."

"But it is. Sean told me how it works with the courts. He may even loan me the money to get out of all of it."

"Why would he do that?" I asked.

"Because he's a good man." She paused. "He's good to us."

"Rosary, he's dead," I said, straight with no chaser. "He's dead, honey."

Silence.

"Did you hear me?"

Silence, then a click.

"Rosie!" I shouted.

She hung up before I could get her phone number and aunt's address. I also wanted to tell her we would keep her and the baby safe.

Someone knocked on my door again. I jumped.

"Angel, it's me," Sanchez said. "Are you okay?"

"Yep, I'm good. . . ." I slid out the bath and tried not to slip on the floor with my wet feet. "Just thought I saw a spider."

"Okay, well. I'm right down the hall," she said.

I hurried and put on my clothes. I needed to tell Maxim where Rosary was. Statenville wasn't a big town. It was a hop and skip near Uncle Pete and Aunt Mary's. It would be easy to find her now that we know where she was. If only I knew her auntie's name.

I called his cell. He picked up on the first ring. "This better be good, Crawford."

"Maxim, Rosary just called me and hung up after I told her that Sean Graham was dead."

He cursed. "Angel, are you applying any of the interview and interrogation techniques we taught you in class?"

I bit my lip. "I was caught off guard."

"Stop with the excuses and tell me, what happened?"

"All I know is that she's in Statenville, where her aunt is, which is a few minutes from here. She saw us on the news, and Sean provided more than free legal service."

"Do you know what this means?"

I shook my head. "Not yet? No?"

He sighed. I could hear his disappointment with me in his voice. "It means The Knocker knows we're here. The sheriff's office promised me that they would ask for an embargo from the press about our activity here, but from what you just said I now know that was a wash."

"What should I do now?"

"Open your window so I can get in."

I frowned. "What? Are you outside?"

"You think I would leave you alone with a possible mole?"

"Well, you're not coming up into my boudoir. How 'bout I climb down to you, that way Sanchez won't know I'm gone."

"Yeah, that's exactly what I meant," Maxim said.

36

As Sanchez slept, Maxim and I checked into a seedy motel and combed through every out-of-date phone book, newspaper, and high school yearbook I could slip out of the B&B, to find Rosary's aunt. I also did a lot of cyber digging. During my Tuesday class, Deacon had introduced us to some MI6 spy software that could cut our work down to minutes. The only challenge was that we were down here in Swamp Georgia. The Wi-Fi Internet connection was slower than a gopher turtle waddling across the highway. I picked up another phone book and began to read down all the pages under Jacobs or Ingrams I could find. Those surnames were Rosary's mother's maiden name.

In the same class where we'd learned about the British intelligence computer software, Deacon reminded us that the number-one way to locate someone was to find out where home was. For infamous bank robber John Dillinger, home was a movie theater. I began to wonder if Maxim and I could find The Knocker this way as well.

Obviously Garden Ridge wasn't The Knocker's home, because there wasn't a store here, but there was someplace, someone, or something he couldn't live without. I could stay up all night to find out what it was and then shoot him in the eye with his captive bolt pistol once he knew that it was me who caught him. I kinda felt like the Lady in Red, except I was wearing regulation blue.

Around four in the morning something stood out. A name. Giselle Brown. She hadn't showed up in The Knocker's jacket, because they only included bail bonds that were issued. However, I remembered seeing her name earlier at the sheriff's office.

The police department was housed in the city hall, so it had been a snap to gather public records like warrants, bonds, liens. Before Sanchez and I checked into the B & B, I had searched for all things Biloxi James. I discovered there was a record of a bond for a theft charge that was revoked, because the case was dismissed due to dropped charges by the property owner, a Graham Brown. The bond owner's name was ironically Giselle Brown.

Giselle Brown's name appeared again in a credit purchase of a Schwinn bike at a Western Auto Store in Valdosta, Georgia, which was about an hour from here past Echols County. There was some dispute at the store when she bought the bike that resulted in the arrest of one Biloxi James. Again the charges were later dropped. Then I found the name again tonight in a recent Statenville, Georgia, newspaper. A local church had hosted a benefit in honor of Mr. Graham Brown and Ms. Giselle Brown. Elaine was the keynote speaker. According to the caption, Sean Graham was kissing Giselle Brown on the cheek.

I observed the photo more closely. Elaine took great care of her constituents, but Sean rarely was this personal with them. I pulled the article closer and studied Giselle and

Sean's face. They resembled each other. I reached for my phone and studied the pics of Sean's wallet again.

I observed the driver's license. *Sean Graham Brown.*

My eyes widened. I sat up. "Sean was such a stinking liar!"

I jumped, tumbled off the bed and felt a man under me.

"Ow!" Maxim groaned.

I scrambled off of him "So sorry."

"What in hell, woman." He growled lightheartedly, lifted me over him and planted me onto the floor beside where he lay. He just lay there and looked up at me. I tried to pretend like I wasn't wowed by his coolness and strength.

I ran my hand down the back of my head, to calm my hormones. "What are you doing on the floor?"

"Waiting for you to jump me again. It was nice." He sat up and rested his back against the bed. "Now have you found Rosie's aunt or is the swamp heat making you batty?"

"I don't know, but I think I discovered something about Sean that may lead us to Biloxi."

"What?"

"More like who?"

He frowned. "I don't do riddles, so speak plain."

I stood up and over him to get my laptop. I lowered it unto his lap and pointed at the screen. "This woman and Biloxi have some kind of connection. She's been his indemnitor on more than one occasion, she's kept him out of hot water with her husband Graham, and she's also related to Sean somehow."

"Say what?" He sprouted from the floor.

I stumbled slightly back against the bed. "This woman, Giselle Brown, is related to Sean."

"And she's had dealings with Biloxi?"

"For years." I nodded.

He began to pace the room. "Do you think Sean knew Biloxi?"

I shrugged. "But get this. Giselle lives in Statenville, where Rosary said she was."

He stopped and put his hands on his waist. "This can't be a coincidence."

"I don't believe in coincidences. Do you?"

"Do you think this is a longstanding generational feud and has nothing to do with moonshine or Rosary at all?"

"Moonshining and generational feuds go hand in hand down here. Usually south Georgia and Appalachia Georgia moonshiners don't compete for business, because shine season is usually in the warmer months, but lately the winter has been warm longer and if you ran stills down in South Georgia where it's warm almost year round . . . This thing could be territorial and personal. It definitely would explain why Elaine was spared, but why did he kill the others?"

"As soon as I think I have this thing locked up, you throw water on my birthday cake," Maxim said.

"Ha Ha, not funny." I rolled my eyes. "Did you get Sean's toxicology report from the M.E.?"

"Not yet, why?" he asked.

"I find it odd that Sean would sit there and allow Biloxi to push that bolt through his head. Biloxi had to have paralyzed him or something. A captive bolt stunner isn't hard to conceal and easy to run away from," I said. "Biloxi didn't have it when I bumped into him."

"I have no clue." Maxim sat on the bed and pulled his hat off the night stand. "But as for the others, everyone else was shot with a rifle."

"Perhaps he killed anyone who got in the way of his sick plans for Sean."

Maxim looked up at me and threw his palms up. "Who was he to Sean?"

"I think we need to start with *who* is Biloxi to Giselle Brown?"

"Do you think the Knocker will be after her?"

"She lives in Statenville, a short drive from here. Let's get dressed and find out."

"Okay. Get dressed, while I assemble a small team to accompany me down there. I'll call Lowndes County, Lake Park, Statenville, Valdosta, and Homerville cities to let them know I'm coming."

I threw my arms over my chest. "No. I changed my mind. I want to go by myself."

"I'm sorry, Angel. What did you say? You can't do anything without me. You're civilian and I'm in charge of this operation."

"Maxim, she's in mourning. Sean is dead. She doesn't need us scaring her to death. From what I read in this article, it will overwhelm her. She seems really sweet and she's ill."

"I understand your concern, but you have to stay focused. We need to see that woman and if need be protect her by taking her somewhere safe until we catch this guy."

"Okay. Then I'll convince her to come with me and I'll bring her to you."

"Have you lost your ding dong mind?" His eyes blazed. His words stung the air.

"Maxim, I'm a recovery agent. I know how to transport people. It's what I do and I do it well. You can't leave, because there's a manhunt about to happen. And don't even think about having Sanchez tag along or you will most definitely get a discrimination lawsuit on your hands."

"Now hold onto your bra strap. This has nothing to do with you being a female. No man goes alone."

I grinned. "Honey, I'm a woman and in this case my going alone is your best bet. She seems like a sweet lady. I'll be back with her before you guys head into the swamp."

"And what about Biloxi? What if he's there?"

"The woman has kept him out of trouble for decades. He doesn't have a beef with her and if he did, killing a loved one was payback enough. Trust me on that one."

He shook his head. "I'm not letting you leave my sight."

"Okay, then come with me, but hang back when I get close to the property. Put me on surveillance and have your men in place, if something pops off. But y'all can't knock on her door with me. She's not going to tell us what we need to know if we storm in there looking like the cast of *X-Men*."

"What do comic books have to do with this?" His voice rose.

"Y'all, Sanchez, Ty, JD, and you, y'all look like WWF wrestlers and superheroes. I look . . . like you said before I'm a chameleon. I can look like whatever will make her comfortable and Giselle, she's not going to tell what we need to know to somebody that looks like you. Big Tiger hires me to pick up very smart characters, because they wouldn't suspect I was coming to get them. I'm thinking instead of inviting Sanchez and the others down here with us, you should've brought one of the fluffy marshals with you, too."

He huffed. "I must be tired or going crazy to even consider this."

"Just give me two hours with Giselle. If I don't come out, then come get me."

His eyes widened. He looked me up and down. He licked his lips. "Come get you?"

"Let's sleep on it." He huffed and paced for a few seconds then stopped. "I mean. Let's get a few hours of decent sleep. This place is crap and we can't be in here like that. I need to get you back to the B & B."

"No, you can't do that either."

He frowned. "What's wrong now?"

"Well, I don't want Ms. Claudine to think I'm slutty, if you take me back."

"You gotta be kidding me." He began to pace the floor.

"Calm down. It was a joke." I smiled.

"I got the joke; I just don't get you."

37

Sunday, 10:00 AM
Giselle Brown's home, Statenville, Georgia

I found Giselle Brown's home fifteen minutes from State Road 129 South on a red clay road a few miles from one of Uncle Pete's stills. (No wonder he knew this place so well.) I had rented Ms. Claudine's white tented Cadillac Deville to take the trip here, so that I didn't look like an out of towner. Before I hopped out of the car I caught a whiff of pond water. There was a large pond whipping through the Spanish moss and oak trees that framed the entryway to this place. As I walked toward her front porch I could taste the salt in the air.

In hindsight I should have asked Maxim to come with me here instead of having an Echols County sheriff hang back around the fork in the road. Maxim wouldn't let me out of his site unless I agreed to have an LE tag me.

After Maxim took me back to the B & B last night I dug a little further into Giselle and Biloxi's past. I found that she was also the indemnitor of an old bond for Biloxi back when they were in their twenties. It was one of the few court dates he actually appeared at. From what I knew of men, especially men like this, they wouldn't honor the bond unless they honored the woman who put herself on the line for the bond. She was special to him and for whatever reason she was still devoted to him, but she was married to Graham Brown. Perhaps Biloxi and Graham did not get along, because Bill and Giselle had a history. That was the only thing that made sense, because Giselle's behavior was classic jail wifey behavior. A jail wifey was a woman who was either the girlfriend or wife of a habitual jail inmate. Their relationship consisted of conjugal visits, commissary payments, and having to do favors for her man's inmate buddies. I wondered if Sean's affinity to bail people out came from her. This story was getting too juicy.

I didn't share my jail wifey theory with Maxim or that I called her before I came, because I knew he would have been furious with me. Yet, I feared Biloxi might be here, somewhere lingering around, watching her mourn over the loss of her relative. I could have at least shared that hunch with Maxim.

Nonetheless, I had my Kahr hidden underneath my shirt, to help me out, in case Biloxi did appear. Anyway, I would find out soon enough. My only consolation was the fact that I learned in my four years of hunting. I had never been asked to visit an indemnitor's residence and then to find my fugitive chilling inside, waiting for me. My gut told me he was near, but I didn't expect to see him, not until he finished what he started. I suspected Rosary had a part in that plan or that Rosary wasn't in danger from him at all anyway. But if the latter were true then Maxim would be right. She was the rat all along.

I hopped up the steps then stopped.

Her front porch was old, wooden, and painted white with rose vines sketched in whimsical places all around it. I observed it and marveled at the detail. I had been in my home for three years now and still hadn't completed my English garden wonderland in the back nor Bella's princess tree house, and especially my bedroom. It was just as bare and boringly beige as it was when I moved in.

I placed my hand over my eyes and squinted to see if I could see anyone moving inside. "Hello? Is Miss Brown here?"

Then I heard a rustle from behind. I spun around and pulled my gun out at the same time. I pointed it at the noise. I held my breath until I saw there was no threat.

A young-looking, slender woman with flowing gray hair, wearing tortoise shell rimmed glasses and an A-line floral dress, stepped back into a rose bush.

"Ms. Brown?" I asked.

"Who else could it be, Miss Crawford?" she said. "I thought you were coming to talk, not kill me, else I would have disinvited you when I had the chance."

"Reflex. Sorry, Ms. Brown." I lowered my gun, then looked her over. "You're going to hurt yourself if you don't watch your step."

"You say that as if you're talking to yourself, not to me." She grinned, then glided from where she stood as if she knew where every rose thorn was. "Call me Giselle."

"Call me Angel." I extended my hand.

"I only allow friends and people I trust into my home, so either give me a hug or continue staring at my door calligraphy."

"Yes, ma'am." I hugged her, but made sure she couldn't feel me up and find my pepper spray, knife, or where I hid my gun.

However, I found myself enjoying the smell of mint juleps in her hair.

She released her hold of me. "Before you leave I'll give you a bottle of my shampoo, since you seem to like it so much."

If I weren't so brown, I'd swear my cheeks glowed pink. "My condolences about your . . . I'm sorry. What relation is Sean to you exactly?"

She took my hand. "When you called me I assumed you knew. I'm Sean's mom."

I would have fallen off her steps had she not been holding me up. "His mom's name is Marla. I've met her before."

"Marla's my sister. It's a long story. Come inside before my family returns. Then I can't talk about it. You know how family can be," she said.

"Where are they?"

"Most of them are in Atlanta helping Marla with the funeral arrangements."

I nodded and looked around the grounds. The sheriff's car was within view. I smiled in his direction to let him know that I was okay.

Giselle coughed. She must have noticed my feet glued to the floor. I was still numb from the bombshell news she just gave me.

"I'm not getting any healthier, Angel. Let's go."

Once I stepped into her home I realized Giselle was an illusionist, whether she wanted to admit it or not. From the outside her home looked like a charming, off-the-beaten-path bungalow hidden with a purpose to keep Georgia's unique architectural history alive. As I walked from the porch to the foyer, I soon realized that the only thing aged in this house was her silver hair. Hardwood floors and Japanese and East African accents meshed with modern minimalist furniture. She had an artist studio in the sunroom with a lot of bird cages. From the looks of it, she was a bird cage designer. I remembered seeing a birdcage in Sean's office and at Flappers. I think she designed the furniture, as well.

She motioned for me to follow her into a living area. She lifted a tray of lemonade ice tea and mint juleps off a table and continued walking.

"Before I make my confession, I would like to know why did you leave your esteemed career to chase troubled people?" Her voice had a bit of grit and honey in it.

"Tired of harboring other people's secrets." I looked at her. "You can identify with that."

"Touché." She sat back and smirked. "It's a shame what happened to your brother-in-law. Did finding his killer and clearing your sister's name bring you and your sister closer?"

I didn't shift in my seat. "Don't believe everything you read in papers. Trust me."

"You two don't get along?" she asked.

"We do, but it's never the way I want. There are limits and I don't know why."

"Limits." She nodded. "Marla and I aren't twins, but I understand what you mean. Although my sister raised my son, I still hurt that he's gone just like any mother should. Unfortunately, I made a mistake that she won't let me forget."

There was a sadness in her eyes that reminded me of myself. I checked my watch. I had promised Maxim I would bring Giselle back in three hours. I had about ninety minutes left, including the drive back.

"Giselle, why was your sister raising your son?" I asked.

"I was fifteen; she was twenty-one. She was married and I wasn't. She had a good reputation and I didn't then. Best decision I ever made. Look how Sean turned out." She sipped her tea.

"What about Graham? Why would he agree to this?"

She frowned. "Our brother was the one who arranged the adoption. What do you mean?"

"He's your brother?"

"Of course, he is. Who did you think he was?" She looked at me intently, grinned, then slapped her leg. "Honey, you're not a good comedienne and this isn't *Flowers in the Attic*. My brother is Sean's uncle, not his father."

"Then who is?"

She looked at me. Tears fell down her cheeks. "It doesn't matter anymore. Now does it?"

"Well, I think it does." I stood up. "You're going to think I'm crazy, but I would really like you to come with me now."

Her eyes widened. "What? Where? And why would I do that?"

"I think you may be in serious danger."

"Honey, I don't know what you're talking about."

"Have you been watching the news? There is a manhunt for the man who killed Sean. The manhunt is down here. The killer is down here, probably coming for you."

"Oh, I don't watch the news and neither should you."

"This isn't in the news, yet. I'm working with the marshals to bring Sean's killer in."

She turned toward me. "Is bounty hunting taking a recession hit? I thought that job was pretty much guaranteed. Your uncle will have a cow, if he heard that."

"I'm not afraid of Uncle Pete, but you should be afraid of what will happen if I don't move you and your family somewhere safe. By the way when will your relatives return?"

"What has that Congresswoman done now? Do they have Marla hemmed up in Atlanta? What's going on?"

"Don't get overly excited, Giselle. I know you're weak."

She looked at me then squinted. "Why do you think I'm

in danger? Is this because of the congresswoman? I feared the job was more dangerous than Sean let on, now he's dead, and we are left to grieve like cockatiels in a cage."

I placed my arms on her shoulders, to comfort her. "Giselle, it wasn't Sean's job as Congresswoman Turner's aide that got him killed. It had something to do with his restaurant bar and a gentleman you had quite a past with it." I took Biloxi's picture out of my coat jacket and handed it to her.

She took the photo and handed it back to me. "Leave my house."

"Excuse me, but this man, a man you knew for some time, murdered Sean."

"Leave."

"Ma'am, he murdered your son in a very brutal way. Yet, you're not angry about it?"

I paused and looked around the room again. A bottle of Sean's signature specialty brand from Flappers sat on a coffee table and beside the bottle sat a silver baby rattle with Lucia engraved on it. I gasped. "Lucia? You know Lucia?"

She grabbed the rattle and placed it in her pocket. "Before you go I want to tell you the truth about Biloxi James."

"Where's Rosary?"

"It would change your mind about searching for him." She continued as if she hadn't heard me.

"Giselle . . . ? Where is my friend?"

"Biloxi did not kill Sean." She shouted at me. "He wouldn't. He couldn't if . . ."

I nodded. "Maybe you can straighten all this out at the sheriff's department office, but I need to know where Rosary and Lucia are."

"I should have told him. I should have told him who he was a long time ago, but Marla and Graham . . ." She said between coughing spats.

"He who?"

She coughed louder, stumbled and began to hyperventilate. I lunged forward to catch her and pulled my phone out my pocket.

I called the sheriff who was waiting outside. "I need an ambulance NOW."

38

Sunday, 9:00 AM
Georgia Moon B&B, Folkston, South Georgia

When we were children Ava and had I spent most Sunday afternoons at South Georgia Medical Center. Aunt Mary was a part-time ward clerk on the weekends. While she worked, she would either drop us off at the South Georgia Regional Library or Skate Rink. Between *Peanuts* movie marathons, summer reading, playing Pac-Man roller derby, and chasing moonshine marauders with Uncle Pete, we had our Sunday dinners here.

As I watched EMS wheel Giselle to triage, the memories of those good times flooded me. I found a quiet spot in the lobby, sat in one of the burgundy lounge chairs, and called Uncle Pete to find out if Aunt Mary had returned.

"I have nothing else to give you, Angel, and you better not have messed up my trucks," Uncle Pete mumbled.

I shook my head for thinking he would sound civil when I called. "Where's Aunt Mary?"

"She's not here," he said, then hung up.

I pulled the phone from my ear and looked at it. "No, he didn't."

"No, you didn't," Maxim growled from behind me.

My knee twitched. I turned around slowly. "What's wrong now?"

"You were supposed to be bringing Ms. Brown to me, not to the hospital. Explain yourself."

Maxim was dressed in his U.S. Marshal formal gear, well, his version of it. He had his badge serving as a belt buckle and wore a dark pair of jeans and a blue, long sleeve, golf shirt. His U.S. Marshal badge was etched on his shirt across his left breast. He carried his Stetson in his hand. He wore no jacket.

I walked toward him. "Maxim, you're not going to believe what I found."

"Found?" He scowled. "I'm not believing you at all, right now."

"Hold on, now. I was doing my job. I went to get her. She didn't want to come. She—"

"This isn't bail recovery, Angel. They don't have a choice." He lowered his head and sighed. "What am I thinking? You're not one of us. You're not even done with Uncle Deacon's course."

"Will you let me explain before you start with the insults?" I hissed. "Giselle Brown is Sean Graham's mother."

He grabbed my arms. His brows furrowed down to his nose bridge. "Please tell me you're joking."

"After you just insulted me . . . why would I joke with you, let alone not walk out of here and let you look like the jerk you seem to always rise to be. And take your hands off me."

He held me with his arms and eyes for a few seconds before he released me. "Angel, put yourself in my shoes."

"That's not why you asked me to join your team, yet I've done more than the rest."

He cleared his throat. "Are you sure Ms. Brown is Sean's mother?"

"If you don't believe me, get a written request from Marla or Giselle yourself."

"Giselle's sister adopted him?"

I nodded. "Yes and Graham Brown wasn't Giselle's husband. He's their brother. You may need to have a seat before I tell you who Sean's father really is."

His eyes wondered as if he was thinking and then they brightened.

He gasped. "Do you think he knows?"

I shook my head. "Or he's more demented than I thought."

"Did Sean know?" He shook his head. "Never mind. The only person who could tell us is Rosary and who knows where she is."

"There was a baby rattle at Giselle's with Lucia's name engraved on it. I think she's been there or is there . . ." I thought about it and then snapped my fingers. "Giselle said that her family would be coming back soon."

"Do you think?" he asked.

I bobbed my head. "Call someone. Rosary's there!"

A nurse in Hello Kitty scrubs came out to greet us. "We're taking Ms. Brown into a room upstairs. With her weakened heart we want to observe her overnight. Ms. Crawford, she would like to see you once we have her settled in."

I turned to Maxim. "Can I stay?"

"You have thirty minutes with her before I speak with her. Meanwhile, I'm sending Sanchez here to watch Giselle overnight. When she gets here I'm escorting you back to Folkston. You will write up a report of what happened here and stay there. I can't have you acting on your own for anything else."

"And what about Rosary? Shouldn't I be the one to—"

He tilted his head, clutched his jaw, and placed his hands on his waist.

"Right. No more acting on my own," I said and then mumbled. "Although you gave me the go ahead to see Giselle."

The nurse cleared her throat.

Maxim waved his hat in the nurse's direction. "After you, Ms. Crawford."

Giselle sat in her bed with a hospital night gown on and the sweater she wore in here. I felt guilty when I met her eyes.

"Giselle, I didn't mean to upset you this badly."

"If I felt that way I would have asked you to come." She smiled and patted her hands on an empty spot on the bed.

I sat beside her and she grabbed my hands. "Are you sure what you said is true?"

I could feel Maxim's presence behind me. I pointed behind me. "Giselle, this is Marshal Maximus West. Maxim for short. I don't want to offend you or make your heart flutter again, but I want you and your loved one's safe. Do you mind him being in here, too?"

She shook her head. "No," she whispered.

Her hands trembled.

"Giselle, perhaps you should get some rest and we do this another time," I said.

She squeezed my hand and smiled. "No, I can't rest until you help me understand this. Did Bill kill our son?"

"Most of the evidence provided to us points in that direction. I'm sorry."

"And you're here to either put Bill in prison or kill him?" she asked.

"Yes, Ma'am," Maxim said before I could.

I turned toward where he stood and gave him the side eye. He didn't have to be that short.

He stepped forward and shook Giselle's hand. "Nice to meet you, Ma'am. I hope my frankness didn't offend you."

"No, Sir. There are too many more pressing things that

got my nerves bad right now." She patted her chest and shook her head.

"Ma'am I'm going to step outside for a short minute, while you and Ms. Crawford chat. I need to call Deputy Marshal Sanchez. She'll be sitting with you until your family joins you. She'll also be escorting you to a safe location."

She looked at me then at Maxim. "I don't know her. I know Angel. I want Angel to do that. She can't do that, Marshal?"

"I'm sorry, but I need her with me. Don't worry, you'll be in good hands." He grinned, revealing those super white teeth, and then left the room.

She shrugged. "I don't know about that . . ."

"He's right, Giselle. Sanchez will take good care of you. She's been taking care of me, so I vouch for her."

"Sounds like they have you on a short leash."

"Yes, Ma'am, they do, but I kind of need to be," I said. "Since we don't have much time and you need to rest very soon, we need to get this straight. The more you can tell us the better the outcome will be for Bill and you could help us save other lives, as well."

"That's why I asked you to come up." She nodded and sat back against her pillows. "I've made enough messes. It's time I clean them up. I know you understand that, Angel."

"Tell me about you and Bill and how everything got so screwed up?"

She grinned. "When I was young and beautiful like you I thought I was ugly. Black women were told they were ugly a lot back then no matter your shade, your size, your hair texture. Honey, if I knew then what I know now . . ."

She chuckled and looked down at her hand. She wore a ruby diamond ring on her right hand. Maxim returned to the room.

"I met Biloxi James back then. The first words that came

out of his mouth were 'you're the most beautiful woman I've ever seen.' Not black woman, but woman. I knew from the moment that he owned me."

A shiver ran down my left side when she said 'owned.' "You sound like an emotionally raped mistress referring to her master."

"It was more like the other way around. I called the shots and he would do whatever I wanted." She giggled for a few seconds then immediately stopped. "It was the early sixties, not that long ago to me. Down here Biloxi and I couldn't marry, although interracial marriage bans were ruled unconstitutional in '67. We tried, but this was Georgia. Sometimes we have trouble with the federals telling us what to do." She winked at Maxim.

He chuckled.

"Down here it was against society, so we definitely couldn't have children together, cause then we would be caught. Yet, I had to have him, mind and body so . . ." She looked out her window and paused for a few uncomfortable seconds. "Sean came and went."

"My condolences, Ma'am," Maxim said.

"Marshal, Biloxi's not some man you hunt down and bring back to rot in a prison. He's fire. He's ice. He consumes."

"I still don't understand why you would have Lucia's rattle. Are you related to Rosary, too? She said she was living at her aunt's."

"Sean made Rose family and to him I'm his aunt. I never told him. The family didn't either." She began to cry. "He knows now I'm sure."

Maxim folded his arms over his chest. "Why would he send Rosary to you?"

"Her family didn't like black people, especially old moonshiners like us. They threw her out when Lucia came. As fair skinned as Lucia is those people refuse to see themselves in her."

I gasped. "Lucia is Sean's baby?"

She leaned forward. "I guess Sean learned how to keep secrets from me, because you looked stunned. Sean didn't tell you about him and Rosary."

"No, Ma'am. But if he had he would be alive right now."

"I know." She nodded. Her tears fell fast now. "And if I had told Bill . . ."

"I'm not sure if the outcome would have been different," Maxim said. "The love of your life has become a bitter man, who has done very bad things to people, including the people closest to him."

I held her hand. "I think you need to rest now. Do you want me to call the nurse?"

She shook her head. "I want you to get Rosie and the baby. I don't want anyone else hurt and when Bill finds you—and find you he will—tell him that Sean was his son."

"You don't want to tell him yourself?" I asked.

She smiled. "Angel, I know it's been a long time since you've been here, but this is the hospice floor. I'm dying."

39

We waited for an hour for Sanchez, but she was a no show and a no call. Maxim asked the sheriff's department to help with securing Giselle and to bring in Rosary and the baby. Maxim and I headed back to Folkston to find out what was going on with Sanchez. He left Uncle Pete's truck in the hospital parking lot, because I told him to. Therefore, Maxim had to ride back with me in Mrs. C's Caddy. But he wouldn't let me drive.

"Giselle is dying. This roller coaster just won't stop." I closed my eyes and sighed, as we sped back down another state road. "There's so much that doesn't make sense."

"Seems pretty clear to me. Her sister Marla had better opportunities to raise Sean that she did. The family agreed. I see it all the time."

"And what about the moonshine? Sean, the Sean we knew, has been running moonshine all along? I don't believe that."

"I don't think he was the type to run shine. It was beneath him, but he learned enough or overheard enough while growing up that he used as a benefit when he opened Flappers."

"Yeah, but . . ."

"There are no buts. People are human, three dimensional, not black or white. We don't wrap up into tidy, pretty bows. You know this. Look at the people you deal with on a daily basis. Sean snitched about the wrong people and so he's dead. My job is to find out who those wrong people are, so we can get this crap off the streets."

"But Sean was different."

"If you think so," he scoffed. "All I'm saying is don't lose sleep over the psychoanalysis of Sean Graham. He may not have known who is real father was, but he was not a nice guy. He was a prick, actually, and I do remember you didn't like him either."

"True I didn't like him. He let Rosary sit in jail while her daughter was God knows where."

"Actually, Lucia was with Marla. She's been with Marla until Rosary went missing."

"What?" I scooted up in the seat. "She was where and you knew?"

He huffed. "I knew that the baby was with Marla until Rosary took her, but I didn't know the baby was Sean's."

"You must be kidding me."

"No, I'm not. When I brought Sean in for questioning—thanks to your heads-up—he told me that he had hired you to find Rosary, his employee. I knew that was a lie, because your mom had already told the truth, so he had to tell me the deal or go to jail."

I rolled my eyes. "I'm so not believing you right now."

"Don't get mad at me. Your girl Rosary could have told you. You need to ask yourself why didn't she?"

"That will be the first question I ask before I wring her neck." I pursed my lips.

He chuckled. "That a girl."

"So why did Sean lie to me about why he wanted me to find Rosary?"

"His mom was keeping Luc, while Rosary was in jail. He wasn't bailing her out, because he wanted her to go to rehab. She got out early and took their daughter," he said, as they drove. "When my leak informed him that we were about to launch a case against him, he sent her down here to wait for him. He hired you to throw off our scent, but it failed. So he agreed to help us uncover this illegal moonshine ring, if we could put them all in WITSEC. We were going to retrieve her and Lucia when all Hell broke loose."

WITSEC was the U.S. Marshal's Witness Security Program acronym, formerly known as Witness Protection.

"Sean wanted to leave his glamorous life for witness protection?"

"No, he didn't. He and Rosary had plans to run their own white lightning distillery. Legal moonshine, according to him. Yeah, right . . ." He chuckled.

"There are a few whiskey distilleries popping up in the state. Amicalola Falls even has a Moonshine Festival."

"Yeah, well . . . That's how he and Rosary fell in love. He hired her to be a mixologist at Flappers and learned she came from a family of profitable moonshiners. He told her about his background and the Brown family's love of the brew. They traded family recipes and secrets. He felt sorry for her, because she didn't have the opportunities that he had. Sean tried his best to clean Rosary up and clean the mistake of bringing illegal moonshine into the restaurant. He didn't realize how deep they were in until we came calling. When we shared with him the facts behind the Calhouns he knew this was the best thing to do for Lucia."

"Rosary didn't tell me much about her family except that they lived up near The Falls. She used to help getting the mash together. That's how she learned how to make prison hooch. The last time I saw her in jail I was asked to compel her to tell the prison staff member who gave her the supplies to make the alcohol in jail."

"Rosie's family has a lock on North Georgia, especially Grayson, Georgia, where there are no package stores. We hoped Luxe could at least get us in on any nip joints up there or near Winder and Snellville, but we will."

"I thought Grayson was finally getting a package store."

"Not yet. A lot of red tape with the local government."

I snapped my fingers. "And that's how Sean came into play."

He nodded. "Mhmm . . . You see that tax money from alcohol sales could help out the city. Imagine what would have happened if Sean and Rosary could work out a deal to sell only their heritage hooch for a little political nudge."

"Whoa, Maxim."

"This story is better than anything I've ever investigated, too bad it was right under my nose. I can't believe Rosary kept this stuff from me."

"The girl has been taught to keep secrets her whole life. Her life depended on it. Her family isn't the normal kind. They'll kill their kin, if they ever felt threatened. The Calhouns belonged to a large group, who isn't fans of the new legit moonshine business owners. Moonshine is sacrilege to them," Maxim said.

"That's why Biloxi didn't hesitate with killing Sean or anyone who stood in his way."

"We knew that Luxe wasn't the big fish we needed. We still didn't know who the distiller was and neither did Sean, because of the double blind system. We hoped Luxe would give us more information then Sean was killed. You I.D.'d The Knocker and we still haven't found the guy."

"But he's not the distiller you've been looking for all this time?"

"No, he's their hired gun and he needs to be stopped before this crew scares legal shine out of Georgia."

"Wow," I sighed. "I can't believe Sean was planning to leave Elaine and his family behind for Rosary?"

"Yep."

I shook my head. "The things we do for love."

"You don't have to be in love with the child's mother, to want the best for her."

I rolled my eyes in his direction. "Do you have children?"

He nodded. "A little boy and no, he's not with his mom. I have custody of him."

My mouth had dropped too low to pick up off the car floor board, so I tried to roll it back into my face and keep my thoughts to myself until we returned to the B & B.

Sunday, 4:15 PM
Georgia Moon B&B, Folkston, South Georgia

Sanchez wasn't in her room when Maxim brought me back and someone had been through my room. My Running of the Brides team outfit was thrown around the room and my folded tees sprawled along the floor against the pink carpet, stepped on. The hairs on the back of my neck stood up.

"It's a good thing that you didn't have anything expensive." Maxim pulled some blue latex gloves from his pocket and handed them to me. "Put these on before we go inside."

"I think I need to see if Ms. Claudine is okay first."

"Angel, you need to see what's missing first before the team arrives. Remember I have a leak."

"But it's obviously Sanchez." I stood under the threshold. "Why would you think that?"

"Okay. Let's deduce from the evidence we have. Sanchez didn't respond when called, she's nowhere to be found, and my room has been ransacked. I was hoping she wasn't the leak, but clearly she had to be, with the meddling, jealous behavior—"

"First off. There's no reason for her to disappear during a manhunt, even if she were. Besides . . ." He stopped checking and looked at me. "What jealous behavior?"

"You didn't see how she looked at you when you talked to me?"

He shook his head. "Why would I see that? She's a lesbian."

I did a double take. "Mama, say what?"

"Sanchez has the hots for you." He bent to his knees and looked under my bed.

"No, she doesn't." I pouted.

"Cinderella, did you lose your slipper?"

"What?"

He stood up and lifted a silver sparkled ladies shoe. "Is this your shoe?"

I squinted at it and then shook my head. "Although the Dollar General is très chic, they don't sell Louboutins. It's definitely a few dollars out of the store's range—about a thousand dollars, to be exact."

He observed the shoe and frowned. "Can you call Ms. Claudine up here?"

I followed his orders and followed Ms. Claudine to the room she had rented to me.

"What have y'all done to my room?" she asked, more like she shouted.

"I don't want you to be too alarmed, Ms. Claudine, but an intruder has been in this room."

"You sure it wasn't the lady marshal?"

"That's what we're hoping you can help us determine," Maxim said. "Did you hear any rumbling upstairs?"

"It's a B & B, Marshal West." She tilted her head and pursed her lips. "Most of our patrons are honeymooners or lovers or something close to it. A lot of rumbling going on. My best practice is to put plugs in my ears until my television stops shaking."

Maxim rolled his eye at me then handed Ms. Claudine the shoe. "Is this your shoe, Ma'am?"

"No, it's too high city for me."

"Have you seen it before?" he asked.

"Yes, sir. I sure have." She studied it then handed it back to him. "This shoe belongs to the gal who stayed here before you came. I remember, because she wore them when she arrived. Can't understand why she would leave them behind and how my Girl Friday didn't see them when she was getting your room together. My apologies. We usually take patrons' left-behind items to the lost and found closet."

My leg twitched. I pulled out my wallet and shared with her a picture of Rosary. "Is this the woman who was here before?"

She nodded. "That's her and she had the cutest little girl with her, full of curly brown hair."

"Was she here with just the little girl?" Maxim asked.

"She came with just her and the baby, but she left with a woman. Checked out early, too. I assumed it was her mother, because she was quite happy when she left."

"Did the woman have flowing gray hair?" I asked.

Ms. Claudine nodded.

"Giselle," I said under my breath.

Maxim folded his arms over his chest. "Did the woman drive here?"

"That's the only way to get here unless she walked."

Maxim leaned toward me. "Did you see a car in the yard when you visited Giselle?"

I shook my head. "No, but she could have borrowed Giselle's car. Will she return with the car or get as far as she can away from here in that car is beyond me."

"She hadn't returned yet, because I hadn't heard a peep out of the officer on duty, who is watching the house." He looked toward the ceiling and grunted. "She more than likely told Ms. Brown she was going on an errand and skipped town in her car."

"I know Rosary hasn't been painted as a pretty picture, but she's not that bad and she needs our help."

"Then she should have called you back or contacted the local authorities after you told her Sean had died. She has taken one misstep after the next. I still can't believe Sean Graham and this woman had a connection, let alone a child together." He walked away from me, thanked Ms. Claudine for her assistance, and showed her out the door.

There was some truth in what he said, but he didn't know Rosie like I did. She was sweet and loved Lucia more than anything. I had an addiction for sweets, so I empathized with her alcohol addiction. Most importantly she wasn't a thief and she hated being in jail. "What if she did come back to Giselle's and noticed the sheriff parked near the house? What if your security detail scared her off?"

He turned around toward me. "Are you blaming me for why this plan isn't working?"

"No, I'm saying Rosie's a professional skip. She knows how to spot Boys in Blue."

"What if she did?"

"Then she bounced, but the good thing is she's a creature of habit. She hadn't gone far, because she's run out of options. She can't go back to Atlanta without answering to her family and possibly losing Lucia to Sean's family. And she doesn't have enough money to hide anywhere else, so I think she's either going to call Giselle to find out what's going on or hang around until the coast is clear."

"But Giselle is in the hospital," Maxim said.

"That's why we need to go back and leave a message or relieve the patrolman of his duties."

"You're going nowhere. JD and Ty are with the volunteers in the swamp, so that leaves me to do it unless Sanchez returns." Then he smirked. "I promise I won't look like a super-hero when I catch up to Rosie."

"And what do I do, while y'all save the world?"

"You get the pleasure to keep Ms. Claudine company and move into another room. Oh and call your boyfriend. He called the sheriff's office looking for you earlier."

"I need to call Bella and check on her."

"Do that." He nodded. "And look . . . you've had a big day. What you discovered about Sean, Ms. Brown, and Biloxi is short of amazing. We will use this information toward our advantage."

My phone buzzed. I looked at it, thinking it was Justus or Mom. But it wasn't.

I gasped. "Maxim, it's Sanchez."

"Well, answer it."

"Wow, I hadn't gotten reception since we got here," I said as I answered it.

"Angel, it's Sanchez. I found the Knocker's still."

"What? We've been looking everywhere for you." I patted Maxim's shoulder.

"I know, but there was something you said before that stuck with me. I had to check out a hunch and it paid off. I had to ditch your uncle's truck and walk at least a mile into the woods, but . . ."

"Sanchez, where are you? Can you hear me?" I asked.

"Yes."

"Why didn't you leave word with one of the guys, so that we knew where you were?"

"I did," she said. The phone reception was choppy. "I told—"

Then the phone went dead. I tried to call her back, but got no response.

Maxim touched my elbow. "Where is she?"

"In some woods, she said she told someone where she was heading."

He frowned. "I don't feel good about this."

"Honey, I haven't felt good about all this commotion since you drove into town," Ms. Claudine said.

Ms. Claudine startled us. She had returned from downstairs. Maxim frowned at her.

"Maxim, do you want me to go look for Sanchez?" I asked.

Maxim's brow furrowed deep into his nose bridge this time. "No, no, no, no. She'll return soon enough."

I nodded at him, all the while knowing that I wasn't leaving her out in the woods alone.

40

Sunday, 6:00 PM
Georgia Moon B&B, Folkston, South Georgia

The cottage now swarmed with every law enforcement officer near the Georgia Coast. If Biloxi wanted to hop a plane and leave the country, or kill Rosary and Lucia, he could, easily. We were all occupied with other matters.

"Well, I could let you hold my car again, but I don't have you on my insurance," Ms. Claudine said to me.

"The feds will pay for it, if something were to happen to it."

"Really now, then make sure you don't ruin my pearl interior."

"Ms. Claudine, you don't have a pearl interior."

She winked and handed me her keys. "I do, if you total my car."

I kissed her cheek. "I owe you big."

"Give me some of your uncle's chacha and we're even."

I left Ms. Claudine in her front yard, while Maxim and the team weren't paying attention. I didn't have a clue where I was heading. All I had was Uncle Pete's map, some bottled water, my taser, my Kahr 45 pistol, some nunchucks, a pair of handcuffs, a billy club, a rifle, a pack of chewing tobacco (don't ask), a flask of Uncle Pete's muscadine chacha, and my cell phone. Then I called Justus.

"I knew you would call me, if Marshal West told you to," Justus said with less sarcasm in his voice than I thought. He chuckled. "I'm so glad to hear your voice."

"I'm sorry it took me so long to call," I said.

"You haven't been gone that long and I'm not a fool. You're on a manhunt. You need to stay focused."

"Wow, I can't believe you're this understanding."

"Why shouldn't I be? You're coming back home to Bella and me right?" he asked.

"Of course, I am." I smiled.

"Then hurry up and save the world, brave Angel, because I want to kiss you badly."

"I promise to get back as soon as I can, if you promise me to stay away from your fawning church ladies fan club and that rat Detective Dixon."

Detective Francine Dixon was Salvador's partner and had become a pain in my backside during Ava's short stint at Dekalb County Jail. She had a thing for Justus and made it a point to rub her crush on my man in my face.

"What are you talking about?" he asked.

"I'm sure she's been sniffing around your office, since she heard I was away."

He chuckled. "After all this time you're still jealous of that woman."

"I'm not jealous of her, more like vigilant. She's a wolf in designer suits. Don't have her around my baby."

"Whatever you wish." I could hear him laughing under his breath, but I didn't care. I meant what I said.

"I wish I were home," I admitted and then noticed the detour signs for the Okefenokee Swamp.

I continued driving past the detours.

"I know you can't tell me what's going on at the manhunt, but I do want to know how you are doing."

"I'm good. I'm about to drive into a fire."

"I thought I knew all the current slang, but I don't know what 'drive into the fire' means?"

"It means exactly that I'm driving toward the Honey Prairie Fire in the swamp. Will call you later." I hung up, and yes, Justus was screaming everything but Hallelujah on the other end.

Sunday, 6:00 PM
Honey Prairie Fire, Between Folkston and Okefenokee
Swamp, South Georgia

When Ava and I were young girls we learned about fire safety from Smokey the Bear and a bunch of afterschool television shows. One thing I remembered was that most fires were caused by careless people, who didn't mean any harm. They just weren't paying attention.

However, one summer when Ava and I were ten and spent our vacation with Aunt Mary and Uncle Pete, we learned another truth. Sometimes folks set fires to set fires. On my second day of P.I. class I learned that most arsonists set fires to hurt someone, to tear something down, and to cover up another crime. In Uncle Pete's case he tried to cover hurting Aunt Mary by starting a fire. I bet the quarter tank of gas in Ms. Claudine's car that whoever was behind these fires were using it as a camouflage to hide the brew that needed to meet deadline before the Knocker came to collect.

As I cut on Ms. Claudine's fog lights and made my way farther down the darkest, dankest, smoggiest road I had ever seen, the puzzles to the pieces surrounding Sean's death became clearer to me. Rosary's family killed Sean to tear her back down. She was trying to clean up their very proud but black market way of life and she had the nerve to try to do it with a fed, well, a congresswoman's aide.

Because there wasn't a cell phone tower in this area, I couldn't use my GPS on my phone to locate Sanchez. So I had to rely on my gut, Sanchez's last phone call, and years of stalking boyfriends in the dark. Uncle Pete's gray truck peeked between the fog and smoke and then tucked back into the clouds just a few yards ahead. I slowed the car down and put on Bella's swim goggles. They were in the bottom of my purse and a godsend.

Although we weren't near the evacuated area closest to the fire, the smoke was thick enough to burn my eyes and tickle my chest into rhythmic, dry coughs.

I had a little trouble locking Claudine's car door because it was dark, she didn't have a remote key, and the buttons inside no longer worked. When I finally got it locked I noticed someone standing at a dirt road clearing in the woods to the east.

"Sanchez?" I coughed.

I'm sure she couldn't hear me from this distance, but I could see her. I felt for my Kahr and began walking toward her. I wondered if JD and Ty were nearby.

"Ma'am, I don't want to shoot you and you don't want to be dead." A low and rich southern man's voice knocked me out of my skin for a second.

I gasped and stopped. It was him. The Knocker. I had never been face to face with a hired killer, especially one whose work I had witnessed. Most of the men I picked up were tough, not sociopaths.

Like in a trance I crossed the road and began to walk toward him. It was eerily quiet. All the LEs were everywhere but here, because he had designed it to be that way. Yet, I wasn't entirely afraid of him. I knew he killed his only son. If my bullet didn't kill him, telling him that fact definitely would.

"I just came to get my friend, Bill," I said.

"Let me save you the trouble and money. I'll throw what's left of her in the fire when it arrives."

A shiver ran through my body. "Did you kill her?"

"No, she killed herself. Someone should have told her that you don't peek inside the worm. Those things can explode when the cap is off. Maybe she didn't pay attention to your uncle's notes."

I kept my knees from shaking. "Yep, that would do it."

He grinned. Even through the fog I could make him out, clearly. Biloxi "The Knocker" James held the accent of a country music legend. I'm sure he serenaded Giselle all her good years with it, too. And then there was the matter of his face. Biloxi James had a face that screamed beautiful enigma. Even in the moonlight his baby blue eyes were reminiscent of a cherub in an Italian Renaissance painting. How could he possess a stare that looked so innocent and yet have witnessed so much brutality at his hands? He was tall and statuesque. I had to crook my neck and slant my head to the side to get a good look at him, because the moon refused to leave the shimmering around his shadow. And there was his skin . . . it was so smooth. His cheeks held the color of a fleshy peach. It complemented his lips, which were plump enough to cause a kick in my left thigh. I noted all of that, as he walked toward me, as we stood off at both ends of a leafless oak grove arch. Bits of ash flew around us.

"Biloxi, did anyone tell you that you were too pretty to be a stone-cold killer?" I asked.

He smiled and flashed a handsome set of teeth for a man his age. "Even from this far away I can tell you're a heartbreaker."

"Hmm . . ." I shrugged. "Too bad we're meeting on the wrong terms."

"I know on good authority that me and you meeting, darling, ain't never gon' be on bad terms." He stood as still as the old trees that flanked our showdown.

It was so quiet that the winds didn't whisper a mumbling word. I almost regretted meeting this devil on my own.

"And where did you hear that from, the snitch in the U.S. Marshal's office?" I asked.

"You'll learn soon enough."

"Enough of the riddles." I shook my head. "You and Giselle are two peas in a pod."

He frowned. "What about Giselle?"

"I saw her today and she is still protective of you. Why? I have no clue."

"Did she tell you she was dying?" His voice cracked.

His eyes bounced when I mentioned her name, but he didn't look away or bat an eye. But it didn't matter. I found his weakness.

"She told me something worse," I said.

"What could be worse?"

"Why don't you ask her after you kill me?"

He chuckled. "Do you think I would be talking to you this long, if I were planning to kill you?"

"I don't know. I don't know why you didn't kill me at Garden Ridge."

"Because I had done what I'd come to do. I don't kill for the thrill."

I rolled my eyes at his sick rhyme. "So why did you kill innocent Terri."

"She got in my way. Foolish girl thought she could shield that Brown boy. But he wasn't going anywhere. I apologize that she was a casualty in that."

I clinched my fists to fight it off. "How much do they pay you to torture and kill like that?"

"Nothing." He shook his head. "You don't charge family to do a favor."

I became nauseated from holding in what I knew. "Why did Sean have to be killed?"

"That boy had been gunning for me since he was born. I didn't know why until the county began to talk about putting a bill on the last election ballot to approve Sunday liquor sales in this county." He spat on the ground.

"Nothing suspicious there. The entire state has been dealing with Sunday alcohol sales."

"It didn't stop. That Brown boy was making deals in Atlanta to push backdoor deals through, but we made sure it never made the ballot. Then the federals began peeking around here, searching for stills, IRS audits, and talk of zoning for another package store."

"You can't put that on Sean."

"Oh, I got proof."

"The leak." I nodded.

"No, the girl. The mutt, Rosie. Her mom's folks are good people, but the girl got her daddy's blood in her. She couldn't keep her mouth off the hooch and married men. After she got into some trouble that embarrassed her folks, they ran her off the mountain and into The City. It was no coincidence Sean took to her the way he did. He had Brown's knack for seizing opportunities."

I scrunched my nose. "What kind of opportunity?"

"The recipes. He got that poor girl convinced that he would clean her up and make a lady out of her, if she showed him how to make shine." He scoffed. "She made a fool of him, just like she's done everybody else."

I waved my hands in the air. "I'm confused. What does it matter if Chatham County had liquor sales on Sunday?"

"Then what need would we be?" I whiffed smoke from the forest fire floating on a breeze coming from behind Bill's back.

"We've had stills here for generations and no one has bothered us before, because it was understood that this was what we do. On the weekends, after a long week's work, we made white lightning and shared it with our family and friends."

"You do more than share. You sell it. Shoot. Y'all make over a million dollars a year slinging hooch."

"Angel, this stuff ain't cheap to make."

"Please tell me you didn't kill Sean Graham because he was competition."

"No, of course not. Rosie's family is competition. This joker wanted to make shine legal. LEGAL. Destroy our whole industry. I couldn't let that happen. I hope Giselle understands." He lowered his head.

"Where's Rosary and Lucia?"

"I don't know and I don't care. With that Brown boy gone she can't do anything but run back home or live with her child's father. If she knows who that is."

"Sean was Lucia's father."

"Well, that's a shame."

"And you will regret killing Sean."

"Angel, don't test me." His voice grew louder. "I killed Sean Graham because he had no home training and respect for what we do. He had hypnotized Rosie into thinking she was something she would never be and made a mockery of what moonshining is. You can't make this legitimate, regulated, and measured by federals. That's not our way of life. That's not what we do. His family should have set him straight a long time ago."

"Maybe he's stubborn like his father." I clutched my mouth with my hand. I shouldn't have said that.

"Maybe, who's to say?"

"I can't believe you're this stupid."

Car lights began to appear through the fog.

He turned around and observed the car then turned back to me and smiled. "Darlin', I'm afraid our time is up."

"So you summoned someone to kill me. Is that what this is, because it won't work. I'm taking you and whoever that is into custody."

"Darlin', I assumed the marshal had a crush on you and that's why he had you tag along. So let me tell you the truth. You're good, but you're not that good. So please stop reading my trigger finger. I might change my mind about killing you, although you're quite pretty to tease." He grinned.

I wanted to slap the grin off his face. "I don't want to kill you either unless you try to kill me first."

"Well, this is your lucky day," he said.

"And why is that?" I asked.

"Because the same little birdie who told me you were here paid me to not kill you."

"What do you mean? You didn't come here to kill me in the first place?"

"No, sugar. I want to stand here in this burning swamp and count the breaths you take before you reach for that gun resting in the small of your back. Our little birdie told me you were a fast draw."

"Man, you do realize we're in the twenty-first century and not in some cowboy Western standoff."

He scratched his jaw. "Well, then, how come it seems like it?"

"Why didn't you kill me when you had the chance?"

"Because I needed you now . . ."

The driver of the car had finally turned off the car and turned off the lights. My heart began to race. I didn't want to die out here like this.

"I need someone to witness my death."

I stepped back and frowned. "You want me to kill you?"

"No, I want your boyfriend to think you killed me."

I heard footsteps coming toward me, but I couldn't make out who it was without turning my eyes away from Bill. Then I heard a huge thump. From my periphery I knew it was a body. It took everything I had to not toss my last meal on my shoes. I prayed for Sanchez's soul and for mine.

"You want me to tell him that you're dead? I'm confused."

"No." He chuckled. "The poor dead guy on the floor is me and you will be you."

"You're faking your death and you're killing me, so that you can run off and live as an alias? It's not going to stick, because the dental records will tell that you aren't that dead man on the ground."

"That dead man doesn't have any teeth and besides I'm not from here. My records aren't in the state public records." He grinned. "Pretty smart huh?"

"Clever, but why do I have to die?"

"Because you're going to be the hero. You're going to kill me, but die by my gunshot wounds. Your daughter will be set for life for your heroics."

"You need me, in order to fake your death. That's why you lured me here."

"I didn't lure you here. You're nosy and you want to be the hero. Your uncle should have taught you that family was more important than ambition, but I guess you learned the opposite from that fool."

"It's in the blood. We are what we are . . ."

I still tried to see who was standing behind him, but couldn't. Whoever was there intentionally hid their face from me. I began to wonder if this was our leak. The only thing I could do to find out was to stall their plot to kill me. I kept talking.

"I just wish Sean knew that he was more like you than Giselle Brown."

Biloxi cocked his head. "What did you just say?"

"You heard what I said. Sean Graham Brown was your son. I don't understand why you never saw it, not even when you looked him in the eye and blew out the other one."

Biloxi's eyes lit up. "You're lying."

"Call Giselle and ask her. She's at South Georgia Regional. Room 418. I checked her in before I came here searching for Sanchez."

"She never told me anything like that."

"Why should she tell you? You've become more criminal. How many times did she bail you out of jail before Sean was born? Why do you think Sean spent so much time down here? I bet he even knew about you."

"That boy was nothing like me." He growled.

"Not entirely. He took care of his kid, even if being with his daughter's mom was a problem." I gasped. "I forgot. You don't know that Lucia is your grandchild?"

He no longer grinned.

"Your son, who resembles you the more I think about it, wasn't like you. He was trying to free his child from some foolish generational curse that you all continue to inflict on yourselves." I paused once I noticed who was standing behind him. "While you're trying to preserve what is overwhelmingly a lost way of life, he is trying to ensure the legacy of your family in a way that is not shameful."

"I remember when you were a little girl, hanging onto every word your father preached, but he is dead. He kept confusing this world with Heaven."

My blood pressure must have risen, because I felt a pop between my eyes. Then I heard the sound of grass crunching behind me.

"Get down! Get down!" JD shouted. His voice came closer. "Get down, Angel!"

But I couldn't move. Biloxi's grimace held me captive. He then pivoted to his left and shot something. Before I could take a breath my hands zipped around me and fired. Biloxi turned back to me. He stepped back, looked at the blood oozing from his chest, and fell face up.

"Sh, not again . . ." I ran toward him.

By the time I got to Bill he was coughing up spittle with blood. I grabbed him up and applied pressure to his wound. I didn't care that his blood was spilling onto my white blouse.

"Darlin', I thought you said you weren't going to kill me," he said.

I double-clicked my Bluetooth earpiece. "Dial. Fire."

I said that through my earpiece. I needed a medic and my Southern drawl had a bad way of messing up names on the computerized service, but "fire" never failed.

"Don't bother." Biloxi grunted. "I'll be gone before they get here."

"What were you shooting at?" I asked.

"The marshal that has a crush on you." He quaked.

I gasped and looked to my right. Maxim was face up on the ground and not moving.

"Was Sean Graham really my boy or were you just stalling me?" Biloxi asked.

I nodded. "Yes, he was."

He whimpered and then dead silence except for the yowl of a fire truck approaching and the rustle of the Spanish moss dancing above us.

I left Bill and then ran to Maxim's side. He was grunting and squirming, but not dead.

I caught his hand. "Why did you follow me after I left?"

"Still nursing a crush." He grinned, then winced.

I kissed him on his cheek, then somehow my lips found his mouth. His lips were soft. I stopped abruptly and chided myself. I held him in my arms until the medics came to fly him to the nearest hospital. No one was there to help me ease my guilt for a good half hour.

41

"So explain to me why we're not looking for Rosary?" I asked Ty.

He had taken over the case, since Maxim was now hospitalized for the gunshot wounds. The B&B was now a crime scene, so we were back at the sheriff's office. Tiger and Justus had returned to the station. They were waiting for me in the lobby. The sheriff had me in the interview room. They wanted to close this case and get the correct messaging to the sheriff's PR spokesperson.

"She's either dead or no longer in danger; if the latter she'll come out of hiding once she hears the news that The Knocker is dead," Ty said.

"Fair enough." I huffed.

"Can you believe that Sean was Giselle and The Knocker's son?"

"Please don't report that. The woman can't take much more scandal."

"Man, that's still crazy to me." JD shook his head. "You would kill your own son like that over moonshine."

"Biloxi didn't know. He was crying when he died," I said.

"Man, that's wild." JD shook his head.

"It's sad."

"Well, you did good, Angel." JD smiled.

"I don't think I've done anything." I folded my arms over my chest. "Sanchez is dead. There was also someone else out there with me and Biloxi. I don't know who that is."

I still didn't know who the mole was either, but I kept that information to myself. Maxim was gone and I needed to get back home to my children. The truth would come out about that eventually.

JD frowned. "Are you sure?"

"I'm positive and I think we need to have a chat with the volunteer fireman chief before we close this case."

"Why?" JD asked.

The U.S. Marshal for this region walked into our office. She was a beautiful forty-something, blond, blue-eyed woman. I could see patches of smut on her cheeks. Her team must have been deep in the swamps when they heard of what happened to us.

"Sorry I've missed most of the hoopla, searching for a needle in a fire ball, but I was listening outside and I'm curious to hear your theory, Angel Crawford."

I nodded at her then returned my attention to Ty. "When you said that you called the volunteer firefighters to help us through the swamps I told Sanchez that I wondered if the reason we had trouble finding the stills was because the distiller was a fireman. A fireman could easily alert the distiller that we were coming."

The room became silent.

"The case is closed," the sheriff said.

"The Knocker's case is closed, but I'm talking about the first one, the King Pin Moonshiner."

Ty rubbed his hands together. "Tell me more."

"If I had a million-dollar-a-year-grossing enterprise hidden between the smoke and brush of the Okefenokee Swamp, I would volunteer to save it," I said.

Ty nodded. "I know I would."

JD smiled. "Let's go see."

I turned to the blonde Marshal. "Marshal?"

"Call me Meg." She smiled.

"Like Mary Margaret Meg?" I asked.

"Nope. More like Nutmeg." She stepped toward our digital whiteboard and studied it. "Makes a lot of sense and won't hurt to look. Trouble is the fire is picking up."

"It could be picking up because we're looking for stills and the shiners need to burn any evidence of them," I said.

Meg's eyebrow rose. "Circle the wagons. We're going back out."

Ty patted my back and we followed the other Marshal team back down the super foggy road. Before the night was out we found it, miles of copper stills lined between tall pine trees and marsh.

JD hugged me tight. "You really done it, girl! Sanchez would be ecstatic over this."

"She definitely would." Ty shook his head and smiled.

I stood up. "That's good to know."

"Where are you going?" JD asked.

I sighed. "To a funeral and a wedding. Don't know which one is worse."

The following Saturday, 3:30 PM
Saint Philip AME Church, Atlanta, Georgia

Lately funerals have been my greatest source of epiphany. Devon's funeral I learned about unyielding faith and how I should never judge a book by its cover. The latter point really struck home at Sean Graham's funeral.

Sean's funeral was held at Saint Philip AME Church on

the corner of Candler and Memorial. It was the largest African Methodist Episcopalian Church in the South. The seven-thousand-plus congregation was mainly comprised of politicians, Elaine and the remainder of her staff, college professors, theologian types, and educators. Ava had been here before, so I asked her to tag along.

Since dealing with Sean and his crazy family, I had been clinging extra to her lately. Justus hadn't been hanging around my house like he did when we had begun to date and then Maxim . . . He was in Winn Army Hospital in Fort James four hours away near Savannah, refusing to take my calls. Best thing for me to do was to steer clear of the men in my life.

"So what is Tiger Jones doing here?" Ava elbowed me.

"Sean was one of his best-paying clients. Maybe he's here to give his condolences and pass out his business cards," I said.

"He better have that contract and a check for you." She scoffed. "That's what he better have."

Since I'd returned from South Georgia I noticed that Ava used Tiger's name in just about every conversation we had. I knew she didn't like him, but what was the deal? And why was she now interested in my business?

On top of that, Tiger had changed, too. He had stopped wearing his Big Bad Boys gear or any of his overstretched tracksuits. Today he wore dress slacks, a shirt, a tie, and a vest that somehow showcased his brawn and massive chest. I had rarely seen him dressed up. This was probably the first time he looked handsome for the world.

Ava stepped in front of me like a good ride-or-die chick would do. I felt awkward about her defensive stance. Usually I was the protector or Whitney. This was totally brand new.

"Mr. Jones, the family is over there, if you're here to give your condolences; else she doesn't want to talk to you." Ava slid her hands onto her hips like a graceful and fearless tarantella dancer.

I lowered my eyes to hide my chuckle. She was being a bit overdramatic.

"Pastor Avalyn Marie, could you please move. Leave it to you to get scrappy in church," Tiger said. "I just need to tell Angel something important."

"She can hear you from right here."

A few church members turned around.

I touched her back and whispered, "I think in God's house we could be safe."

"You didn't think that a few months ago when Elvis was trying to make you into chopped liver, but I'll acquiesce." She moved to the right just a smidge.

"Tiger, I need to get home. This service was long enough."

"Just a few minutes, Angel Soft." He eyed Ava. "Alone, though."

She threw her hands over her chest and harrumphed. "Uh-uh."

"Ava, where can Tiger and I talk in private?"

She rolled her neck. "What is it about the word 'no' you two don't understand?"

"Hunters don't quit," I said.

Tiger smiled. "We don't quit, Angel. I won't quit you, so why are you trying to quit me?"

"I never told you that. The last time we talked you made it clear that Riddick was more important to your business than I was."

"Don't go there, because we were in a good space before you went down to the swamps. I told you I'll take care of him in my own way." He glanced at Ava then back to me. "I don't want to hold you up, but I need to know. Will you come back? I'll renew our contract just like before."

"No." I shook my head. "I'm not going back to that. Tiger, I'm not your employee. I work for myself and if you want me to continue doing what I've done for you, then you're going to have to pay me. I'm a private detective also now."

"Thatta girl." Ava cheered softly.

I bubbled up with pride. "Tiger, I'll have Whit draw us up a new contract. Say Tuesday?"

"Angel Soft." He said my name with hesitation.

"I've never taken advantage of you before, so trust I won't with this," I said.

"You know that what we do don't come with much guarantee," he said.

"I'm a mother, Tiger Jones. I'm created to guarantee."

"Fair enough. Tuesday," Tiger mumbled.

"Uh, Mr. Jones. She didn't hear you. Can you repeat that?" Ava asked.

"I heard him, Ava. It's all good."

She relaxed her shoulders then smiled.

"Now that's good news, because I've been holding onto this pew, trying to keep myself from cutting a new groove at Mr. Tiger Jones. You look good."

He furrowed his brow and grinned at the same time. "How you gon' flirt with a player in God's house?"

"I knew it." I snickered. "I knew y'all must have sniffed each other while I was away. That's why you both sound crazy and that's the real reason you're here, Tiger."

Tiger chuckled. "You know you look good, girl."

Ava giggled.

"I can't do this." I hurried outside onto the old sanctuary church steps and prayed Tiger and Ava wouldn't say or do anything else that might send a lightning bolt through this beautiful church.

Sean's family sat in Kelly & Leak Funeral Home Cadillac limos. Five of them lined Candler Road. Rosary and Lucia sat in the first car with them. I frowned. *So now she shows up.*

I ran down the steps toward the limo. I noticed the wheels turning. Rosary saw me coming toward them, waved, then turned back around. *Are you serious?* I ran faster.

"Wait a minute!" I shouted. "Rosie, I risked my life to save you. That's all I get?"

I stopped running and decided not to follow them to the graveyard service. After all, I didn't need her to confirm what I concluded on my own. Sean and Rosary fell in love with each other after they learned that they both had a family history with moonshine. Lucia was born from that love. Yet Sean didn't want to share the good news with his family. He had a good reason. Rosie has issues with a red neck mob family to boot and then somehow he had found out about his father. Sean couldn't spill the beans, not even to his lady love. Rosary took it personal and went back to drinking to quell her broken heart. Sean tried to find a way to straighten her up and get her out of her family obligation without losing the identity he had created so well. It was a big gamble; unfortunately he lost. Lucia would grow up without a father, but at least she didn't have those generational curses. I hoped.

I decided right then to reach out to Gabe's family. They needed to know about Bella and she needed to know who they were.

"Angel, may I chat with you for a minute?" Riddick Avery asked.

I jumped. "You startled me, man."

He stood to the left of me. He carried a pack of cigarettes in his hand then placed them in his pocket. I wasn't surprised by his presence here, because he and Sean were good friends.

However, I was surprised that he wanted to talk to me. I was also surprised that he smoked.

"Since we're standing on holy ground, why don't you tell me the real truth behind the card?" I asked.

He chuckled nervously. "I knew that wasn't going to wash with you."

"So why did you lie?"

"Angel, we were at the Dunwoody Jail for Pete's sake. We could have gone to jail, including your mom, if you had gotten any wilder." He scoffed. "Not to mention that what I have to tell you must be in private. So I fibbed. I thought it was best if I kept that information to myself for a more appropriate time."

"Like today?"

"Yes." He nodded then reached in his pocket for the cigarettes again. I waited for him to take a smoke, but my patience had worn thin.

"Riddick, please, don't play with me," I pleaded.

"That picture was given to me by someone who wants to make contact with you, but he can't."

"I assume you won't tell me who this person is?"

He nodded. "When I sent the flowers I had every intention of telling you who sent them, but with Sean dying and my realizing that Lucy was Sean's baby, I won't do it. I'm sorry, Angel. This is all I can say, so don't ask me anything else about it."

"Riddick, you owe me more than this. Am I in danger? Is my daughter in danger?"

"I'm a lot of things, Angel, but I would not let harm come to you. Like I said before I didn't know Marlo would come at you like that. You have me all wrong." He held both my arms with his hands. "You and Isabella are safe."

"So why won't you tell me?" I began to cry.

He released his hold of me, slid his hankie out of his pocket, and dabbed my eyes with it. "You may never understand my position on this matter, but it is the best thing for you, kid. Move on with your life."

"I'll move on if you do me a favor, one kindness," I said.

His eyes narrowed. "What kind of favor?"

"Cesar Cruz. I know his girlfriend works at Grits Draft House, the same place where your girl Marlo works. And I know that you know that Tiger's butt is on the line. I just don't understand why you haven't picked him up yet."

"Dagnabbit, Angel." He grimaced. "I'll pick him up. Will that make you happy?"

"No." I smiled. "I'll pick him up and you'll be my heavy. That'll make me happy."

Two weeks later . . .
Back to the Georgia Coast

I wish I could say that my life wrapped up into a pretty bow after I killed Biloxi "The Knocker" James and got to the semi-bottom of this mysterious note, but it didn't. Ava and I weren't entirely back to being patty-cake-playing twins as I had hoped, because of Tiger. Something was going on between them and I promised myself I didn't want to know anything about it. Mama spent too much time at my house, which meant her new marriage was about to hit its expiration date. Drama . . . I overheard Whitney (actually, I tapped her line, thanks to Ty) telling Lark that she hadn't taken the bar yet, because she wanted to be a bail enforcement recovery agent like me. As if . . .

Then, to make matters worse, Bella spent so much time now with Ava and Mama I only saw her on school days, except when she needed me to chauffeur her to one of her many BFFs' birthday parties. That was definitely not what I planned for the rest of my vacation.

And then there was Lana's wedding. . . .

Today I wore a violet bridesmaid's dress. I hate violet. Everything else was beautiful. Lana's Amsale dress made her groom cry when he saw her glide down that aisle. Stacy Albright even got off her high horse and accepted her debunked bridesmaid role. Lana had to have an extra groom to escort me. We didn't have to look far. And to top it off, I had the audacity to catch the bridal bouquet and then tried to hide it from my escort when he came over waving Lana's garter belt in the air.

"I think you and I are supposed to be dancing," he said, as I slid into his arms.

"As long as that's all we're going to do." I smiled. "I know you. You may try to sneak a kiss."

He swung me around, then dipped me. "So I shouldn't propose, then?"

I giggled. "That would be crazy."

"But if you're crazy in love"—Justus pulled me up, then knelt down in front of me and presented a diamond and sapphire engagement ring—"then you can't help yourself."

My mouth dropped. I looked at him and then at the crowd gasping around us. I saw Maxim standing in the background. I blinked, but it wasn't a figment of my imagination. He was in the room and smiling back at me. I wondered if he remembered our kiss.

"Will you marry me, Evangeline Grace Crawford?" Justus formally asked. "Make me the second happiest man in this room, save the groom . . ."

I saw people laughing, cameras snapping, Mom crying and ruining her mascara, but I didn't hear anything. I looked down at Justus, back up at Maxim, and I couldn't speak.

Will Angel say "yes" or "no" to Justus?
Who is Riddick keeping Angel from?
Want to know who is the mole?

Then join Angel on her next manhunt in Can't Keep a Bad Bride Down, *coming in July 2013 from Dafina Books.*

DISCUSSION QUESTIONS

1. Would you have let Misty Wetherington go?

2. Do you have a Mrs. Bitter in your life? What do you do to keep her from stealing your joy?

3. Although Justus isn't a tough guy like Tiger or a marshal like Maxim, how does he constantly save the day for Angel?

4. Why does Ava have a soft spot for Rosary DiChristina?

5. For Angel, making sure Justus fits into her world with Bella is very important. What advice would you give Angel to help her feel secure about Justus?

6. Justus lives by the gentleman's code on relationships. Do you think he's old-fashioned or should more men follow his lead? Why or why not?

7. What do you think of Sean Graham? Was he good, bad, or misunderstood and why?

8. Why won't Ava accept Angel's career as a bail recovery agent? Do you agree that Angel could do something better with her life?

9. What do you do with frenemies like Riddick Avery?

10. Do you believe Riddick's explanation for Angel's mysterious gift?

11. Who is the someone bad in *Someone Bad and Something Blue*? Is there more than one?

12. What was the something blue and did you expect it?

13. Do you think Aunt Mary has finally left Uncle Pete or is he hiding something?

14. How do you deal with caustic family members?

15. Do you think Sean knew who Biloxi was?

16. What are your thoughts about forbidden relationships? Bill and Giselle?

17. Since Tiger was the only client Angel had, was he more like her boss than a client? What should small business owners do to ensure they keep control of their business?

18. Was Maxim really that irresistible or was he a good excuse for Angel to be bad?

19. Is Angel cut out to be a private investigator?

20. Should Angel tell Justus what happened on the manhunt with Maxim?

Don't miss Miranda Parker's debut novel—in stores now!

A Good Excuse to Be Bad

Smart, gorgeous, and too tough for her own good, bail recovery agent and single mom Evangeline Crawford moved to the burbs for a quiet life. Fortunately, it's not turning out that way . . .

1

Wednesday, 11:00 PM
Club Night Candy, Underground Atlanta, Georgia

If I weren't so screwed up, I would've sold my soul a long time ago for a handsome man who made me feel pretty or who could at least treat me to a millionaire's martini. Instead, I lingered over a watered-down sparkling apple and felt sorry about what I was about to do to the blue-eyed bartender standing in front of me. Although I shouldn't; after all, I am a bail recovery agent. It's my job to get my skip, no matter the cost. Yet, I had been wondering lately, what was this job costing me?

For the past six weeks, Dustin, the owner of Night Candy and my Judas for this case, had tended the main bar on Wednesday nights. His usual bartender was out on maternity leave. According to Big Tiger, she would return tomorrow, so I had to make my move tonight.

Yet, I wished Big Tiger would have told me how cute and how nice Dustin was. I might have changed my tactic or worn a disguise, so that I could flirt with him again for a different, more pleasant outcome. See, good guys don't like to be strong-armed. It's not sexy, even if it is for a good reason. Such is life . . .

Dustin poured me another mocktail. Although I detested the drink's bittersweet taste and smell, I smiled and thanked him anyway. It was time to spark a different, darker conversation. The fact that his eyes twinkled brighter than the fake lights dangling above his station made it a little hard for me to end the good time I was having with him.

"If you need anything, let me know." He stared at me for a while, then left to assist another person sitting at the far end of the bar.

I blushed before he walked away.

Get it together. I shook it off and reminded myself that I was on a deadline. I wanted his help, not his hotness and definitely not another free, fizzled, sugar water. It was time to do what I was paid to do.

When he returned to my station to wipe my area again, I caught his hand.

He looked down at my hand on his, glanced at my full glass, and grinned. "Obviously you don't need another refill."

I giggled. "No, I don't, but I do need something from you."

"I was hoping you would say that." He smiled and took my hand, then held it closer to his chest. "Because I've wanted to know more about you ever since you walked into my club."

"Great." I couldn't help but giggle back. "Does that mean I can ask you a personal question?"

He nodded. "Ask me anything, sweetie."

I leaned forward and whispered in his ear. "Do you have a problem with me taking someone out of here?"

"Of course not. You can take me out. My patrons don't mind, long as the tap stays open." He chuckled.

"No, Blue Eyes. I'm not talking about you. I'm talking

about dragging someone out of your club. Very ladylike, of course, but I wanted to get your approval before I did it."

He stepped back, looked around, then returned to me. "I don't think I understood you, sweetie. You want to do what in my club?"

"Take someone out."

He contorted his grin into a weird jacked-up W. "And what does that mean?"

"It means that you have someone in the club that I want, and I'll shut this club down if I don't get whom I came for. I don't want to cause a scene, so I'm asking for your cooperation."

He scoffed. "Is this some kind of joke?"

"No, it's a shakedown, Dustin Gregory Taylor, and surprisingly, you're the one who sent me. So I need you to play along with me right now. Okay? Sorry for the inconvenience."

"Sorry?" He stumbled back and let go of my hand. "Who are you? How do you know my name?"

"You're causing a scene, Dustin, and that's not good for business. Why don't you come back over here and I'll tell you . . . quietly."

He looked around the bar. The club was jumping so hard only a few people around us noticed his confused facial expression and his almost backstroke into the glass beer mug tower that stood behind him. He ran his hand through his hair, then walked back to me.

He murmured. "Who told you about me?"

"We have a mutual friend." I pulled out my cell phone, scrolled to a saved picture, and showed it to him. "I'm sure you know the man in this mug shot. It's your cousin Cade. Correct?"

His brow wrinkled; then he sighed. "What has he done now?"

"What he always does, Dusty, robs banks and skips bail. But do you want to know the worst thing he's done?"

Dustin just looked at me. He didn't respond.

"Well, I'll tell you anyway. He convinced your mom to put a second mortgage on the family house, in order to pay his bail the last time he got caught. Guess what? He got caught three months ago and then he missed his court date, which means—"

Dustin yanked the towel off this shoulder. "Say what?"

"Your mom's home is in jeopardy if I don't find him tonight. My boss Big Tiger Jones of BT Trusted Bail Bonds is ready to turn your childhood home into his Smyrna office, if you know what I mean."

"Son of a . . ." He turned around in a full 360. His towel twirled with him. "This isn't fair."

I nodded. "Life can be that way sometimes."

"I had no clue he had gotten back into trouble. He didn't say anything to me, and my mom . . . No wonder she hasn't been sleeping well lately." He rung the towel in his hands, then snapped it against the bar. "I don't believe this."

"Believe me, I understand how frustrating it is to watch your family make horrible mistakes and you or someone you love pay the price for their burden." I thought about my sister Ava. "Dustin, I have to take Cade downtown tonight. We both know that he's here in Night Candy right now and has been sleeping in your back office since his ex-girlfriend Lola kicked him out of her house. So tell me how you want this to go down, nice or easy?"

"Neither." He folded his arms over his chest. "You can't do this, not here. It'll ruin me."

I sighed. "I know, ergo this conversation."

Last year after a stream of violence and crime, the Atlanta Mayor's Office and the Atlanta Police Department issued a new ordinance against crime. Any businesses that appeared to facilitate criminal activity would be shut down. Night Candy already had two strikes against it: for a burglary gone bad that ended in the brutal murder of Atlanta socialite and real-estate heiress Selena Turner, and then there was that cat brawl between two NFL ballers' wives that was televised on a nationally syndicated reality TV show. The club definitely didn't need a showdown between a habitual bank robber and me. I'd tear this place up and anyone who stood between me and Big Tiger's money. I'm that bad, if I need to be.

"Maybe it won't." I touched his hand with hopes that I could calm him down. The last thing I needed was Cade to notice Dusty's agitation. "But you must do as I say."

Dustin leaned toward me. His starry eyes now looked like the eye of a hurricane. I shuddered. Man, he was hot.

"Listen to me," he said. "It's not you I'm concerned about. Cade has made it clear to everyone that he'll never go back to jail. He will fight. Lady, he'll burn my club down with all of us inside before he goes back in."

I patted his shoulders. "I believe you, and that's why Big Tiger sent me. See? Look at me."

"I've been looking at you all night."

"Exactly. This froufrou that I have on is a disguise."

"Didn't look like a disguise to me."

"That's my point, Dustin. I can sweet talk Cade out the back where Big Tiger's waiting for him in the alley. No one will suspect a thing, not even the plainclothes APD dudes hanging around near the champagne fountain."

He looked past me toward the fountain, then lowered his head. "I didn't see them there."

"That's because your attention was on me, just like Cade's will be once he sees me." I grinned. "All I need you to do is to introduce me to him. I'll take it from there."

"Makes sense, but there's a problem." He ruffled his hair again. "Cade's in the cabanas upstairs, but I can't leave the bar. I'll let Ed, the VIP security guard, know you're coming. He'll parade you around for me. What's your name?"

"Angel."

"Angel, that name fits you." He looked at me and then over me. His eyes danced a little; then he frowned. "You're very pretty and too sweet looking to be so hard. Are you really a bounty hunter?"

I slid off the stool, smoothed down my hair and the coral silk chiffon mini cocktail dress my little sister Whitney picked out for me, then turned in the direction of the upstairs cabanas. "Watch and find out."

Night Candy sat in the heart of downtown Atlanta—underneath it, to be more exact—on Kenny's Alley, the nightclub district inside Underground Atlanta. Real-estate moguls, music executives, and Atlanta local celebrities frequented the club whenever they were in town. They also hosted popular mainstay events there. The upscale spot had become so über trendy that unless you were on the VIP list, getting inside was harder than finding a deadbeat dad owing child support. But getting admitted was worth the effort.

On the inside, Night Candy was its name: dark, indulgent, and smooth. Chocolate and plum colors dripped all over the lounge. Velvet and leather wrapped around the bar like cordial cherries. It even smelled like a fresh-opened Russell Stover's box. Dustin looked and smelled even better. I wished we'd met under different circumstances.

The club had three levels with VIP at the top and the best live music I'd heard in a long time: vintage soul, reminiscent of Motown girl groups with a dose of hip-hop and go-go sprinkled on top. My hips sashayed up the stairs to the music until I stopped.

I checked my watch and huffed. In three hours the judge

could revoke Cade's bail. There was no time for errors. Cade had to go down now.

I texted Big Tiger. He had assured me he would be outside waiting for us. Trouble was, Big Tiger's promises had 50/50 odds. I promised myself to hire a male tagalong next time, preferably one as big as this Ed guy standing in front of me.

Whoa. I reached the stairs he guarded. Ed was a massive, bronzed bald-headed giant. He had brawn and swagger. My little sister Whitney would eat him up. Dustin must have given him the green light, because by the time I reached the top of the staircase, he was smiling and holding out his hand to help me inside the VIP lounge.

As he gave me a personal tour of what I called a Godiva version of a party room, I spotted Cade and exhaled. The Taylor men definitely had great genes. I didn't have to take a second look at his Fulton County Corrections Office booking photo to know it was him. He was drop-dead handsome—bald and dark, a bad combination for me. I'm a recovering bad-boy-holic. I hoped he wouldn't give me too much trouble, but the thought of a good crawl with this guy was enough to send me to church first thing Sunday morning.

I melted into a milk chocolate lounge chair across from his cabana and waited for his jaw to drop at the sight of me. And boy, did it. He was talking to a barely clad and quite lanky teenybopper when he saw me through the sheer curtain covering the cabana. I grinned and slid my dress up too high for a woman my age to ever do without feeling like some dumb tramp. I wished I could say I was embarrassed acting that way, but I couldn't. I liked having a good excuse to be bad sometimes.

The sad thing about all of this was that the young woman holding on to Cade didn't notice him licking his lips at me.

After five minutes of his gross act, she stood up and walked toward me. My chest froze. Maybe she had seen him and was now coming over to warn me to back off or to claw my eyes out.

Yeah, right, like I would let that happen. Homegirl better think twice about dealing with me. But I didn't want to hurt her. I didn't get all shiny and done up to scrap with some girl over a fugitive. Besides, I promised Dustin I wouldn't show out up in here. So I gripped the chair as she approached and relaxed when she breezed past. I watched her enter the ladies' room, then patted my cheeks with my palms. I was getting too old for this crap.

As soon as the child left his side, Cade slinked his way over to where I sat. I looked below at the bar where Dustin watched me. I waved my fingers at him until he dropped the martini he was making. *Man, he was cute.*

While I daydreamed of a date with Dustin, Cade stood over me. "So you know my cousin?"

I turned toward him. "Is that your way of introducing yourself to me, or are you jealous?"

He smiled and reached for my hand. "My apologies." He kissed my hand. "I'm Cadence Taylor, but everyone calls me Cade. Don't tell my cousin, but I think you're stunning."

"No, I'm not." I giggled. "I'm Angel."

"I can see that." He sat beside me. "Like a guardian angel . . . no, a cherub."

"More like an archangel."

He clapped and laughed. "Not you. You don't look like the fighting type. You have sweetness written all over you. You're definitely Dusty's type."

Oh, great. Now you tell me. I moved closer toward him. "And you have 'Bad Boy' written all over you."

He grinned. "You don't have to be afraid of me. I'm a good guy when I need to be."

I smiled back. "Can you promise to be good, if I ask you for a favor?"

He nodded. "Anything for you, Angel."

"I'm tired. I'm ready to go home. Can you escort me to my car? I was supposed to wait for Dustin, but I don't have the stamina for this club life."

"Of course, you don't, because you're a good girl." He stood up and reached for my hand. "Surprisingly, I'm not a clubber either. How about you leave your car and I take you for a quiet night drive through the city, then over to the Cup-cakery for some dessert. By the time we get back, Dusty will be closing up this place."

"I don't know. I don't think Dustin would like that so much. Sounds too much like a date."

"Yeah, I guess so." He scratched his head like his cousin, another Taylor trait.

"Besides, your girlfriend would be upset if you left her here."

"What girlfriend?"

I pointed toward the ladies' room. "Her."

"Oh, her. We're not together."

I came closer and whispered in his ear. "Neither are Dustin and me."

He smiled and his eyes outshined the VIP lounge.

"Why don't you escort me to my car and follow me home instead, just to make sure I get there safe?"

He placed his hand at the small of my back. "I can do that."

Because Cade almost carried me out of Night Candy, I couldn't text Big Tiger to let him know that I was coming outside. All I could do was hope he was where he said he would be.

We stepped outside. No Big Tiger. I hit the hands-free Talk button on my phone earpiece and voice-activated Big Tiger's phone number to dial. I got nothing. My heart began to race. Where was he?

"Is something wrong?" Cade asked. His hands were all over me.

I removed his hands, but said nothing. I had no words.

Sometimes bail bondsmen needed women locators to lure a defendant out of their hiding spot. I didn't mind doing it. Honestly, I needed the money, but we had a deal. I brought them out; he rode them in. So why was I out here alone? Well, not entirely alone . . . with Octopus Cade.

Cade watched me. "Are you having second thoughts?"

"I have a confession to make." I scrambled for something to say while fiddling for my handcuffs. They were trapped somewhere under the chiffon.

"So do I." He pulled me toward him. "I can't keep my hands off you."

I wanted to cuff him, but I couldn't, because he had wrapped his hands around my waist.

"Not here, not like this." I removed his hold on me again, but held on to one of his hands.

He smiled until he felt—I assumed—my cold handcuffs clank against his wrists. "What the—"

"You've violated your bail agreement, Mr. Taylor," I said. Still no Big Tiger in sight. "So you'll have to come with me."

He chuckled as he dangled my handcuffs—the ones I thought had locked him to me—over his head for me to see. A piece of my dress had wedged between the clamp. They were broken. My heart hit the floor.

"Unless these handcuffs are chaining me to your bed, I'm not going anywhere with you, sweetie."

Then, quicker than I anticipated, he head-butted me. I saw stars and fell to the ground. A pain so bad crossed my forehead, it reminded me of labor pains. I couldn't scream. I had to breathe through it to ease the pain.

The head-butting must have stung Cade, too, because he stumbled before he could get his footing. I caught one of his legs and clutched it. I closed my eyes and groaned as he dragged me down the alley. Through the excruciating bumps and scrapes I received holding on to Cade, past the onlookers who didn't care to help this poor damsel in distress, I asked myself, "Why wouldn't I let go?"

My forehead and my skinned knees throbbed now. I'm pretty sure Whitney's dress looked like wet trash. To make matters worse, I was angry with myself for putting myself in this position. I couldn't afford to be so cavalier anymore. I knew that before I took this stupid assignment. I knew it while I sat at the bar. I knew it the day I became a mother, but I did it anyway. What's wrong with me? I couldn't leave my daughter alone without a parent. Now I had to hurt this fool to get back to my baby in one piece.

Cade stopped and cursed. My heart beat so fast and loud, I prayed it would calm down so I could prepare for his next move.

"Angel, sweetie, I think we need to have a little talk."

He pulled me up by my hair, my store-bought hair. I wore a combed-in hairpiece because I didn't have time to go to a hair salon and I didn't want to damage my hair. However, Cade's tugging made the plastic teeth dig deeper into my scalp. I screamed to keep from fainting.

"Shut up!" He slapped me. "You stupid—"

Before he could say another word, I grounded my feet then threw a round kick so high and hard with my left leg that I heard his jaw crack against my stilettos. He hit the ground, unconscious. While he was knocked out, I turned him over and handcuffed him again, but from the back this time and with the chiffon visibly gone.

I dialed Big Tiger. "Where are you?"

"Where did I tell you I was gon' be?" Big Tiger's voice seemed crystal clear. "Right here."

Someone tapped my shoulder. I jumped.

"It's a good thing I showed up when I did. You could have killed the man. I'da lost my money and then I would have had to take care of your raggedy bond." Big Tiger laughed, then helped me hoist Cade up. "Why didn't you wait instead of messing up your sister's dress? How many dresses have you slaughtered now?"

I looked at him and growled. "Say that again. I dare you."

"And your face, Angel Soft." He squinted. "I think we'd better call 911 after we put homeboy in my truck."

I walked toward Big Tiger with the intent to give him a right hook across his jaw. When I lunged, I think I fainted. I don't know what happened next and I almost didn't care until the EMS worker asked me whom I should call to let them know I was being taken to the emergency room.

"Call my sisters. Tell them where I am and make sure Ava comes to get me."

Then I faded back to black and it felt good. In my dreams, Dustin was on his knees proposing to me with some chocolates and a pink diamond.

His voice was so clear. "Angel, will you . . . be healed in the name of God."

God?